THE DEVIL'S SECRET

LILIAN HARRIS

This is a work of fiction. Names, characters, organizations, places, events, and incidences are either products of the author's imagination or used fictitiously.

© 2022 by Lilian Harris. All rights reserved.

No part of this book may be reproduced, or stored in a retrieval system, or transmitted in any form or by any means, electronic, mechanical, photocopying, recording, or otherwise, without the express written permission of the publisher.

Editor: Ms. K Edits

Interior Formatting: CPR Editing

Proofreader: Judy's Proofreading

Cover Design: Black Widow Designs

A WOUNDED SOUL ISN'T ANY LESS BEAUTIFUL.

PART I

THE PAST

SIX MONTHS AGO

ENZO

ONE

I don't remember my parents well. Not anymore. Too many years have gone by without them to see their faces or remember how they walked and talked. But I remember some things—like how my mother would leave notes in my lunch box, reminding me how much she loved me, or how Dad would let me have an extra cupcake when my mom wasn't looking. He did that shit a lot. I laugh at the memory, hating that they're gone.

Those memories are what stay. I hope they stay for good. They're the only things I have left of them. The only pieces of our life the Bianchis couldn't take from us.

There's not a day that goes by when I don't think about it—what Faro Bianchi, the don of the Palermo crime family, and his brothers, did to my father and Matteo.

If Dom hadn't watched them die, if he hadn't heard Faro

threaten to kill us too, we'd all be dead.

I think about that sometimes. Like the fact that we're even standing here today. The sheer luck it took for Dom to go looking for Dad the day he was killed.

Death. It's a funny thing. One day you're here. The next day you're gone. When it'll happen. How? No one knows. No one wants to. Some think they do, but they really don't. The unknown may be scary, but knowing the day your ticket is punched is its own hell.

Did my father know his day was coming? What had him killed? We still don't know, but we'll find out. Faro himself will tell us before we rip out his fucking tongue.

After our parents died, we were alone in the world, only having each other. We had no extended family. We hid from the Bianchis, living on the street for a year, stealing, lying, just to survive.

After a year of that, then living at homeless shelters, we thought we'd never make it out, but Dom's chance encounter with Tomás Smith, a wealthy hotel chain owner, changed our lives.

Right before Tomás died, he made Dom the CEO of his company, and gave Dante and me board positions.

My brothers and I also run our own nightclub chain, but not under the aliases Tomás set up for us when he learned of our past. If the Bianchis were still looking for us, we wanted them to know we were back, to come after us if they dared, to wonder when their ticket would be punched. After fifteen fucking years, we're finally going to destroy them once and for all.

They have no idea what we look like. We're different now. In so many ways.

We're vengeance. We're war.

Killers.

Monsters, haunting their dreams before they even get a chance to close their eyes.

For our father's and brother's deaths, they will all pay.

With their blood.

Their screams.

It will all be ours.

We may not be able to bring our family back, but we could sure as fuck see their murderers suffer before we slice their throats.

We'll burn every business they own to the ground—the laundromat, the strip club, Tips and Tricks, run by Faro's daughter, Chiara—it'll all blow up into ashes.

I can't wait to see the look on her daddy's face when he realizes who we are, that we're not those little boys anymore. The need for revenge has transformed us into men we never wanted to become. I bet he'll wish he found us back then and killed us.

Too late now.

The party's only beginning.

We'll get the Bianchi brothers soon enough.

We'll avenge my baby brother and father.

And we'll kill anyone who dares to stop us.

I ready to enter Tips and Tricks, parking my white Bugatti Divo in the lot. Dante's already inside, chatting up Carlito, one of the soldiers in the Palermo family. He's the man who's been chosen to marry Chiara's cousin, Raquel, the woman Dante's been tailing, the one he plans to marry himself.

The scheme is solid, really. Raquel will do anything not to marry that asshole. Dante will offer her a way out, except he doesn't plan to let her go.

I kinda feel sorry for the girl. She didn't do shit to us, except carry the unfortunate luck of being Salvatore's daughter, the consigliere, a.k.a. the adviser to the don.

But Dante wants this. He wants her father to know that the

son of the family they thought so low of back then now has his precious daughter, and there's nothing he could do to stop Dante.

Raquel will be his.

A bouncer tips his chin up in greeting, parting the door as I step inside, the blaring music jumping off the walls as I continue down a short, dimly lit corridor leading into the club.

I immediately spot Dante at a table in between the second and third stage. He leans back into the black leather sofa, Carlito talking while my brother forces a smile, nodding as he glances around.

A snicker slips from me, knowing how much Dante hates the man and how hard this is for him. But Carlito likes to talk when he's been drinking, and we're hoping he lets something about Raquel or the Bianchis slip. That's the only reason Dante forces himself to show up.

"Yo, yo." I approach, clasping my brother's palm while he clenches his jaw. I instantly know he's pissed at me for taking so long to get here. Me being around makes this more tolerable for him.

"Sorry, man, I got caught up with Candy. She's got a big appetite to feed." I wink.

His eyes lock with a glare, but I just grin. I love fucking with him. But Candy does have a big appetite and well—so do I.

Carlito's sitting next to Dante with a beautiful blonde stripper on his lap, his hands on her hips. I watch her, trying not to stare but doing a shit job of it. Her jaw is sharp and angled high as she gyrates on his thighs, swaying her head to the side.

Her eyes, though, they're vacant, like she doesn't want to be here at all, like her body is there, but her mind, it's somewhere else entirely. Who could blame her, though? I wouldn't want to be anywhere near Carlito either if I were a chick.

I focus on her for far too long, fascinated by her, akin to the distance in her gaze. I feel like that sometimes, my mind and body aren't in sync, like I was meant to be someone else. But here I am, Enzo Cavaleri, a man with too much hate in his heart. A heart that will kill, a heart that's coursing with more venom than I want to taste, the acid already dripping down my throat, poisoning my thoughts.

I hate it all. But normalcy ain't in the cards. Not for me. Not for any of us. Not yet anyway. The women and liquor are how I manage to get through it all. Sometimes it works. I don't feel anything else when I'm fucking, when I'm drinking.

But after it's over—shit. That's the worst. That's when it all comes crashing down—the loneliness, the self-hatred, the need for violence, to murder the ones who ruined us.

It'll end soon. When we kill our enemies. When we let their blood rain on this city. We won't stop until the Bianchi brothers are all dead.

So this girl? I understand her. I get it. We may be different, but we're also the same. Doing things we wish we didn't have to do. Wanting something else, but knowing we'll never have it.

She pivots her head toward me, her serious gaze caught with mine as though realizing I'm thinking about her. Her brows furrow for a split second before her lips wind into a sultry smile, one I return willingly, hiding behind it. If I didn't know any better, I'd guess her smile is as fabricated as mine. Though it probably doesn't seem like that to the shitheads here, too drunk to notice or give a fuck that the girl taking off her clothes for their pleasure is sad as hell.

"Hey, the brother is here," Carlito slurs, leaning toward me over Dante, and I reluctantly stop staring at the woman, too gorgeous to be anywhere near him.

"Hey, man," I reply, glancing at the bastard, clasping his sweaty, outstretched palm, wanting to rip it off his body for merely touching her. "Patrick." I use my alias, a name Tomás set up for each of us. Dante goes by Chris here. We couldn't use our real names in case this idiot talked to the Bianchis about us. We don't want them to know we're among their people, gathering intel before the attack comes.

"I remember," Carlito yells over. But I wouldn't be surprised if he had forgotten my name. He's usually drunk off his ass by the time I show up. I only join in for my brother's sake.

Dante can be a little short fused, particularly with the likes of Carlito. He's damn close to losing his temper, especially when Carlito talks shit about Raquel. I have bets on Dante slitting his throat by the end of tonight. I'd pay to see that.

"You want a dance too?" Carlito continues, his smile displaying a set of yellow teeth. "I can share." He slaps the woman on her ass, and for a mere second, her cheeks hollow with the grit of her teeth, before she sways her hips on his thighs again. "Your brother is buying." Carlito's shoulders roll with a laugh. "You may as well take advantage."

My stomach stirs with revulsion at the way he just said that, like she's a damn piece of meat he's offering me a taste of. I rip my attention from him, my eyes drifting back to the woman, and instantly, hers fall to mine, and our connection—that intangible, unrelenting link—it's there. I can feel it. Among all these people, I can hear her talking with a mere look in her eyes, winding the power of her gaze through mine. The crowd. The noise. It all falls to a whisper, as though she had magically turned the volume down.

And the only thought going through my mind is that I need to know her. Her name. Her favorite fucking color. Why she works here with these assholes? I want to know everything.

"I'm good right now," I tell Carlito, unable to tear my gaze away from her, and she sure as hell isn't looking away either. Carlito is too drunk to notice or care.

Dante usually pays for everything. It's his way of buttering up the prick, and Carlito's more than willing to take advantage.

"He hasn't even opened his wallet once," Dante says into my ear. "The son of a bitch drank one entire bottle of cognac and is guzzling the second, and still hasn't given me anything we can use. But I swear, if he talks about fucking Raquel while his boys watch one more time, I'm gonna bash him on the head with that bottle, then make him swallow the glass. And I know what I said last time, to hold me back and shit, but fuck that, let me kill him."

"Damn, man." I chuckle, finally looking at him. "You sound like you got it bad. Protecting her honor and shit."

His face bends with a grimace as he backs up a couple of inches. "I don't."

"Okay, liar."

"Whatever. I just can't stand the thought of that nasty-ass fuck thinking he can have a woman like that, let alone do the kind of shit he plans to do once they're married."

I glance back at Carlito, whose hunger is back on the stripper's ass, while her eyes carelessly roam around the club, glazed with the same layer of cloudiness I saw before.

I wonder what she's thinking about. Is she counting down until she can go home? Does she have someone to go home to? I envy that. It'd be nice to have a woman to come home to. Someone who's not after my money or my cock, just me.

I keep staring while her eyes wander straight ahead. She's gorgeous, with all that wavy golden hair spilling down her back. Her curves built for a man, a man like me.

Before I could turn back around to my brother, her bright blue gaze fixes on mine, and I'm unable to look away from her eyes once again. They're the color of the hottest fires burning like the sun. They're beautiful. Warm. Inviting. Deadly as hell.

A woman this stunning.

This sinful.

Sure knows how to destroy a man.

Both of us are caught in this trance, where nothing else seems to exist, at least not for me. It's as though she can read my thoughts, knowing I can see her, truly see her, not just her body, which I definitely see too.

Is she wondering about me? Does she think I'm a prick, like all the rest here?

Strip clubs are normally not my thing. As much as I love women, I don't care to see them take off their clothes for everyone in the room. I want them to strip for me alone because they want to, not because they have to.

Carlito's hands are back on her hips, sliding to her stomach, pushing himself closer. I want to wrench him off her. I wanna break his fucking bones.

I drag in a long, deep inhale instead, attempting to steady the rage.

Her jaw strains for a brief second before she flips her head back seductively, her long, thick hair spreading over his chest as she grinds on his dick. He glides his hand up her thigh, too close to the thin red thong that barely covers her.

She's not that into you, asshole. She's just pretending. Not like a fucker like him would care anyway.

She clearly hates this job, and I wish I could help somehow.

Once the song is over, she curls around, kissing him on the cheek with a grin as she rises, and he hands her two singles with a slap on her ass.

Is this cheap motherfucker joking?

Two. Fucking. Dollars?

Dante's right. He should kill him.

Now I'm the one who wants to pick up that bottle and bash it over his head.

She peers down at the crumbled-up bills in her hand and stuffs them in her panty before walking away, while he talks to the men seated beside him.

I ball a fist tightly.

I should end him right now. Dante will forgive me for taking that away from him. Eventually.

"I'll be right back," I tell my brother, who nods once, carelessly staring ahead, thumping his head to the beat, rolling closer to Carlito in hopes of getting more info out of him, no doubt.

I follow the woman who had the unfortunate luck of dancing with that cocksucker.

"Hey, miss, wait up," I call loudly over the blasting song.

She turns on her high heels, appearing only a few inches shorter than my six-four. Her brow arches, a smile flirting over the slant of her full red lips. She's in a fucking see-through bra. I'm really trying hard to look at her face instead. Attempting to be a gentleman in a place full of naked women ain't easy. I may not like coming here, but I still have eyes.

"Yes, handsome?" She props a hand on her hip, her long black-painted fingernails curving over it. "Would you like to buy a dance, too?"

"Maybe next time." I smirk. "I only came to give you this." Reaching into my pants pocket, I retrieve my wallet, opening it up and taking out a few hundreds. "This is for you." I outstretch my hand.

Squinting inquisitively, her eyes dart between me and the stack of money. "Is this some kind of test or something?" She takes a few steps closer, that fake flirtatious mask she just wore is now gone. Instead, I find a dash of fear interspersed with annoyance.

"Do I look like a teacher to you?" I grin. "That idiot back there gave you two damn dollars," I explain. "This is my way of fixing it."

She gives the money a curious look, peeking back up at me.

"I hope you know we're not friends," I add. "That asshole and me. I mean, not even a little. I don't keep friends like that."

She fixes me with a softened stare, her lips twitching. "You're cute. And for some strange reason, I believe you."

I lower my arm, the money still in my grasp. "Cute?" I nod contemplatively, my mouth bending with a smile, loving hers. "Not the word I was hoping for, but coming from you, I'll take it." I angle in closer until I'm only a hand away. "I have a feeling you don't throw out compliments that freely."

She nears her lips to my ear, and I have to battle to keep my palms at my sides instead of her hips. "Am I that easy to read?" Her breath skitters up my skin. Heated. Enticing. I don't know if this is her way of setting me off, but it's working.

"You are to me." My voice rises over the smooth column of her neck, my hand losing the fight as my fingers inadvertently graze her hip. Just a touch. That's all I've had. And yet, my fingertips tingle, like I've never touched a woman before.

"Really?" That one word is feathery soft, drenched in an erotic tone, the sound going right to my cock, making it throb, chafing in my jeans.

"Mm-hmm." My pulse jumps a beat.

"What else can you tell about me?" She tips her head sideways, giving me more of her throat, her words louder now, straining over the hammering of the music.

I draw back, needing to see her eyes, needing to drown in the waves of her gaze. "I can tell you're probably lonely. And you clearly hate working here. You're only doing it because you don't have a choice."

I lift my free hand to her face, the money still clutched within it, as my thumb cruises down her cheek.

Her chest rises and falls like a wild storm, her lips parting as my eyes settle on hers, our gazes melded as I continue. "You show the world only a tiny part of who you really are, keeping the rest hidden, afraid if they saw the real you, they'd run like hell." I let my thumb brush over the corner of her mouth, and her brows pull so tight, I can taste her raw emotion like it's etched into the marrow of my bones. I lean back into her ear for a moment, dropping my hand from her face. "So how'd I do?"

Once I level my attention back to her, her sadness, it's still there, but only for a stolen moment, then her face slips into that smile she disappears behind.

"Wow, you ahh—" She swivels and stares down at her feet for a second too long before focusing back on me. "You have me all wrong. I—ahh—I love working here and am doing it willingly." A shallow breath's caught in her remark. "So unless you want a dance, I have to go back to work."

She whirls around, not giving me a chance to respond. But instead of marching away, she pauses, fastened in place. Even without her needing to tell me, I know all of what she just said was a lie.

I stroll up, my front only an inch from her back. I slide my hand up her arm, my fingertips caressing her smooth, bare skin, and her shoulders sway with harsh breaths. "I'm sorry if I offended you." My whisper comes gently over the shell of her ear.

"You didn't." Her words are set with an edge, but there's a

vulnerability within it.

"I did." I pause. "Friends shouldn't hurt each other's feelings."

She slowly pivots, a line forming between her brows.

"We're not friends and you don't know me." There's no anger there, just pain, and I instantly want to take it all away.

"How about we change all that?" The question sits heavy in my throat, like it's dreading the answer.

Her forehead creases, her face contorting with annoyance. "Are you trying to mess with me? Did they send you?" Her slightly widened eyes casually dart across the room. The fear is all around her like an aura. "You can tell them to fuck off! I'm not that stupid."

The anger's trapped in her features as it takes a hold of me.

Are the Bianchis doing something to her? Is that who she's scared of?

It has to be them. Dante has told me she's their favorite, and I'd bet a bullet that's who she fears. Those fucking bastards taint everything they touch. But I won't allow them to hurt her. Not anymore.

"Hey." I tip up her chin with a finger. "I don't know who you're talking about," I lie. "But whoever they are, tell me where I can find them, and you'll never have to be afraid of them again."

She exhales weakly, her eyes on me again, her chin trembling, then she smiles, fighting the very pain she just revealed. "I'm sorry. Ignore me." She sighs in a huff. "I'm being stupid. But I should go though. I'm up on the stage soon."

Reluctantly, I drop my hand away, realizing she won't tell a complete stranger the truth. I have to get to know her better and gain her trust. It's the only way I can help. "Are you gonna give me your name before you leave me forever?" I tease, hoping for a genuine smile this time.

"I guess I can. Not like it's a secret." She laughs and it's beautiful. "I'm Joelle. You?"

"I'm En—"

Fuck.

I want her to know me. I don't want to give her some fake-ass name, but I've got no choice.

"You're En?" She slants her face.

"Nah, I'm Patrick. Enrico is my dad." I hope she buys it.

"Well, Patrick. I do have to go. It was nice meeting you."

Looking around, I don't see anyone directly around us. I stretch out my hand discreetly with the cash in it. "Take it."

She finally does, and when she sees the amount, her eyes bug out. "Ahh, that's like two grand."

"Is it?" My lips jerk, knowing it probably is. I didn't count it.

"Are you sure that's all for me?"

"It is. And you're taking every penny. Keep it somewhere they can't find it."

Her lower lip is caught in her mouth, and I can tell she's not sure if she should take the cash, doubting that I'm not one of them.

"I won't tell them," I reassure. Knowing the Bianchis, they probably steal the tips from the women.

"Thank you," she finally says, subtly sliding her hand to mine and grabbing the money.

"When can I see you again?" I know I want to, and not just because I want to find out what the Bianchis are doing to her, but also 'cause I kinda like being around her. She intrigues me.

"Well, you can see me every night on stage." That inauthentic grin is back.

"That's not what I meant. I want to hang out, away from this place, like over coffee or…dinner?"

"I can't." The reply is quick. Sharp. And her gaze falls to the ground.

"Fine, fine." I roll my eyes, an amused smirk slipping on my face. "You play a hard bargain. Lunch, then?"

She looks up from below her dark brows, fighting a laugh.

The need to touch her, let my hand fall to her face, to tell her I can fix whatever or whoever's harming her, takes hold of me. That brokenness within her eyes, I want to consume it, like a roaring flame. Extinguish it until it no longer bleeds into her soul.

"Why would you want to see me anyway?" She bows her head. "I'm no one."

"Hey..." In a mere blink, my body goes flush against hers, a finger tilting her chin up until she can't do anything else but look into my eyes. "Who the hell told you that? You're far from no one." Her throat trembles with emotion and it breaks my damn heart. "I may not know you, but I can tell you're special." I let my thumb trail the base of her jaw. "So I don't want to hear that shit coming out of your mouth again. Got it?"

She nods into my hand, her expression muddied with an ache. "You have to know," she goes on. "I can't see you outside of this place, even if I wanted to." She pauses, and my pulse drums in my neck. "And I kinda want to."

My nostrils flare. "Are you being held prisoner?"

Her palm goes to my bicep, and she leans into me. "Don't ask me things I can't give you answers to." The confession wafts over the music, her breath scurrying over my neck. "If you want to see me"—her gaze drifts back into my eyes—"it can only be here when you buy a private dance."

I have to get her alone. If buying a dance is the only way I can get to know her better, to find out what's going on, then I'll do it.

If the Bianchis are hurting her, they'll die twice. Once for my family and once for her—this woman. This stranger. Someone I barely know. But someone I want to know more than anything.

"I don't just want a dance. I don't want whatever you do with every asshole here."

"Look, Patrick…" Her shoulders sag, her breathing filled with dejection. "I don't know what you want from me, but a dance is all I can give you."

There's more there, more she wants to tell me, that she's probably dying to tell someone, but she's fighting it like hell.

"You working tomorrow?"

"And the night after that." A warm, soulful smile stitches up her lips.

"Then I'll be here."

"I guess I'll see you tomorrow." She lifts her hand in a small wave. "Bye, Patrick.

"See ya, Joelle."

She walks away, tucking the money in her bra as she disappears behind the stage.

JOELLE

TWO

He was the first man to ever look at me. Really look at me.

As more than a stripper. As more than a whore.

That's what I am, though. A whore. I have been for too long. Nine years long. I don't know who I was before. Not anymore.

That woman has long disappeared into a dark abyss where I can no longer hear her or feel her. She's someone I can never be. Was I ever her? Was it all a dream I made up to erase the agony of my current life?

No. I remember it all. My family. My friends. My son.

Robby.

God. How I wish I could hold him. Love him like a mother would. But *he* took him. From the moment he was born, he was theirs.

The monsters. My tormentors. That's who they are.

They run my life. This club. Their teeth have sunk so deep into every facet of my existence, I'll never scrape them off. They've imprinted their mark on my soul. I'll never escape them. How could I? They watch the house I live in, with cameras running twenty-four seven. The whole place is covered with security night and day.

Every girl watched like I am, I'm sure. Every one of them is just like me. Someone who never had a choice. Someone stolen. Robbed of her life. Of her family. Of her dignity and self-respect.

They call us sluts.

Whores.

They beat us.

Rape us.

They control us.

If it weren't for my beautiful boy, I would've found a way to die. He's the only one keeping me tethered to this world, instead of finding myself sinking into another.

He looks so much like me. From the moment he was born, I saw myself, and to this day, at seven and a half, he has his mama's eyes and my hair too.

I don't think I could've handled if he looked anything like his father. A shudder rolls down my arms, the tiny hairs popping up. God, even the thought of that man sharing DNA with my baby makes me violently ill.

My mind drifts to Patrick as I stare at myself in the mirror, trying to find the pieces of the woman he saw, or at least I hope he did. If anyone could find her again, maybe I could too. Maybe there's still hope for her.

For me.

Was he genuine? Was he really looking for a friend or was he like every man here, wanting to sleep with me for free? They try. They want everything.

They can pay for that too, though. It's on the menu if they ask.

We're not supposed to talk about it, and my boss, Chiara, has no idea it happens, but her father, the one who owns the club, and Agnelo, the one who's in charge of us, allows it to happen.

Well, allow is a loose term. His people kidnapped me and my two friends and made us work for them.

We were locked in tiny cages, the size made for dogs. We were barely fed. We showered once a week or when they needed us for work. Once they decided to make us permanent somewhere, such as a strip club, or their members-only sex club, then we were put up at shabby houses they own, usually multiple girls in one home.

If any girl tried to run, to talk to another about anything related to what happened to us, they were killed. I've had roommates shot to death right in front of me, their bodies never to be found. That's what the men told us, that our bodies would be gone forever, that our families would never even find pieces of us. That fear, it worked, and we kept quiet, not even talking to each other about anything.

For me, it's even worse. They have my son. They always use him as leverage. If I don't do what they ask, they'll kill him or sell him to some pervert, and I'll never see him again. I can't let them harm my baby. I'll do whatever they want. However they want it.

They call me Joelle, but once, I was Jade Macintyre.

"I really don't want you going, Jade," Mom says from behind me, her tone gripped with worry. "Do you really need to go?" She leans a hip against the doorframe of my bedroom as I peer over my shoulder, folding the last few items of my clothes and laying them

into the suitcase.

Once I zipper it up, I walk up to her and place both hands on her shoulders. "I'll be okay, Mom."

She shakes her head, fingers pressing into her temple.

"I'm nineteen," I continue. "I'm not your baby anymore."

"Oh." She huffs with a grumble, playing with the edge of her short, blonde hair, framing her jaw. "Thanks very much for reminding me."

"You're being dramatic," I tease, the corner of my mouth lifting. "I'll have my phone. You can call me anytime. Okay? Stop worrying so much."

"How can I stop worrying when you're planning on driving around the country like a crazy person? Who does that? Why couldn't you do something else? Like skydiving? Swimming with sharks? There are so many other reckless possibilities."

"I need this, Mom. I'll be in school for so many years. And I'll have Elsie and Kayla with me."

"Again, not feeling any better, young lady. Can I come with you? I'm quiet and fun. I can hang with the cool kids."

I let out a laugh, the kind that has your whole body shuddering. My mom is fun, but she's always been more mom than friend. She knew when to let me fly and knew when to keep me close within the safety of her wings.

She had to be both mother and father to my brother, Elliot, and me, who's three years younger. My father left when she was pregnant with him, and we've never seen him again. No cards. No letters. Nothing. He met another woman at work and started a family with her instead, forgetting the one he already had.

But we've survived without him just fine. My mother was more than he could've ever been. She worked two jobs to keep us fed and housed. She made sure we had new clothes, healthy food. She was our rock and still is. That's why I'm planning on going to med school once I finish college. Not only do I love kids and can't wait to work as a pediatrician, but I want to make money to help her for once instead.

"Great, Ma." *Elliot's voice travels as his feet prod across the tiles.* "So, you're going to abandon the one child who isn't leaving you for the one that is? Nice one."

Mom turns as he makes it beside her. Her arm wraps around him, bringing him into her side. "I'd sneak you into the luggage. Obviously." *She rolls her eyes.* "Just don't tell your sister," *she half whispers while her gaze is on me, the edges of her pale blue eyes crinkling from the smile radiating through them.*

"Yeah, okay. You're both staying here," *I tell her.* "I'll be just fine on my own."

"Good." *Elliot coils his mouth into a playful smile.* "I didn't want to come anyway. You're too loud and annoying."

"Me?" *I screech.* "Ha! Look who's talking." *I prop a hand on my hip, twisting up my brows.* "Remember the time you put shaving cream all over my lips while I slept and sprinkled it with cinnamon. Who even does that?"

Elliot hysterically laughs, while Mom lets him go, her rounded eyes flying between my brother and me. "When did this insanity happen?"

"While you were at work one morning." *I glare at my brother, remembering how pissed I was when I sneezed, and the cream flew into my mouth. He ran so fast while I chased him, shaving cream dripping down to the floor.*

"I always miss the good stuff." *Mom frowns.*

"How about we get some shaving cream now and re-create the scene, hmm, Elliot?" *My eyes zero in on my brother.* "But this time, it's your ass who's grass."

Elliot gets ready to run.

"Oh, stop, you two," Mom chides. "You're leaving tomorrow for two ridiculous months," she says to me. "Why don't the three of us have a nice day at home with a movie, too much popcorn, and lots of ice cream?"

"Okay, but I pick the movie," I say.

"Um, no!" Elliot grimaces. "I'm not sitting through some stupid chick movie."

"It's called a chick flick, doofus."

"Whatever it's called, I'm not watching it."

"I wasn't even going to pick a girlie one, relax. Sheesh."

"Fine. Whatever. Pick something good."

"I'll make the popcorn." Mom takes a step back, heading for the stairs. "Hopefully that'll shut both of you up for a while."

"Hey!" we both mutter in unison while she grins facetiously, waving as she disappears down the stairs.

∞

That was the second to last time I saw them before I left in my Jeep the next morning, all smiles, my two friends waving to my mom and brother as we drove away. I never thought that would be the last time we were all together.

They're states away from where I am. I'm to have no contact with them, or Robby and I will be killed. I'd cut my own throat before I let anything happen to my son.

My focus is on doing whatever they say and trying to find a way to get Robby away from their grip, and eventually run away with him.

I realize that dream is far-fetched, but if I don't visualize our escape, if I don't try to come up with some kind of plan, I'll feel even more hopeless than I do already. But how? How could I not only get away, but save my son in the process?

They only allow me to see him once a month at an undisclosed location, and that only began when I tried to kill myself shortly after he was taken from me. They have a driver pick me up, put a hood and blindfold over my eyes and take me to where he is. Every time it's a different place, and every time I only get to see him and hold him for ten minutes. Once they say we have to go, Robby cries so hard, while I sob on the floor as one man in a mask drags him away, and another pulls on my body, my soul already gone.

It's like a never-ending wound, festering, eating into the agony that's always building with a fresh coat of pain.

I have no one. No real friends. No boyfriend. And even if I were allowed to have a man in my life, who'd want me anyway? I sleep with men for money. I can't fall in love.

Love. It's laughable really. How would a man feel, knowing what I've done? What I have to do? What I'm not allowed to stop doing?

The center of my chest burns from the shame, from the disgust of my actions, even when I don't have a say.

I've been drugged. I've been beaten by those who pay to do whatever they want to me. They've captured my tears, the cries, begging them to stop, but they never do. They rather enjoy my suffering.

After a while, I learned to stopped screaming, not giving them what they wanted. They'd hurt me harder because of it, hoping to break me, but my mind went somewhere else. Somewhere they aren't. Somewhere beautiful. Somewhere my son and I can be together, along with my mom and Elliot. We're happy, watching a movie with too much popcorn and lots of ice cream. Yeah, that's what we do. Maybe, one day, we can actually do it. Together.

Something tickles my cheeks, and when I look into the mirror, sitting in the dressing room, I realize I've been crying. I don't even cry loudly anymore. I haven't been able to do that for years. The tears sometimes come silently, but I rarely feel them on my face or in my heart. It's like I've become numb. And maybe that's a good thing.

So whoever this Patrick is, however nice he seems, I need to stay numb. I can't develop any sort of feelings for any man, friendship or otherwise. There's no point. I can't tell him who I am. I can't be with him. He's nothing but a customer, a gorgeous customer, but still, someone I can't know.

Patrick, with his thick, mahogany strands and strong jaw, is nothing more than any other man whose money is the only thing I'm after. It's the only way to keep my enemies happy. He can have what he pays for and nothing else.

My heart seizes in my chest when I remember how he looked at me, those emerald eyes analyzing me as though burrowing into my brain, into my heart—it was unnerving.

He read me like an open book, as though he's the one who typed the pages. No matter how badly I wanted to convince him that he was wrong, it's like he knew my thoughts. *Knew me.*

Was I really that easy to read? Could the monsters see it all too? Or are they not even paying attention?

We hate them, but we pretend we don't. We have to pretend, or we die.

Patrick may think he knows me, but there's so much he never will. I won't allow him to. Those chapters have been burned, their ashes forever gone.

Just like I am.

ENZO

THREE

The next day, I return to the strip club as promised, but without my brother this time. I don't want him to know about my thing with Joelle yet. What he doesn't know can't hurt him.

As soon as I walk into Tips and Tricks, I see her. There are three stages here, and she's in the middle one, her eyes closed, a yellow sparkling bikini top and a matching thong molded to her curves.

Goddamn. I know I told myself I'm not into this shit, but I can't stop staring at her. She dances like no one's watching. The music is her only spectator as she grabs the pole, wrapping her thighs around it, gliding down as though making love to it.

She mesmerizes me without even trying.

Every bastard here has his eyes set on her. They all want her. They're all fantasizing about her body. I flex my jaw, a fist forming at my side as I lower myself into an empty leather sofa.

She spins, the pole sandwiched between her ass cheeks as she rocks her hips to the sultry beat, her back to her audience. Her hands drift behind her, unclasping the damn bra that I want to immediately slap back on her body.

No one should see her. No one but me.

Fucking hell. I've never felt an ounce of jealousy over any other woman. It's not something I ever thought I was even capable of. But here I am, needing to carve out the eyes of every man here.

But I can't. She's not mine. I have no damn right to be jealous. But I am. So fucking jealous. I can literally feel it weighing me down.

Her bra drifts to the floor and then she twirls, her round tits, those deep rosy nipples for all to see. The men start whistling as she winks, spinning around the pole, facing her fans.

I need out of here. This was a fucking mistake. I don't need to know her. I don't want her friendship or whatever the fuck I said to her.

I'm not here to help some woman who works for our enemy. We're here to destroy them. That's where my focus should be. But as I stand up to go, she catches my eyes from across the room.

Her lips part, her brows lifting a fraction, and it's as though I could hear her intake of breath. She stops moving, her fingertips still wrapped around the pole.

I can't seem to look away either, caught in a daze. With every other woman I've been with, and there have been way too many to count, I never cared. There was no connection. Never anything besides some good fucking. But her, I don't know. I'm drowning in her eyes, getting lost, and nothing has ever felt this good.

The men start booing, and that causes her to wake up, mouthing *sorry* before picking up her dance again. I instantly want to pick up a bottle and bash it over every one of their heads for insulting her, but that would cause quite the scene.

I head for the bar, not wanting to see her dancing for those assholes, but not being able to leave either.

I lift a finger, calling over the bartender.

"Hey, what can I get you?" a young brunette asks, her cropped top barely covering her.

"Whiskey. Neat."

"Coming right up." She winks, but I ignore it.

While she gets me that drink, the song ends, and I don't even want to see if Joelle's dancing to the next one.

The bartender returns with my order. "Enjoy." The flirtatious undertone is there, but it does nothing for me, and she's definitely the kind of woman I'd fuck.

"Thanks," I mutter, leaving a tip.

"I thought you left," a voice says from behind me, the one belonging to the woman I should want nothing to do with.

I down the liquor in one shot, needing the burn to sustain me, to keep me from grabbing that delicate neck of hers and kissing her like I've wanted to from the moment we met.

I push the glass down on the bar, still giving her my back.

"Are you mad at me?" she continues, her hand snaking around to my front, riding up my abs, those long nails running over each one. Her body moves closer now, her tits splayed over my shirt. "I bet I can make you feel better, handsome."

My palm catches her wrist, gripping firm, yet softly, as I sharply turn. "What the fuck is this?" I snap, barely containing my wrath. She's treating me like all the rest of them. Like I'm here for her pussy. Like this is some game.

She tilts her head to the side. "What do you mean?" But that little sexy smirk tells me she knows exactly what I'm talking about.

I lower my mouth so close to hers, I bet she can taste my liquor on her tongue. "I'm not here to be treated like your groupie."

She scoffs, trying to yank her hand out of my grasp, narrowing her gaze. I flash her a glare, finally allowing her to take her hand back.

"I thought you came today to buy a dance, or did you change your mind?" There's a spark lighting a path in her eyes, making my cock throb. That's what I want to see—fragments of the real her, not whoever she pretends to be for the crowd.

"I didn't change my mind." My tone's clipped, wanting my hands on her, wanting to know the sounds she makes when a man makes her feel really good. But for the first time in my life, I'm not after that. The goal is to be her friend, to get her to trust me enough to confide in me so that I can help her.

"So, what kind of dance would you like?" She pops a brow. "A private one?"

"How much?"

"A grand for thirty minutes."

I cross my arms over my black, long-sleeved T-shirt. "I'll take an hour."

"There's so much we can do in an hour." Her red-painted lips twist into a smile. "You sure there's nothing else I can do for you in all that time?"

A taunting chuckle breaks from my chest before my palm dives for the back of her neck, pulling her to my lips. "Are you offering me your pussy?" My other hand slips to her hip, fingers squeezing the hard edges and the softness in between. "Is that what's for sale?"

Her fingers brush over my shoulder, settling on the back of my head, her sharp nails biting into my scalp as she draws away just enough to look into my eyes. "Everything's for sale if the price is right."

Why are you doing this? Why the fuck are you lying to me as though this is what you want?

But even if I were to ask, she wouldn't tell me the truth. She doesn't trust me yet, but she will. She and I will get to know each other, and I will learn everything I need to.

"We'll start with a dance…" My mouth nears hers, and I wonder what she really tastes like when she drops that façade. "Then we'll see where it goes."

Her lips tip upward, her eyes delving into mine, unrelenting, tightening with my own ruthless gaze.

She grabs my hand, softness enveloping my calloused fingers. "Come with me." I follow as she pulls me into the back, a dimly lit area with multiple curtained-off rooms greeting us.

She heads for the one that's empty, a long L-shaped upholstered sofa on one side, with a circular table beside it, and a pole all the way across. She closes off the curtains, picking up a bottle from the bar in the corner.

"Have a seat." She points to the sofa. "Don't be shy."

The music from the main area travels through the speakers in the ceiling above as she saunters over to where I still stand, the bottle in her palm, my fist clenched at my side.

"You don't have to take off your clothes for me, Joelle." My attention wanders to her face, those full lips, those high cheekbones. She's too beautiful to be stuck doing this. "I'll help you, whatever you need."

Damn it. It's like I can't turn it off, wanting to rescue her and shit. What the hell is wrong with me? Maybe I read her wrong. Maybe she wants this.

She palms my chest, her gaze threading with mine, and then she pushes me down onto the leather below. I don't resist. I go down willingly. Her body settles over my thighs, the bottle tipped to her lips as she takes a long sip, her eyes never leaving mine.

"Stop worrying about me." She flashes me a serious look. "Here." And then the tip of the bottle is at my mouth as she lifts it up. "Maybe this will help relax you."

I jerk the bottle away from her as soon as the first taste of whiskey trickles down my throat, drifting with a steady burn. I take another sip before shifting forward, a hand winding around her back as I drop the liquor down onto the table to my right.

As soon as the glass hits the surface, both my hands are laced through her hair, fisting, pulling, yanking roughly as I groan with desire clinging to every messed-up inch of me.

My cock is hardened steel as I look up to find her gaze tangled with need, the same web I'm trapped in. When she lets out a sensual exhale, her head falling back, I arch my hips in between her, wanting inside.

The song changes, the beat turning sensual, and so do her hips. She circles them around me, my hard-on jerking from the way she moves, from the way she looks at me.

I ease a fraction, lowering her face to mine, her lips brushing over my mouth, my hands around each one of her hips now as she rocks against me.

"Are you doing this because you want to or because you have to?" I need to know. This only works if she wants it.

Her features soften, her gaze wandering between my eyes and my lap as her hands go to her bra.

I find them, clutching both in my large palm.

"No," I insist, edging my hand up her back until the span of my palm is around her neck. Lowering her so close, I could kiss her right now. "Answer me, Joelle. Tell me if you want this. I need to hear it. And don't you lie."

Her movements slow.

"I'll still give you the money even if you stop. I promise." My fingers snake through her hair, holding her tightly to me. "I don't know what it is about you, but I just... I don't know..."

"Patrick, I—" Her breaths fall over my mouth, her lower lip stroking over mine. "This is my job." She tries to push herself back, but I don't let her. She can say whatever she wants just like this, where I can taste her words, wanting to taste the rest of her in between. "This is what I do. I don't know you and you don't know me, and honestly, you don't want to know me." She pauses. "I'm not a good person. If you knew the kind of stuff I've done, you'd probably never want to see me again."

"None of us are good, Joelle. We've all done things we're not proud of." I slip my palm up to her cheek, cupping her gently like I've been wanting to, and instead of recoiling, she burrows further into my touch. "Whatever you had to do, I'd never judge you for it. Because I bet you anything, I've done worse."

Taking in a long breath, she lets out a sad laugh. "I don't know why, but I believe you."

"You should." I stroke her full lips with mine. "I don't lie."

She forces a long sigh, pushing away from me, and this time, I let her go.

"I've never had a dance at a place like this before." I attempt to lighten the mood. "You'd be my first."

"You mean you've never had a stripper grinding on your dick at a fancy club before?" She giggles all sweet. "I'm flattered."

A deep-chested chuckle breaks free with a groan as she shifts over me, my cock straining, my lower lip trapped between my teeth, forgetting where we are and why she's really on top of me. "I never wanted one before you," I admit. "But I like the way you dance, Joelle. I don't want you to do it for me because it's your job,

I want you to do it because you want to." My hands fall to her hips, my thumbs massaging with slow circles. "So, until that moment happens, when I come here, we talk. We hang out. That's it. And you get to keep your clothes on."

A harsh exhale rushes out of her chest. "Patrick," she whispers, fear looping in her voice, on her face. "They'll know."

"Are there cameras in here?"

She shakes her head. "Only in the hall."

"Then they won't know. I won't stay a minute past my time, and they'll still get their money. On top of that, I'll pay you two grand each time I come here, and every penny will be yours. Got it?"

"Why are you doing this?" Her brows slant into a frown as her gaze falls tenderly to mine. She palms the side of my neck, my pulse loudly thrashing in my ears, my heart weak for this woman.

She wakes up every part of me. The man. The boy. The hero. And the villain. With her, I'm all of them at the same time.

I shrug. "My brother once met a man, a long time ago, who helped us when we really needed it. I have a feeling you need that too."

"I do," she breathes. It's the first real thing she's said, and the way she says it, the shudder in her voice, goddamn, it breaks me as a man.

"You have no idea how badly I want to kiss you." A hand slides up her spine, fingers parting through the luscious curtain of her hair, weaving deeper as I lean her forehead to mine.

"Then do it." Her tone lowers with a tremble, the words skating past my lips. "It's been a while since a man kissed me. Really kissed me. Really looked at me the way you do."

"Fuck, Joelle. I want to." I yank her back, my control practically breaking. "I want to so badly, baby, but I can't."

"I figured." She scoffs, trying to push off my lap, but I don't let her, gripping her hips, and keeping her just where she is. "A guy like you would never want a girl like me, who does the things I do."

With my palms returning to her waist, I fasten them tighter. "You think I don't want to kiss you because I'm afraid of where your mouth has been?"

She shrugs, avoiding me.

"You're damn beautiful, you know that, and even more irresistible when you're doing that thing with your lip."

"What thing?" She narrows a playful gaze, popping up her chin.

"You know what thing." My fingers go to her mouth, and I place each one of my thumbs at the corners and pull down. "That."

"It's called a pout." She rolls her eyes on a laugh, shoving my hands away, then I'm laughing too, grabbing both her wrists as she inadvertently rubs her pussy over my cock while she moves. As she does, she moans. It's low, but goddamn I heard it, and nothing ever sounded so good.

Her eyes widen as she realizes what she did, that awareness thickening the air around us, the addiction, the attraction building in my body, in hers too. I know it's there.

If I had just met her, I probably would've fucked her already, but I can't. She wouldn't be like the rest, a random hookup, a booty call I need just to get off. I wouldn't use her to hide the torment stitched onto my soul. With her, I'd feel. For once, I'd feel something. Something real. Something worthy.

And I want that. Maybe my heart is capable of beating for someone else, but now isn't the right time.

My life's been riddled with too much loss. I've never wanted to tie myself to someone else—another person to care about, only to lose them, like we lost our family.

Danger is all around me, too great to ever involve a woman I'd grow to care for. Once our enemies realize we're alive, they'll do whatever they can to cause us pain, and what better way than through the women we love. Joelle will be safer never being with me.

"I'm sorry. I...ahh, should go," she stammers, trying to wriggle her way out of my lap, her cheeks flushed with what I think is embarrassment from that sexy damn moan she gave me.

"I didn't say you could go." I run my palm up and down her back, thrusting my hips up so she can feel the effect she has on me.

She bites into the corner of her lower lip, squeezing her thighs around mine.

"Any man would be lucky to have you, you know that, right?" My hand coasts up to the back of her head, my fingers twining in the soft strands of her hair. "But I'm not that man. There's too much in my life that I wouldn't want to harm you, to touch even a single hair on your beautiful head. That's the only reason I can't kiss you. Because if I do, I'm gonna want more." I let my lips fall against her cheek, just keeping them there. I breathe her in with a gradual close of my eyes. "More of you. Of this." I suck in a deep breath as she whimpers, her hips rolling over me, my balls aching to feel her come undone.

"I'm fighting so damn hard not to rip off your clothes and fuck you like the animal I am." I gaze up, her lips parting with a weighty exhale. "But you're different from the other women I drown in to forget the darkness. You're the kind of woman who'd help me find the light."

I bow my hips, rougher this time, her eyes sinking into mine, my other hand closing in around her delicate throat.

"Don't do that," she gasps with a tremor in her voice, her ass running circles over me.

"I'm not doing anything," I strain, my cock growing harder the more she glides her pussy over it. "You are. You're in control, baby. Take what you need."

I fist her hair, pushing her chest toward my mouth, kissing the spot in between her tits. "Take it all. Use me," I growl. "Make yourself come."

"I can't," she cries, but it's not a denial, she's trying to convince herself.

I trail kisses down her neck, sucking on her skin. "You can. I'd enjoy watching you, knowing it's me you're using to do it."

"Patrick, you don't under—oh God…" She licks her lips, unable to stop her hips from moving, her eyelids fluttering, her mouth forming a perfect O.

"Whatever is holding you back, forget it all. What matters is what we're both feeling right now."

I drive my cock deeper, rocking against her, giving her something I know she needs.

"Yes, please don't stop," she cries, her breathing scattered, her fingernails digging into my shoulders.

I can't tear my eyes away from her face, her features twisted with pleasure, her exhales rapidly falling from her lips.

She looks like a fallen angel, corrupted by the devil on earth. And I am him. In my heart. In my soul. There's endless darkness there, too great to drive away, even by someone as beautiful as her.

She rolls her hips faster, my painfully throbbing hard-on straining heavily inside these damn jeans. "I want you so goddamn bad. I want to watch my cock stretch your sweet pussy with every damn inch."

"Oh fuck," she cries. "I'm so close." Her face drops to the spot where my neck meets my shoulder. Her lips shuddering against my skin is the most erotic damn thing I've ever experienced.

I grab the back of her neck, yanking her away, gritting my teeth as her gaze seeps into mine, her brows pinched tightly.

"You want that too, don't you, baby? Wanna feel me inside you?"

"Ye-yes." The words fall with a shudder, her hips gliding faster.

"That's it," I urge. "Give it to me. Let me hear you come."

"Oh God, Pat—"

"Enzo," I correct. "Call me Enzo. That name is my real one, and it's only for you."

There's confusion and lust riddled on her face, but all I know is I don't want someone else's name on her lips. The only one that belongs there is mine.

"Enzo..." She hums my name like a song, her mouth slipping closer, her lips fluttering over my own. "I'm, I'm—"

Her words die out as I take over, my palm still around the back of her neck, my eyes on her as I shift, pounding harder, deeper, not giving her an inch to move out of my grasp. She screams my name, the music too loud for anyone to hear her.

Her body spasms, again and again, and once she's gone still, I round both arms around the small of her back and hold her. I just hold her close, our hearts beating against one another.

Right now, within these bare walls, we're just two people held together by time and space. Unbreakable. Yet utterly alone.

JOELLE

He left over an hour ago, the man with two names, a mystery like the rest of him seems to be. I still can't forget the moment we shared.

I don't think he realizes the magnitude of it. Why would he? I'm sure he's made plenty of women come, their bodies willing, wanting. But not me. I've not wanted anyone since I was taken when I was nineteen.

The men who touch me, they don't do it for my pleasure. They're nothing but a job I'm forced into. The first few times, I cried during and after. I cried so long, they beat me for it. But soon, my mind and body became numb. It was my only way of escaping the misery, the intrusion into my body and my heart.

I don't even touch myself, not since it all began. Whenever I've tried, my hands would tremble, my body growing ice cold, freezing my desire until the idea became detestable, reminding me of the shame and disgust pervading my body. But with Enzo, I wasn't thinking. For once—I felt.

Him.

Myself.

My body.

I felt it all.

I forgot who I was. Who I was made into.

I wasn't a whore. A slut.

With him, I was just a woman crushing on a man whose eyes looked at me like they saw me—the girl I used to be, instead of the woman I am now.

There wasn't simply a craving behind his gaze. I recognize that look easily. No, Enzo looked at me like a sculptor looks at his creation, like a painter looks at his model. Whoever he is, Enzo, Patrick, someone in between, it doesn't matter. He's not like them. He can't be.

I don't know why he likes me, but he does. And after the way he made me feel today, I want more of that. I want him to look at me that way again, just once more if that's all I can have.

I want him to help me forget where I am and what I do. I want him to help me remember who I was. And maybe I could remember her. Be her again. Maybe he can pull her out. Maybe he can save her.

If only.

JOELLE

FOUR

"Put this on," a man who was sent to pick me up the following day says, scratching his long gray beard specked with brown. "The boss wants you in this dress and those heels you wore last time."

I nod, picking up a black mini dress that will barely cover my ass, the glistening silver high heels lying on the floor beside it. I pick that up too, taking both to the bathroom.

"Where the fuck you think you're goin'?" His voice crawls with venom and my entire body breaks into hives, like it's swarming with ants.

I turn, rapid heartbeats firing off in my chest. "I'm gonna go change."

"Yeah…" A callous grin creeps up his face. "Right here." I swallow against the bile slamming into my stomach, slithering up my throat.

"I prefer to change in the bathroom."

He laughs, his shoulders rolling. "You *prefer*." He chuckles louder. "Bitch, take your fucking clothes off. I'll get to see your cunt later anyway, but at least right now, it's all mine."

My pulse thrashes with hard spasms as I drop the clothes, and they tumble to the floor.

It's just another job. He's just another customer.

My fingers fall to my leggings, and I blink back the tears piercing into my eyes.

Don't show him your pain.

I suck in an inaudible breath, sliding my pants down to my hips. He parks himself on my sofa, spreading his thighs wide, as wide as the grin he still wears.

He lifts a finger, pointing it in between his legs. I know what he wants. There's no point in fighting it. He'll get what he wants anyway.

Fighting has gotten me nothing but wounds, both the ones that go away and the ones that stay, scars I'll carry for as long as I'm alive.

I move to stand in between him, dragging my underwear and pants all the way down my legs, trying hard not to bend my chest close to his. Disgust pools into my empty stomach, nausea swirling, battling to get out.

Fight it.

Be strong.

I inhale low, pulling a breath of healing. Of salvation. They can't have my suffering. Not ever.

"Your shirt. Let's go," he chides, his eyes narrowing. He waits for me to bare myself fully, knowing I despise every moment. But I'm just a whore. That's all he sees.

When the shirt is off my body, his eyes roam every inch of me, and unlike Enzo, he looks at me like I'm a shiny object made just for him to enjoy.

"Mmm, mmm, mmm. It's no wonder the boss fetches top dollar for you." His hand reaches for my hip, his fingers creeping up and down, my skin prickling with dread.

The back of my nose burns with tears I won't shed, so heavy, it engulfs me. But I can't. I don't cry. Not for them.

"Turn around," he demands. "I want to see your ass."

I do what he says, and that's when I feel his sweaty palm groping my ass cheek, twisting harshly like I'm not a person but a thing he can manipulate however he likes.

"Bend over."

I choke on his words. "We'll be late. Faro will be mad," I try to convince him, hoping it scares him enough to leave me alone.

"You're not here to have opinions, Joelle. Don't worry about him. He told me I can test drive you for myself."

No.

My heart pounds harder, faster, making me sick all over again. I tremble where I stand, feeling so alone.

He rises, his hand in my hair, yanking hard. "I said, bend the fuck over before I grow impatient."

When I refuse to move from the sheer shock of what's about to happen, he flips me around and slaps me hard. My entire face burns. I grit my teeth, not giving him the satisfaction of knowing he hurt me.

"You whores never learn, huh? Don't worry, I'm gonna teach you some manners."

He grabs me around the throat and throws me onto the floor. My body hits the wooden floorboards with a heavy impact, and I stifle the whimper from the pain to my back.

His belt buckle clacks as he undoes it, zippering down his jeans once the belt hits the floor.

"Face down." His tone is clipped. "And don't make me ask again. Don't want to mess up that pretty face. Not that the customers will care with a body like that." He laughs with such hideousness, I flinch.

I spin around, doing what he wants. There are two kinds of men who come to fuck women like me. Those who want to look at me, wanting some weird connection, or those who want to treat me like a slut.

With me, all their desires can be achieved. That's what I'm there for. Less than human. A toy. I'm there to serve, and I do it well. I act. I perform. But right now, I can't seem to become that person.

As I lie there, facedown, staring at the floor, I think of Enzo. I think of the man who looked at me like I meant a damn, and as the savage behind me roughly enters my body, a tear rolls down my cheek.

He grunts as he clutches my hair, and the tears trickle only for me to be their witness, falling silently down onto the floor. I don't make a sound. Not of pleasure. Not of anything. I never do, not even when I'm crying alone. The droplets of agony, they don't stop. They leak for the life I once thought I'd have, for the love and family I'll never get to experience. They leak for the young girl I once was.

Women like me don't get a happily ever after. Our life is riddled with never-ending pain. If only I had listened to my mother and not left that day. What would my life be like now? Would I have had a family? A loving husband?

But I wouldn't have Robby, would I? And even still, I'd give it all back because all that boy has known is pure evil. That's not a life I'd want for my sweet baby. I wish I died when they first took me. I wish I could go back and make them injure me badly enough that I wasn't here right now.

The man groans as his pace increases, while I wish I could crawl into a hole and die.

What would Enzo think of me now? He'd never want who I really am. He thinks he knows me, but he doesn't know a damn thing.

The man is finally done, the sound of his zipper echoing through the hollowness of my heart.

"Get dressed. We're gonna be late."

I quickly wipe the tears away, rising off the floor, and grabbing the dress and shoes I left behind.

"Fix your damn face!" he barks, baring his teeth. "You look like fucking shit." He rushes toward me, gripping my hair. "You stupid bitch, were you crying, knowing we have clients to see?" He bares his teeth. "I should kill you for this."

"You'd be doing me a favor. And you know what the best part would be?" I grin into his smug face.

"What?" His stare widens with a flare of his nostrils.

"Knowing Faro would kill you too."

He shoots me a venomous look, his chest expanding while I stare at him unblinking. He knows I'm right. Faro has done it before when one of his men played a little too rough with one of us.

We're money, and Faro doesn't like anyone messing with his money. His one brother, Agnelo, is the one in charge of the women, but Faro is the actual boss. What he says, goes. He always shows his face at their private sex club, which is where this asshole is gonna take me.

There, we do everything. Anything the people pay for.

Shows. Privates. The sickest things one can imagine.

Some of the girls are regulars there, while others, like me, pull double duty. We go when we're needed, when we're specifically asked for.

I rush into the bathroom with the shoes and dress in hand, finally able to be alone. I quickly put on the clothes, slipping into the heels before looking at myself in the small oval mirror.

The house isn't big. It's a two-bed, one-bath home, which I recently shared with Laina, my roommate, a girl who was taken around the same time as me. But a few months ago, she disappeared.

When I once asked the men who drive me to the club about her, they said she won't be coming back anymore, that if I knew what was good for me, I wouldn't ask any questions.

I know when not to be stupid. I know she's dead. She has to be. Why else wouldn't she come back? They wouldn't house her anywhere else. There'd be no reason to. She and I didn't talk about anything we weren't supposed to, so why kill her? If they heard anything through one of the cameras, we'd both be dead. Something must've happened while she was working.

The club is a place full of men with dangerous appetites. They could've done something to Laina, and then Faro could've ordered her body to be disposed of.

There's a loud bang on the door, and I startle with a gasp.

"Hurry the fuck up!" the man hollers. "If you're not out in one damn minute, looking as good as you did when I first came in, you're going to answer to the boss."

My fingers fumble when I reach for my makeup inside the drawer. I rip off some of the toilet paper and wet it in the sink, wiping off the mascara stains under my eyes, applying a fresh coat before adding some concealer and liner to my lower lashes. I look as good as I can.

He bangs again, louder this time. I open the door just as he's about to raise his voice. As soon as he sees me, he assesses me for imperfections. "That'll do." In his fist is a black hood I'm all too familiar with, along with a black eye mask.

"Put it on." He holds out his hand and I take the mask, slipping it around my eyes, the world turning pitch black. His hands are on my face now as he slips the hood over me, ensuring I see nothing as he grabs my upper arm and drags me out of the house.

The chill of the evening violently hits my body. I shiver, my nipples beading as the door of his car clicks open and he throws me roughly inside.

The leather's cold beneath my thighs and it practically turns my body into ice as I tremble, wrapping my arms around myself.

The door bangs to a close, then another, and a few seconds later, the car speeds down the road. Sharp turns and uneven gravel send my body side to side, the black nothingness making the rough drive even scarier. The fear of dying overwhelms me.

I think of my son, wondering where he is, who he's with. The only thing Agnelo told me was that Robby wouldn't be kept in a cage as long as I obeyed.

I can't get much out of my son when we see each other for those short minutes, especially with the men listening. But once, when we hugged, I asked if he's in a house and he whispered, *yes*.

I was relieved, as relieved as I could be, but I still don't know what is being done to him. Who has my son? My heart squeezes in my chest like brick after brick of heaviness sitting over it. I'll never stop worrying about him. I don't know how to.

The car stops and my stomach sinks with heavy dread. I push against the tightening in my throat just as a door shuts with a loud thud and footsteps creep closer. The cold air greets me once more, a rough hand pulling me out, and I almost stumble, catching myself.

"Let's go," the asshole says, jerking me.

When his feet move, the footfalls crunching over the gravel, mine do too. I fight the shudder rolling up my arms as he leads me to hell, a door creaking until the frigid air is replaced by a warm current and sounds of people talking in hushed conversations drifting from all around once we make it down a flight of stairs.

The man's hands are on my face again as he pulls off the hood and blindfold. My eyes adjust to the sight before me, the dimmed lighting, the men with women beside them.

As we move further in, I see the children. I turn away with a cry, unable to stomach the sight of their faces, the pain behind their eyes. It's permanently sewn into my heart. Some of them are as young as my Robby. Tears swell into my eyes when I think about all that they've endured in their short lives. The horrors they've witnessed. Their poor families.

"You're entertaining three tonight." He looks over his shoulder as he says that. "They're gonna share you and they won't be as gentle as me." A vile sneer slithers to his mouth.

My gut churns, panic setting in, the air escaping my lungs in a hurry as I try to get it back. I should be used to this. The violation. The abuse. But every time, it's as though it's happening for the first time.

I'm still that girl who ran on the road, away from the men who were about to alter her entire future. Still the girl who was raped by a man who gave her a son, then took him away. Still the girl who screamed for help as multiple men took turns day after day.

I'm her and she's me. We're one and the same. And I don't know who's worse off. The girl who didn't know what was about to happen or the woman who now does.

I enter a room where three men sit, their expensive black suits and loafers matching the black upholstered leather sofa. They're only a little older than I am, maybe in their late thirties.

As soon as they see me, they rise, their sinister smiles like multiple daggers to my chest. I bleed, yet they can't see the droplets spilling from my flesh, from my very existence.

The man who brought me here shuts the door behind him, and I'm alone now. With them. The men who hold the power.

Each one takes a menacing step closer, a shot glass in the hand of the one in the middle, his eyes as dark as his soul.

"Let's have some fun, boys," he tells the others. "I paid for the full package."

And then, their hands are everywhere.

ENZO

FIVE

I've never actually looked forward to hanging out with a girl before. Normally, they call, or I call. We fuck, then we're done. I don't know them, not really. And they sure as hell don't know me. They know whatever I allow them to know, and it ain't much.

With Joelle, it's different. I want to see her, and it isn't for sex. It's her. I want to see *her*. Even if it's only at her job. I'll take whatever I can get.

I park my car in the strip club lot, step out, and walk over to the bouncer who lets me in. Continuing inside, I don't see Joelle at first, scanning the whole damn place.

Maybe she's on break or some shit. I march over to an empty sofa, and as I'm about to take a seat, I spot her in the far corner by the back. But she's not alone. She's with a man.

His palm grips her upper arm, his face hard, brows tight, mouth moving a mile a minute while she remains quiet.

My feet are already moving, needing to rip his beard off his damn face and feed it to his corpse. He dares to put his hands on her? It won't go unanswered.

"Drop your fucking hand off her," I bark out, practically growling like a damn animal. She pivots right, finding me marching up, her stare growing wide.

She shakes her head a little, mouthing *no*, but I ignore it. I don't know who this man is, but he won't be touching her. Ever again.

The asshole doesn't drop his hold. He tightens it instead, and she flinches.

He's gonna die. Slowly.

"Hey, pal. This is a business conversation," he mocks with a tilt of his upper lip, too much hostility in his tone. "Why don't you take a hike, huh? She's not in service right now."

"Fuck, man." I scoff with a shake of my head. "It's like you're asking to die."

He finally releases her, a glare radiating from him as he moves in on me, his face nearing mine. Luckily he let her go when he did, because I was about to slice his throat open like a fountain with the knife in my pocket. "Are you threatening me, you piece of shit?"

I grin so wide it fucking aches, and as soon as his fist comes at me, I grab it, twisting it hard as he lets out a groan. Violence fills my heart, not seeing a man, but prey. *My* prey.

"No!" Joelle pleads, her hand on my shoulder, her softness tearing through the harshness soaking my veins. "Please don't do this." Her warm exhales fall over my neck, her words a whisper in my ear. "I work for him. They'll hurt me if you hurt him. You have to let him go. Do it for me. I'm begging you!"

Her safety, that's the only reason I drop this asshole's hand.

He grumbles in pain, rubbing his wrist, eyeing me with a snarl, about to come at me until Joelle palms his chest.

"Stop it!" she tells him. "He's a high-paying customer. You think the boss is gonna want you to mess him up? Why don't you think with your brain for a change?"

"Bitch, you think you can talk to me like that?" He readies a palm, intending to slap her, but I pin him with a growl, putting myself right in front of him.

I should end him. I can make it quick. Somewhere quiet where no one sees me. She wouldn't even know.

"You ever call her a bitch again, I will cut that tongue from your mouth."

"This fucking guy." He laughs. "He's still talking."

"Patrick. You're here for a private dance, right?"

"Yeah," I say, my eyes still on this man. "Let's go." *Before you see what I'm truly capable of.*

She grabs my hand, pulling me backward and I move with her.

"I'll see you around, pal," he spits out, staring, and the hint of that threat has me wanting to finish what I started. I begin pulling out of her grasp, glaring back at the fucker.

"Don't, Enzo. Come on, forget him. For me."

My breathing quickens, and I focus on her to stop myself from killing him. The only reason he isn't dead is because of her. When I eliminate them all, and I will, I'll do it when my need to spill their blood doesn't affect her.

Finally, turning around, we head to the back. "How the hell could I forget him putting his fucking hands on you, talking to you like that?" We step into an unoccupied private room, and she closes the curtain.

"If I'm used to it, then you'll have to learn to tolerate it too."

"Fuck that!" My palm tightens over her cheek. "I'll never allow anyone to speak to you that way." She places her hand over mine, a haunted look in her eyes.

"What are they doing to you, Joelle? Don't lie to me."

She pulls in a long inhale, her body practically wilting. "Why can't you just let things go?" She bows her head. "I don't want to lie to you." Her gaze finds mine again, her eyes bleak. "But I can't talk about it. So just drop it, okay?"

There's too much pain clouding the features of her face. The truth she won't admit is there, submerging her in hell. I want to take it all away, to end the lives of every single one who's made her feel this way.

"Come," she says softly, dragging me to the sofa.

I attempt to steady my racing heart, my barraging breaths. She needs that. I know she does. We sit side by side, her fidgeting with her long, red fingernails, me bouncing my foot on the floor like a damn lunatic.

"Hey." She draws my focus to her, her palm landing on my knee like a lightning bolt, zapping me to life.

"Yeah, baby?"

Her eyes, that angelic face, her grip around me, the need to be her protector, to save her, it's all there.

Why her? What makes her so special?

Who the fuck knows? We can't control how we feel about someone. Sometimes feelings, they just happen, unexpectedly. And meeting her, wanting to know her, it's unexpected all right.

"I'm your baby now? I thought you were looking for just a friend." A smile tugs at her mouth as she comes to straddle me, draping her arms over each of my shoulders. Her whole face lights up, and fuck, it makes me want to be a better man, to make her look this way every day, knowing I did that.

I snicker. "I call all my friends baby."

She lets out a raspy giggle that goes right to my cock.

I curl my arm around her back and pull her closer, staring up at her. "You're my favorite though."

"Oh yeah?" She bites her lower lip on a laugh. "You've got a hierarchy of babies?"

"Mm-hmm, and you're at the top of the list. You're on top of a lot of my lists."

"Lucky me. Or is that what you tell all the girls?" Her gaze flirts with mine, her voice dancing with an erotic current that makes me hungry for more.

"Only the pretty ones," I tease, my lips twitching with amusement. "But you're more than just pretty, you're damn special. I may not know you well, but I can't explain wanting to be around you." I let the pad of my thumb brush over her mouth, locking her gaze with mine. "I never felt that shit before, never wanted it. Not until you. And that's the damn truth, baby girl."

She forces her blue gaze down to my chest, like she's trying to hide that she feels the same.

"Look at me," I demand, softly nudging her chin up with the back of my fingers. "Don't hide."

This time she doesn't.

"I've never even hung out with a girl before, unless I was fucking her," I confess, and for once, I'm afraid of being judged for it. "And I *do* want to fuck you, by the way, you know, in case you get some weird-ass ideas. *Again*." I shoot her one of my crooked grins.

Her eyes roll and she laughs. "Duly noted."

Lifting her hand, my lips land on the center of her palm, just as she holds my cheek with the other, her mouth lowering there with a tender kiss.

I pull in a harsh breath. "That's the first time I've ever been kissed like that." I throw in another confession. "That's officially my favorite kiss."

"I'm sure you've had way better kisses than that." Her voice goes low and raspy.

"Nah. None of them meant shit." I roll my fingers up her spine, curving them into her hair, holding back a groan, my cock throbbing. "Not until you."

She shuts her eyes, her brows pulling with…with what? Regret? I'm too damn afraid to ask. She doesn't even know me, or everything I'm going to do in the name of my family. She's sitting with a monster, and she doesn't recognize his face.

Will she fear me? Hate me? I guess we'll find out. Because Joelle, she's not going anywhere.

My other hand drifts to her knee, my fingertips gliding up, and when I glance down, I almost jump off the seat.

"What the hell is that?" Anger swells in my gut, not meant for her.

"What are you talking about?" When she glances to where I stare, she tries to get off my lap, but I clutch her tightly, refusing to let go.

I grip her jaw, pulling her face gently toward me. "Baby, who left those bruises on your thigh? Tell me who fucking did that."

"Enzo, please…" She sighs with a drop of her shoulders. "It's nothing. Let it go."

But I can't. I won't.

"Joelle, all you have to do is give me a name. That's all. They'll never find his body. I promise."

Her eyes go round. "You'd kill? For me?"

I lower her lips to mine, inhaling her heavy, scattered breaths. "Without an ounce of hesitation."

"You can't," she murmurs. "There are too many..."

"Too many of them?" I finish for her when she won't, my lips stroking over hers.

She exhales, defeated.

"I know who you work for, Joelle. I know what they're capable of. I swear to you, baby, they'll all die, and you and me, we can be a thing after it's over. If you want it."

Shit, that was fucking stupid. The girl is gonna think I've lost my mind, talking to her like this. But maybe once things are safer, we can try. The thought grips me with hope of something more, something better in my fucked-up life.

She moves back enough to look at me. "I want that so much, but I just ca—"

I press a finger to her lips. "Don't say no. Not yet."

Not ever.

She nods, a frown taking hold. "I can't let you kill for me. I can't have that on my conscience."

"They were dead before we ever met. Now I have even more reason to make their end painful."

Her chin trembles, but she tightens her jaw, steadying the ache forming behind her eyes, like it's hiding. Like she's its keeper. She tries so hard to be strong, but slowly it'll destroy her. Pain always does.

"You don't know what you're getting involved in," she says, all evidence of her sadness is now a distant memory.

"I can say the same about you. But here we are, baby. And I'm not going anywhere."

JOELLE

He holds me like he's always meant to. Like his arms are the safest place on earth. But it's all a desperate illusion my mind has created. I'm not safe with anyone.

"Are you going to tell me who hurt you?" he asks for the second time, refusing to give in. I want to tell him, I really do, but I can't. I have to think about my son and the repercussions to him if I do.

I wish Enzo could find those three men and make them suffer for what they did to me last night. I want him to beat the living hell out of the bearded man who drove me to them, the man who I now know as Roman, the one who was scolding me for not doing my very best work with those men.

After they were through with me, they complained to Roman. He told me he wouldn't tell the Bianchis if I fucked him again. That's what Enzo walked in on.

I've never seen Roman before the night he showed up at my place, but Faro likes to change the men around. He doesn't want anyone to get attached to each other.

I don't know how a man like that has a daughter as nice as Chiara. She's oblivious to everything her father is doing, all the women and children he's destroying. She hates him too. She's told me so plenty of times.

Chiara is as good of a friend as I have. If my life were different, I could see us being friends outside of this place. We mainly talk here at the club. The people in charge don't allow us to have anyone over or go anywhere. It's part of the rules they have set for us.

The gym and work are the only places I can step foot in with the shitty car they provide us, monitored with a locator so that we don't get any ideas. My body is my job, and they make sure I keep it in prime shape, or else they'll have no use for me.

They also supply us with the basics like food, clothes, and toiletries. We get no money. They even take our tips. They want us dependent on them for everything we have. They fill our gas tanks too. We get a basic flip phone that we're only allowed to use for work purposes. None of us would ever dream of calling for help.

Every week, I have a woman come to my place and do my nails. They want us to look as good as possible for their clients. The better we look, the more money they get. That cash I've gotten from Enzo so far, I've managed to hide it in a tampon box, hoping they never look there.

Some of the clients at the sex club are men with more money and power than anyone should have. They're politicians. Celebrities. You name it. With us, all their wildest dreams can come true, as long as they're willing to pay for it.

My mind drifts to the night before, to the three men and what they did. My pulse races, envisioning it as though it's happening all over again.

"Let's see how well she can take this." One of the men laughs, after they've all had a turn with me. He twirls a large baton in his hand, like he's performing a circus act, while two others hold me down by my wrists.

My breathing grows agonizingly heavy, my eyes remaining on him as he walks up closer, the thud of his footsteps slithering up my flesh with piercing dread, and when the baton lands softly on my inner thigh, I flinch.

"Bad girl," he croaks with a grin so wicked, it sours my soul. Before I realize what he's doing, he lifts it up in the air and hits my thigh with it, again, then again. He hits me a few times more while I scream through the gag in my mouth.

The other men fondle my breasts even as the beating stops, and then, he shoves the baton inside me.

"Joelle?"

I hear the distance of his voice—Enzo's voice.

"Joelle, you're shaking. What's the matter? Talk to me, baby."

I clear my throat, ridding myself of those thoughts, my body still trembling. Enzo gazes at me so tenderly, the agony, the tears, they scream and claw to get out, but I won't cry. If I start, I will sob in his arms until there's nothing left.

With him, I'm vulnerable. For once, someone cares—someone sweet, powerful, beautiful. And he wants me, or what he thinks he knows about me.

But the ugliness is still buried deep where he can't see its tattered ruins. Will he still want me then? No. He won't. No matter what he says, no matter what he thinks he wants. He wouldn't want a whore. And I am one.

ENZO

SIX

Something happened to her. Something bad. She was afraid to tell me, and the way she was shaking in my arms, her mind elsewhere, it was obvious she had been harmed. I didn't even need to see those black and blues on her inner thigh to know that.

I wait in the parking lot for that motherfucker with the beard. He doesn't know it yet, but tonight will be his last night on earth.

I don't know if he's the one who did that to her, but it doesn't fucking matter. He's dead for merely grabbing her, talking to her the way he did, like she was nothing, and he was the one in charge. We'll see how in charge he is with me.

I finally catch him come out of the club, heading for the parking lot. Once he's in his car, I start to tail him. I can't do shit here. I have to find a quiet place.

My brothers would kill me if they found out what I'm up to. That I may ruin our plan for the Bianchis. But I won't. I'll be careful. I can't let his actions go unanswered, no matter what. He will pay.

The streets are immersed with silence at this time of night, and I keep some distance between us as we drive down a wide two-way road, streetlamps on both sides.

He makes a sharp right and I do too, finding myself on an unassuming one-way street this time, with a heavy wooded area to our right, large trees blanketed by darkness. The perfect location.

The guy slows. I think someone's finally realized he's got company.

Night-night, motherfucker.

Retrieving my black leather gloves from my pocket, I slip them on before picking up the knife from the passenger seat, the same one I had on me earlier.

His vehicle slows to a halt, and he steps out, a bat in his hand. I should put a mask on, in case we get company, but fuck it. I want him to know exactly who's going to kill him.

I reach down for the gun at my ankle, closing the knife and sticking both in my pocket as I get out, shutting off the lights in my car.

"You little asshole," he jeers, tapping the bat in his hand. "You really thought you could follow me, and I wouldn't know?" He chuckles. "You young cats think you're some tough shit these days, huh?"

I don't say a word as I move up on him slowly, my loafers crunching over the gravel, the noise resonating through the air.

"You just gonna stay quiet before I beat your fucking ass to the ground?"

I take another step, yards between us now.

"You in love with Joelle or something?" He keeps moving toward me while I do the same. "She's got a fine-ass pussy. I don't blame you." He draws up his upper lip. "I had some the other day. On the house." He winks.

He doesn't see it coming. Not until it's too late. The bullet from my gun punctures him straight through his esophagus, the silencer on. No one hears him fall to his knees, gasping for breath, mouth parted wide, eyes even wider.

With the weapon in my hand, I step closer, his hands covering the hole in his neck, blood seeping, slicing in between his fingers.

"This is a lot better." I pat his head, placing the gun back into my pocket and removing the knife. "Now, what were you saying about her pussy?"

He gurgles up blood in response.

"Oh, right." I snicker. "You're preoccupied. No worries. You don't need to talk. You just gotta listen." Circling around him, I run the pointy edge of the blade up his back. "How does your blood taste? Hmm?"

He lifts a trembling hand as I make it to his front. I near the weapon to his eye. "You must be proud of yourself for doing what you did to her." My body buzzes with the rage pounding through it. I could barely contain it, my teeth grinding so hard, they could shatter.

"You'll never get to touch her again." Each word is neatly wrapped in fury, the tip of the knife quietly slicing under his eyes. "It must've been you who put those bruises on her."

He shakes his head, trying to speak, but all that comes out is a choke and the spitting of his blood.

"She begged me not to kill you for what the Bianchis can do to her as payback, but no one will know it's me. No one will suspect it. They have so many enemies. I'm only one. And I'm sure a fucker like you has plenty of his own."

He continues to stare, hacking, strangling on his own demise. My other hand reaches for his pants, unzipping it. He must suspect where the knife will go next because he fights me as I try to take them off.

"Let's make this quicker, shall we? I have places to be." I rear the knife, stabbing the top of his hand. He quickly jolts it away, unable to scream, to call for help while I pull down his pants. "Not the way I wanted to spend my evening, but we do what must be done. And this, I'll gladly do for what you did to her. You will suffer. Painfully."

After his tiny dick is visible, I line my blade at the base. But before I start to cut, I grip his shirt in my fist, nearing his face, his blood dripping over my hand. "I'd make you suffer for days if I had the luxury of time, so for now, this will have to do."

Then I slice.

He chokes, screaming in silence. There's no one to hear him begging for mercy. I've never cut a dude's dick off before. Add it to my growing list of talents.

The savagery roaring in my veins is untamable. Images of what he did to her slam into my mind over and over until I realize his dick is completely off.

"Open your mouth, motherfucker. I'm gonna give you something good to chew on."

He sobs soundlessly, his chin quivering, the pathetic tears of a coward rolling down his round cheeks, some caught in his beard, those charcoal eyes drenched with a massive dose of regret.

"Okay, since I'm such a good guy, I'll help you out." I pry his mouth open, my fist with the knife in it pushing against his upper teeth as I stuff his dick down his throat with the other.

"Chew," I demand as he tries to spit it out. "I said chew." I keep my voice low, the tip of the knife nearing his eye socket.

And then he does. The motherfucker chews his own damn dick. Well, as good as he can with the bullet in his throat.

"This would make a pretty picture, don't you think? I bet your mother would love one as a keepsake."

I remove my cell from my pants pocket and snap a pic, the flash glaring against the darkness, the only other light coming from his car.

If Joelle ever needs to see it, I'll have the photo ready for her. I want her to know that I'll always be there to do whatever the fuck I can to keep her safe, even when she doesn't want me to.

He gags, his eyes rounding.

"I should take each one of your eyes and make you swallow them too, but I don't have the time. Lucky for you."

Grabbing the back of his shirt, I lift him up over my shoulder, and his dick falls out of his mouth, right onto the ground.

Opening my trunk, I throw him inside. We can't forget the dick though. I return to pick it up, then stuff it down his throat again. He should be dead by the time I get home. I won't end him with a bullet. I didn't lie when I swore he'd die slow. I want to prolong every miserable second.

Luckily, I've got my Royce SUV today. I would've hated to bloody up my Bugatti.

Shit, I'm really going to have to explain this to my brothers. I can't hide it from them, especially when I need our personal cleaners to get rid of the body and the evidence.

Getting behind the wheel, I begrudgingly call Dom and Dante.

"Yeah," Dom answers first, Dante joining seconds later.

"I was getting my damn beauty sleep." Dante yawns. "Why the fuck are you calling this late?"

"I got into some shit," I say, jumping right to the chase, putting them on speaker as I drive off.

Dom's breath is harsh, like a friggin' dragon.

"How many times did I tell you not to fuck without a condom?" Dante groans. "I'm not helping you pull crabs out of your dick." He chuckles, entertaining himself.

"Speaking of dicks… I have one in the trunk."

"What the *fuck* did you do?" Dom's question is harsh.

"Damn, bro, let me finish. Shit." I exhale sharply. "I meant I got an actual dick in the car."

"Is he fucking making sense to you?" Dom asks Dante. "Because I'm about to strangle him."

"Shit, I'm too tired for this." Dante yawns again. "Enzo, spit it out already."

"All right, damn. But you two won't be happy about it."

"Why the hell am I not surprised?" Dom's voice is even yet clipped.

"There's a dying dude with a missing dick in my car." I pause. "I need his body and all that shit disposed of, like right now. I just texted you the location of where it happened," I tell Dom. "Send them there first."

"You have got to be kidding." Dom's exhale comes roughly through the line. "Of all the idiotic shit you've done in your life, this has got to be the worst."

"Wait." Dante pauses. "You really cut some guy's dick off?" Then he's laughing. "Fuck, bro. How was it?"

"Not as bad as I actually thought it'd be, but I kept thinking about my own dick. I mean, I wouldn't want that to be me."

"I'm glad you guys are enjoying this," Dom cuts in. "Who the hell was he and do *not* lie to me."

"Some asshole from the strip club. He got a little too rough with one of the girls and ya know, shit happens."

"Why were you at the strip club? You hate that place," Dante throws in. "Wait a minute, is this over that blonde chick you were talking to the other day when I was with Carlito?"

"Maybe."

"Damn, baby bro fell in love with a stripper."

"Chill. No one's in love with anyone, but I couldn't let him hurt her anymore. I had to end it. He's just another dirty Palermo fuck. I was doing the world a favor."

"And what about Dad and Matteo!" Dom cuts in, his tone edged with a sword. "What if your actions fucked everything we've been working toward? What then? You couldn't wait to get rid of him until we ended the Bianchis?"

The only thing on Dom's mind is killing the Bianchi brothers. I get it. I understand why he's pissed. "I did what I had to do, and I'd do it all over again," I tell him. "It all worked out anyway, didn't it? The guy's missing his dick, and no one but us knows about it. Our plan is safe." I turn left, only a few miles from his place. "So go and relax. Maybe have a shot of something strong before I get to you. Or I can call Candy. She gives good head."

Dante strangles on a chuckle, trying, yet failing to hold it back.

"Hurry the hell up," Dom barks. "The cleaners are on the way to the location, then they'll come by my place."

Dom hangs up, but Dante's still there.

"I still can't believe you chopped off some guy's wiener," he throws in.

"Yeah and made him eat it."

"What?" His chuckle hits heavy, and he's unable to control it now that Dom is off the phone.

"It's a long story," I point out. "Well, not really."

"Bro, you're my hero. Must've been fun."

"Tell that to the guy in my trunk."

JOELLE

SEVEN

I haven't seen Enzo for a couple of days since the incident with Roman. Did he decide that was too much? Will I never see him again? The thought wedges through my heart with a sharp spasm. He's the only good thing that's come into my life recently. I can't lose him now.

I walk into my dressing room at the club. Paulina and Sienna are already there, preparing for their dances, fixing up their hair beside each other.

Sitting on an unoccupied chair in front of a mirror, I stare at the girl staring back at me, not liking who I see. I know I shouldn't allow these men to make me feel that way, but it's not something I can control. I hate myself. I hate what they've done to me. What they've turned me into.

The girls begin to whisper with each other, causing me to

wander their way, finding their hushed voices and wide eyes darting behind me.

What the hell are they looking at? Did I grow wings or something? Hell, that'd be nice. Maybe I could find my son and fly us out of here.

I'm sure Paulina is talking shit about me as always. It's what she does best. I shake my head with exasperation, and as I do, a strong yet gentle hand lands on my arm, brushing up to my shoulder like a feather.

My breaths hitch, my mouth parting inadvertently, warmth spilling down my arms. I don't have to look behind to know whose touch that is. The one I missed desperately, even though it took me feeling it again to realize just how much I actually did.

"Enzo?" I whisper his name with bated breath, like I'm afraid he'll vanish if I say it any louder.

"It's me, baby." Those words cruise with a sultry husk, his palm on the back of my neck, fingers dipping into me as he tilts my head to him with a firm grasp.

"Miss me?" His lopsided smirk wraps me up in warm intoxication, lustful desire filling into every hollowed space.

"Like you have no idea." The confession feels bitter on my tongue. I don't deserve him or his kindness, yet I can't seem to push him away either. If I do, it'll only hurt me more, and I can't handle another dagger to my heart. I can be careful. I won't let Faro or his men know that Enzo is not simply a customer.

"Is that your boyfriend or something?" Paulina asks with too much curiosity.

Shit.

"Mind your damn business." Sienna lightly swats her on the arm.

"I'm just asking. Geez." She flips her shoulder-length brown hair back with her long fingernails, rolling her eyes a bit too dramatically.

Enzo releases his grip on me, and I can tell he senses my shift in demeanor from the thoughtful expression he wears as he looks at me. He knows what Paulina is trying to do. He's not stupid.

I turn my attention to the girls. "He's not my—"

Enzo bends his mouth to my ear. "Let me handle this."

He's moving toward the two women as they eye him like their favorite ice cream flavor. I bite on the inside of my cheek, the center of my chest heavy, my gut tossing. If Faro or Agnelo so much as think I have a man in my life, Robby and I are as good as dead. Or worse, they'll sell him to the highest bidder or make him work the club.

"Ladies." He nods with a smirk so devilish, it'd have any woman's panties on fire. I hope that's enough to convince them we're not together, which technically, we aren't. So why do I suddenly feel this slam of jealousy from the way they look at him? "I'm Patrick. Nice to meet you."

We never discussed why he has two names, but I have a feeling whatever the reason, it's got danger written all over it.

There's an air to him, both civility and madness, draped like a mask over his face. He may be gentle with me, but I've found the monster lurking behind the softness of his gaze.

The girls peer up at him, eyes practically falling out of their sockets. He looks like an ad for a fashion magazine. A long wool coat falls to his upper thigh, his hair slicked back. As he smiles, his cheekbones appear more angled. I'm not at all surprised by their reaction. We don't normally get men as hot as he is.

"As much as I'd love for Joelle to be my girlfriend, she's not. I came back here so I can get that dance I paid for." Picking up each of their hands, he kisses the top of it, then strolls back to me. "It was nice meeting you both, but we have to go now."

"Bye." Sienna practically sighs.

"Lucky bitch," Paulina mutters under her breath, loud enough for me to hear it. She's never liked me. I don't know if it's jealousy due to the amount of attention I get from customers, but she can't stand me.

"You shouldn't have done that," I whisper to Enzo as we walk side by side to one of the private spaces. "How did you even get back here by yourself?"

I undrape the curtain and we enter one of the empty rooms. With my back to him, I head straight for the liquor, grabbing a bottle of vodka and pouring myself a much-needed shot to calm my nerves.

If Paulina says something... Oh God.

He lowers himself onto the sofa, leaning forward, legs spread, elbows braced on the top of his thighs. I try hard not to stare but fail miserably. His eyes flick to mine.

"The bodyguards were too busy kicking some guy out to notice me sneaking back here," he explains, cracking a smirk. "Aren't you happy to see me?"

The way he asks, it's as though he already knows the answer. "Of course, I am. But you don't understand what could happen if they find out about us."

I lift the glass to my mouth and let the burn roll into my throat, savoring the hum of heat coasting down the length of me.

"Come here," he beckons, that deep, throaty echo increasing the pace of my heartbeats.

I pop a brow in challenge, staying exactly where I am, pouring another shot. This will definitely be the last one if I plan to dance without falling on my ass later.

He rises to his feet, his fingers falling to the buttons of his coat, undoing them one by one, before gently placing the coat down on the sofa. As he treks closer, his eyes tangled with mine, he rolls the sleeves of his black button-down all the way to his elbows, the veins trapped within his skin on full display.

"Are you going to be mad the whole entire hour?" He's in front of me now, the drink forgotten. "Or could I convince you to forgive me?" His voice curls with a deep rasp, a palm enveloping the back of my neck, pulling me harshly to him, close enough for my heartbeats to echo with his. I go willingly. I always do. Because he's the only safety I've ever known.

His breathing rolls like a deep wave over my lips. The hardness of his chest, the smell of his woodsy cologne, it all causes my core to tighten, wanting something I didn't think I'd ever be capable of.

He's a life force to the wrecking of my soul, a trigger shooting me up with hunger—with a craving so raw that for a moment, I forget who I am.

Sex has been nothing but a job, a complication in my life that I've come to hate. But he's not them, those men. Maybe that means I can be with a guy without allowing the abuse to define me. Maybe one day, he and I could be together like he said.

But that hope is doused by the sudden realization that I'll probably never get out, that my son will be theirs. Forever.

My throat goes dry, and my breathing turns shallow. Reaching for the shot glass, I squeeze it between us, downing every drop.

He watches me drink it all, taking the glass once I'm done and placing it on the bar. His hand finds my jaw, cupping it possessively, a thumb brushing over my lips.

My brows squeeze as I relish in the tender touch of a man I've never known. And not just a man but Enzo.

"I'm sorry for coming to find you," he admits in a whisper. "When I didn't see you out there, I…" His words are lost before he finds them again. "I was afraid something happened to you. That's the only reason I went back there."

My pulse jumps a beat.

"You were worried about me?"

"Of course I was, baby."

"Thank you." Tears fight to fill my eyes, aching to show their face. No one worries about me anymore. I forgot how good it felt.

"Don't thank me yet," he says, low and husky. "I still have to make it up to you. And I'm damn good at that."

"Oh, really? And how will you manage it?" A smile creeps to my mouth.

His eyes delve into mine, my insides humming with a beat of arousal from the way his gaze grips the very essence of me. I'm drowning in the greenest eyes I've ever seen, lost to the fall, never wanting to be found.

"I could start with this…" His mouth lowers to my lips, hovering over them, breath to breath. Like he's drinking me in, savoring me, without actually doing it. It's the most erotic thing I've ever felt. I tingle all over.

I need this kiss. I want it like I've never wanted anything before. My heartbeats pound in my chest, his thick fingers massaging my hip.

Make me feel it. Make me feel something again.

"Shit," he mutters. "If I kiss you now, I won't stop."

Don't stop, I want to scream. Take me. Have me. Fuck the consequences.

But I regret even thinking those thoughts. What kind of mother am I? He's right. We can't do this. Being alone with him under the pretense of a lie is bad enough. Anything more and they're bound to find out. My body is their paycheck, their property. I don't belong to myself.

"It's fine," I say, walking away, and he lets me go. I move toward the stripper pole at the opposite corner of the room. "It's for the best."

"Joelle…" There's regret tethered there. "I'm sorry, it's only because I—"

"Look, Enzo, Patrick, whoever you are, it doesn't matter, okay?" I grin, the façade like bulletproof armor. Except it's not. It's fragile, no matter how strong I think it is. "How about we just sit and talk," I continue, clearing my throat. "Maybe you'll even want that dance after all? Or maybe…" I grip my hand around the pole and swing, lifting my feet into the air. "Maybe you'll want more."

He moves so quickly, so expertly, I don't even have a moment to inhale when the span of his large palm wraps around the front of my neck, his thumb pressing against my weighty pulse as his eyes hold mine like two missiles pinning me into place.

My body practically liquefies, my breathing ragged as my tongue swipes in between my lips, unable to look away.

He pushes my back into the pole with the hardness of his chest, my spine lining up against the cold metal.

My skin breaks with a shudder and it's not from the chill to my skin. It's him. This madness. This fury he creates within my heart. A whirlpool of emotions, and all I want is more.

His chest expands like that of a beast, his jaw flexing, ready to devour me, the lust, the need for the taste of darkness absorbing the emeralds of his eyes.

It's as though he's shrouded in both heaven and hell, a man split in between two worlds. In this moment, it's easy to see both sides of him. But I'm not afraid. Neither man would harm me.

His touch, it's filled with possession, a man torn. Wanton. It's there in his gaze. I can practically taste how badly he wants me. I want him too. I want this. But he's right, we can't.

We're souls lost to a world filled with the ashes of our future. Not meant to be. Not in this lifetime.

"Don't act like that with me," he warns, tightening his palm around my throat enough to make my core hum for more. "I'm not them. I'm not here for your pussy, Joelle. I thought we already established that." He leans into my neck, his lips ghosting up my skin.

A trembling pant slips out of me, my hands on his back, nails sinking into the hardened muscles that flex beneath my touch.

"No games, Joelle." His voice pulses with a sultry rhythm. "I don't want who you pretend to be. I want you. The real you."

I let my fingertips skirt up his back, rolling up into his hair.

"You can trust me, baby," he breathes. "I'll never hurt you."

His lips leave a tender kiss at that spot right under my earlobe and my body breaks out with a tantalizing shiver, my nipples hardening under the thickness of my black sequin bra.

I don't know how to respond. I can't tell him the truth. There's no way I could trust anyone with my secrets.

"Baby?" he calls, backing away, his thumbs now at my cheeks, wiping under my eyes.

Was I crying? God, I can't even keep it together.

"Did I say something wrong?" he asks, his brows drawing tight, concern filling the tenderness written all over his face.

I shake my head. "No." I lean over and kiss his knuckles. "I was just thinking stupid stuff." A bitter laugh escapes me. "Could we sit? The hour will be up soon, and I want to spend a little time with you before you go."

"Yeah." He attempts a smile, but it never quite reaches his eyes. Grabbing my hand, he gently squeezes as he leads us to the couch. When I take a seat beside him, his arm rolls under my ass and brings me over his body, my thighs straddling his. His fingertips cruise up and down my hips as he looks deep into my eyes, and my heart—it shatters.

I want you so badly. Every bit of me aches.

"When we're together," he says. "My lap is your permanent seat."

I force a grin. The way he stares at me, it's like his entire face brightens. It's like I'm the only woman on earth who could ever steal his heart away. That I'm his already. That nothing matters. But it does. It all matters. And I hate it.

Why do I have to meet him when my world is in ruins? Why is the universe trying to punish me more? Haven't I been through enough? Why dangle him right in front of me, only to take him away?

"Well, I much prefer to sit elsewhere." I tease away the pain boring a hole in my chest.

He pops a brow as I stare down at him—all man, the masculinity and power dripping from every pore. His hand reaches for my neck, his fingers crawling up until he cradles my jaw with a commanding grip.

"Try it, Joelle." The darkness from his tone oozes with an erotic undercurrent.

"I don't want to," I whisper, my heart skittering with quickened beats.

"That's my girl."

His girl. I almost burst into tears. It means so much to me and he doesn't even know it.

He glides his knuckles softly down my cheek. "You're so beautiful."

My heart squeezes, an ache forming behind my eyes. How I wish we were normal. Two people falling for each other. But that is not our fate, and it may never be.

I palm the side of his face, wanting my hands everywhere, to discover all his hidden secrets. The ones I know he has.

We all have them.

But for some of us, they're filled with too much obscurity, seething into the wounds we carry in silence.

JOELLE

EIGHT

"**W**ake the fuck up," someone yells, the male voice distant, cutting through the fog of sleep draping over me.

I groan, my face still planted on the pillow, burrowing further. *This is a stupid dream. I want to go back to bed.*

"I said wake up, you lazy bitch!" a man roars, his hand on my arm, fingers roughing into my skin, my heart beating so fast, it climbs up my throat.

As the stranger yanks at my hair, dragging me out of bed, I realize this isn't a dream at all, but a very real nightmare.

I let out a scream into the shadows, the walls caging my cries, my hands fighting as I fall to the ground, knees slamming into the tiles with scorching pain.

"Be careful," someone else says from behind us, turning on my bedside lamp. "If she breaks a bone, Faro is gonna kill you."

"Yeah, yeah." He hauls me up to my feet by my arm, and I discover a brown-haired man, around my age, his eyes small and round, his height towering over me. "See, she's in one piece. Isn't that right?" he asks with a sinister chuckle.

"What is this?" I muster out the question, my legs and scalp aching.

"The boss wants to see you. You have two seconds to put on your shoes."

"I need to get dressed first." I run my hands up my bare thighs, my pajama shorts riding up my behind. "Could I get some pants at least? I'm only in a tank top."

He snickers. "Yeah, and no bra." His eyes zero in on my nipples. My face heats with shame.

"Let the girl get pants, man. Why you gotta be such a dick?"

"You're soft," he tells the other one. "If you don't treat a whore the way she's supposed to be treated, she's gonna go and think she's in charge." He considers me cruelly. "Isn't that right?"

Before I can answer, his hand flies out, curling over my stomach, pressing my back to his front. I feel the bulge there, and grit with disgust.

My brows squeeze as I stare at the other man, his blond hair illuminated by the light flitting from the lamp beside him, his body against the wall as he casually observes.

He has a young boy's face, maybe no older than twenty. His eyes skitter down to the floor as the guy behind me pinches my nipple, his fingers climbing down, fitting them at the juncture between my thighs.

My insides twist as he presses into me there from above my shorts. The violent need to find a weapon and squeeze the life out of him overwhelms me.

Enzo.

I call to him, even while knowing he can't hear me. If he did, these men would be dead already.

"Come on," the blond one says. "Faro said to be quick. Do you wanna piss his ass off? Because I sure as fuck don't."

"Fine. Whatever." He finally drops his hands off of me. "I don't want her dirty pussy anyway."

The words cut into my skin, pouring acid over the wounds already there. I fight against the sadness, running to my closet, quickly grabbing sweats, throwing it on in a matter of seconds, before slipping into my sneakers.

"Let's go," the dark-haired one says, waiting for me to exit before they follow me out.

As we leave my place, the morning light still flashing past the clouds, I wonder what sort of nightmare I'll be entering into next and why there's no mask on my face.

We arrive at a large two-story estate and climb up the three steps, the two black doors greeting us before they open. An elderly woman, her black hair pulled up into a tight bun, donning a maid's outfit, says hello before politely letting us in.

The place looks bigger inside. The cathedral ceiling has a huge gaudy, crystal chandelier hanging at the foyer, a spiral staircase in the center.

"This way," the man who touched me snaps, jerking my wrist and shoving me forward. We enter another room, and Faro is the first one I see, a black robe on his round, short body, head full of grays.

I've never been inside his home. I never wanted to be. This isn't good. He wouldn't have me here unless it meant something bad.

My gut flips.

"Ahh, there she is." He extends his arms, smiling, but it never reaches his eyes. "Welcome, welcome." He gets off from the brown leather sofa, making his way to the bar at the corner to my right, my eyes following his every move. "Drink?" he offers, but it's not sincere.

"No, I'm okay. Thank you."

The sound of him pouring the honey-colored liquid into the crystal glass, his back to me, crawls up my flesh like roaches.

Something's coming. I can feel it.

Panic swells inside me, my muscles going rigid.

The two men lock the doors behind them with a loud bang, and when I look back at them, something catches my eyes, and I gasp, my limbs trembling as I hold back a scream.

We're not alone. There's someone else here. Someone I hadn't noticed before.

When our eyes meet, she smiles ruthlessly, running her nails up and down the tops of her breasts, hidden under the white robe she wears.

I need to run, to escape, but I'm frozen in place, trying not to react, even when every inch of my body is bathed with undulated fear.

What did she do!

"Oh, I see you've seen Paulina already." Faro's voice is a sharp bite and I immediately look back at him, dread swirling inside me.

He sits where I first found him, sipping on his drink, the light of the day splitting through the curtains on his left. "Paulina was telling me some interesting things about you." He glances at her, but she stares at me instead, a calloused grin growing on her face.

I remain still, like an immobilized statue, praying no one takes a hammer and shatters me into fragments too broken to be put back together.

"That man who came to the dressing room. Who is he?" Faro interrupts the scary thoughts zapping through my mind.

"He's no one." I keep my tone even, unaffected by her glare poking holes into me. If I don't react, he may buy it. "He's just a guy who pays for dances. Typical Paulina." I roll my eyes. "Always finding trouble where there is none."

"She's a liar, Faro! That's what she does. She lies," Paulina screams. "You had to be there. You had to see how—"

He raises a hand to silence her.

"Who's the liar, Joelle? Hmm? You or Paulina? You know what happens to the motherfuckers who cross me, don't you?"

"I wouldn't do that, Faro. Paulina is jealous. She hates me. That's what this is." I take a confident step toward him, a smile tugging on my lips. "Some of these men get possessive, that's all this is." I let the grin widen, hoping to sway him with its flirtatious edge.

Paulina growls, rising to her feet, running for me before I see her coming. With her palm centered to my chest, she pushes me down onto the floor.

In a flash, I prop myself onto my elbows, a snarl forming over my mouth, my breathing pummeling out of me as we stare each other down. While she's too busy looking tough, I swipe out a foot, kicking her knee, causing her to fall flat onto her back.

I pounce, punching her gut. I would've left a nice mark on her face, but Faro would murder me for that. She doesn't need her legs to fuck.

"Should we stop it, boss?" one of the men asks from somewhere. I can't see him.

"If I wanted you to, I would've said so. You have a brain in there or somethin'?"

"Sorry, boss."

"I'm gonna kill you!" Paulina shouts as I clutch her small, delicate neck in my palm.

"Try me, bitch," I pant. "You don't know what I'm capable of when I'm shoved into a corner."

I pretend to be weak when it allows me and my son to survive, but mess with our lives and that person will see a side of me they won't like.

I could kill her right here, right now if I wanted to. I could choke the life out of her for the betrayal. We're supposed to stick together against *them*, but she went and fucked Faro and gave him info on me. For what? To get ahead? To be favored?

What did that ever fucking get me other than more abuse, more rapes. Is that what she fucking wants? Women like her disgust me. This is my life. My son's life!

Before I have a chance to stop her, she raises her head up and throws it against my forehead. We both groan as we connect hard, and she finds the opportunity to get away, climbing back up.

I fight through the pain, rolling away as she tries to kick me in the face.

Jumping to my feet, I run, shoving her hard with both palms until she flies across the room...right into a large coral vase, cracking it into thick pieces of glass.

Oh no!

I stand there, chest heaving, waiting for her to rise, to fight me.

"Come on, Paulina. Don't give up now." Silence envelops the room. "Paulina?" My stomach dips as I release a stuttered gasp. Why isn't she doing anything? "Get up!" I call, tiptoeing, the trudging of my sneakers adding to the inching of fear sliding up my body. "Paulina?" I murmur, my eyes darting to Faro, a sneer on his face as he sips on his liquor, like he's watching a theatrical performance.

I continue the path to her, my breathing shallow. And when I finally reach her...

No.

My body shakes with a tremor, my knees bucking as I stumble, almost falling on top of her. But a hand holds me up.

His hand.

"Well, this is a problem." Faro snickers from beside me as we both stare at Paulina, a thick shard of glass sticking out, punctured through the back of her neck, a pool of blood around it. Her eyes are open but there's no life there.

I killed her.

"Wha—I," I stammer, unable to part my gaze from her, my heart rate speeding to an abnormal pace.

"You what, hmm?"

"I—I di-didn't mean to." I shake my head, my throat swelling, tears on the verge of storming down my face.

"Well, you fucking did it, you stupid bitch," he barks out, his glare as evil as the rest of him. "Not only did you cost me money, but now I have to clean this fuckin' mess."

"Please, Faro!" I don't know what I'm begging for. *Don't punish my son. Don't kill him.*

His hand falls to my hair, roughly pulling it with his fist. "I should get the cops to arrest you for murder. Then, you'll never see your son again. And he..." Faro grins. "He'll be the new favorite. Like mother like son."

"No." The tears quietly rain down. "Please don't do that. I'll do whatever you want. Just don't hurt my son."

"Yeah, you bet your ass you will." He tugs, making my scalp burn. "That man from the dressing room, you make sure you never dance for him again. He's not allowed anywhere near you. I can easily get rid of him, but…"

He releases me, moving back to the couch, and sits down. "I want you to be the one to do it. I want him to know it came from you and make it believable. Or I swear to God, I will end you and your damn son."

"It's done." I breathe heavy, knowing I have no choice but to get rid of Enzo for my boy. And yet, my heart, it feels like it's being ripped out. "I—I'll make sure of it."

"Oh, you better." He takes a long sip of his drink. "Now get the fuck out." He waves a hand dismissively. Then the men drag me away, while I stare one last time at the woman I murdered.

A mother.

A daughter.

A sister.

A whore.

Now a killer.

I'm all of them.

ENZO

NINE

Arriving at the club, I tag along with Dante, who came when Carlito texted for us to join him. I was planning on seeing Joelle whether my brother was gonna be here or not, considering I couldn't stop by last night due to some business that needed taking care of.

Dante doesn't know the extent of our—I don't know what the fuck to call it. Relationship? Whatever label Joelle and I attach to us, it doesn't matter, I don't want my brothers to know I like her, especially Dom. He'll think I'm distracted from our plan. But I'm not.

In six short months, we'll enact our revenge against the Bianchis, and in the meantime, we've been setting everything up. Synchronized perfection. That's what we're after. Nothing can go wrong. Nothing we can control that is.

They won't see it coming. Hell, they probably think we're dead. We've been training for this for years now, utilizing Roger, one of our men, who owns a martial arts school. He made our body a weapon, preparing us for what's coming.

I get out of my Royce, waiting for Dante as he gets out of his car, making it over to me.

"Maybe your girlfriend will be here tonight." He bumps my shoulder with his, chuckling low.

"Yeah, yeah, go worry about yours. Joelle and I are friends."

"Right, tell that to your dick."

"What the fuck you know about my dick, bro?"

"Just sayin'. You don't kill for just anyone."

I keep my mouth shut as we head inside, not wanting to be too damn defensive or he'll catch on. As soon as we enter the main area, we find Carlito there with two other made men, strippers on each of their laps, drinking shots as their hands fall on the women before them.

Carlito spots us walking up. "There you fuckers are! Took your asses long enough." He roughly throws the woman off him and she practically stumbles as he comes to a stand, clasping each of our palms. "I gotta introduce you to my cousins," Carlito continues, not giving a fuck that he just disrespected that woman. "This is Riccardo and Tommaso. Boys, this is Patrick and Chris."

They greet us with a tilt of a chin. We take a seat, me next to that fuck, and my eyes immediately scan for my girl. She isn't out here. I don't know what the hell I'll do if one of them makes her dance for him. Nah, I do know. Their dicks won't be the only thing they'll be eating if they touch her.

"All right, ladies and gentlemen," the emcee announces. "Let's welcome the one you've all been waiting for, Miss Joelle! Give her some love!"

The place erupts with whistling and applause. Carlito parks his ass back down, leerily staring onto the stage while I glare at him, wanting to pop his eyes out and squeeze them.

The room darkens to almost black, the music changing into something with a bit of danger. The stage erupts with a mist, and then she appears, like an angel finding her way through hell.

The lights return to a dim as her hands glide up the pole, her eyes closed, while she sways her hips softly for a moment, then she swings around.

I face her head-on, but we're toward the back with a few tables before us. If she looks this way, she'll see me.

Joelle climbs up, her legs split in the air before she grabs the pole with her thighs and rolls down the length of it while upside down. As she does, her palms touch the floor and her gaze lands to mine. With all the assholes here, their cocks probably hard for her, I'm the one she sees.

She continues to dance, glancing at me when she can, her tits out now for every unworthy asshole. I want to carve out their eyes for merely looking at her. I want that body naked just for me, but I can't demand that of her. She's not even mine, is she?

Damn, I've never felt this possessive about a woman before. It's a new feeling, but one I'm liking. Though I kinda hate it right now, knowing I can't do a thing about it, like throw her over my shoulder and tie her to my bed or some caveman shit like that.

"She's fucking hot, isn't she?" Carlito shouts over at me. "I'd fuck her right in front of Raquel. Maybe that'll get that sour bitch jealous."

Don't kill him. Don't kill him, I repeat like a chant, my fist tightening at my side.

"What did he say?" Dante whisper-shouts into my ear. He must've noticed my change in mood. We're good like that. My brothers and I know each other a little too well. That comes with the territory though. Growing up, all we had was one another, and we quickly learned to pick up on each other's cues.

"He said he wants to fuck Joelle in front of Raquel to make her jealous."

"I'm gonna gut him like a pig on Christmas."

"Do people eat pig on Christmas?"

"What the fuck does it matter?"

"'Cause your shit makes no sense." I chuckle. "I don't know where you come up with some of the crap you say."

"Whatever, man, this isn't English class. How about you shut up and watch your girlfriend instead of worrying about what I say."

I continue laughing at his irritation as another girl jumps on the stage now, her red hair as long as Joelle's. They say something to each other, the redhead's eyes going to me for a moment as she nods. Then they're both dancing on the same pole.

What the hell was that about?

I watch Joelle until the song ends, and both women climb off with two others replacing them.

"You boys drinking?" Carlito asks.

"Nah, we gotta drive," Dante answers, leaning over me.

Carlito nods once, his attention on the stripper he had on his lap before he threw her off, pulling her back on top of him, dollar bills sticking out of her hot-pink G-string.

The redhead struts her hips, heading straight for me. When she's real close, she bends to my ear. "Joelle told me you wanted a dance."

"She what?" I pause, jaw straining. "No, sweetheart, I don't need one, thank you though."

"She asked me to come. She insisted."

I open and close a fist at my side.

What the hell is she doing?

"Excuse me," I tell her, getting to my feet so I can find Joelle and ask her what this is all about.

I head to the back, knowing she's either in the dressing room or dancing for someone, which I don't wanna fucking think about right now. I'll look through every goddamn square foot of this place until I find her. She can tell me to my face why she sent another woman to dance for me.

Reaching the dressing room, my hand lands on the doorknob with every intention of going inside, not giving a shit if it'll make her mad. She won't be pissed for long when I'm through.

Tonight, I'm gonna show her just how much she means to me. I'm done holding back. We'll figure the rest out together. She won't belong to anyone but me. If I have to kill every man who tries to take her from me, then that's what I'll do. I'll keep her safe. No one will touch her.

The knob twists, turning all the way before I push the door open. It takes me a second to process what's happening inside, what I'm actually seeing. It almost cripples my resolve, and I find myself reaching into my pocket, retrieving a knife.

Joelle continues to kiss a blond guy, his palms on her bare ass. She's completely unaware that I'm standing right here, my heart downright breaking. I didn't even know it could do that.

Suddenly, she turns her head toward the door, finding me there. Her face pales as she fixes her bra, no longer showing me what she was so eagerly showing him.

"Who the *fuck* is that?" I snarl, baring my teeth, the knife in my grip as I advance, almost halfway to them, wanting to see that man bleed all over the goddamn floor.

Her lower lip trembles, her features twisted up, but she doesn't move, she just stays there. And that cocksucker has the balls to stare me down.

"You better talk quick, Joelle, before I kill him."

"Yo, who the fuck you think you're talking to?" The guy tries to stand and come at me, but Joelle shoves his shoulder back.

"Babe, give us a minute, okay?" she tells him.

"Did you just call him *babe*?" I could hear the blood rushing in my head, the pulse at my neck pounding in my ears.

She ignores me, kissing his cheek while the need to murder something, anything, ravages for space in my heart. My entire body tenses, about to go off like a bomb. I'm going to kill whoever the hell he is.

He rises once she climbs off him, scoffing at me as he passes with a look that says he's won a game I had no idea I was even in. If it wasn't for Joelle in front of me, that blade in my hand would've ended up in his neck.

Once he's out the door, I close the knife and place it back in my pocket. Before she has a moment to say a word, I'm on her, my body pressing into hers, pushing her up against the wall.

"Talk," I explode, venom tangled within the word. "And I swear, it better be good."

"Get the hell off of me!" She attempts to force me away, her palms shoving at my chest.

"Wrong answer." I grip both of her wrists and pin them over her head. "What were you doing with him?" My face slides to hers, my lips so close to her mouth I can capture it, kiss her ruthlessly. Savagely. Like she deserves.

"Tell me I misunderstood what the hell I just saw." I back away only enough to see her, to see the truth in her answers. "Tell me that was some damn joke." My voice lowers as she gazes up at me, her brows pinched tight, her chin quivering. "Because otherwise, I swear, you'll kill me, Joelle."

"Enzo, don't do this." She begs for something I don't understand. Her eyes light up with the fury of her tears, shining within them, blue oceans replaced by stormy seas.

My palm roughly clutches the back of her neck with one hand, while holding her wrists with the other.

"Who was that man, baby? Tell me," I breathe, the question dripping with emotion. "Fucking tell me now."

"I—" she stammers, tears rolling down her cheeks. "H-he… he's my…my boyfriend."

"Bullshit," I whisper over her lips. "That's fucking bullshit. You're lying."

She sighs with a deep pull of a breath. "I'm not. I'm sorry. You're a great guy, but me, I'm not a good person. I never was."

I laugh bitterly, my fingers straining into her flesh, her pulse throbbing against the pads of my fingers, my chest expanding with every rough exhale. "I don't believe a damn word that's coming out of that pretty mouth."

"Enzo," she urges. "Listen to me!"

I stare back into those eyes.

"That guy, he really was my boyfriend. He's been my boyfriend for years." She avoids my gaze, wandering onto the floor. "I was only after your money. The more I make, the happier my bosses are. You were nothing more than a customer."

My vision blurs, my entire body ringing, flames of rage sweeping over me until I'm consumed.

This can't be happening. She's fucking lying.

There's no way she was pretending this whole damn time.

But what if she was? What if you finally let someone in, and all she did was pretend?

My grip on her weakens, my heart weakening with it.

She has the decency to look defeated.

I let her go completely.

"I'm sorry, Enzo. I—I hope one day you can forgive me." Tears flood her eyes.

I smirk, staring at her with disgust. I can practically feel it dripping off of me in ripples. "There's nothing to forgive. You're forgotten already. A distant fucking memory I'll gladly wipe away for good."

"Enzo," she softly cries. "Be happy."

I take one last long look at the woman who managed to break through the cage of my heart, only to shatter it in the end.

I walk away.

When I return, and I will return, she won't recognize the man I've become.

JOELLE
ONE WEEK LATER

As soon as he was gone, my body crumbled into a million tiny pieces. But I had to do it. I had to break both of our hearts. I had to let him think I'm a monster, a cruel one.

I wanted to scream out the truth, but I couldn't. I had no choice. I lost the only man who's ever given a damn about me. The only one who made me feel alive for the first time in so long, and deep down, I know I'll never feel this way about anyone again.

My plan was well thought out. I knew the moment I sent Sienna to dance for him, he'd reject her and try to go find me in the back.

I was ready for him.

One of Faro's men, the one from the night I killed Paulina, who stood back and watched while his friend violated me, was to pretend to be my boyfriend. When I told Faro the plan, he sent that guy. At least it wasn't the other one.

The plan for Enzo worked. Too well.

I saw the pain rivaling with maddening wrath in those heavenly eyes. He hated me. I felt it. I betrayed him. That's all he saw. All that I let him see.

Even if, in some alternate world, we could have had something, that died the moment I broke him. He'll never forgive me. He'll never trust me again. It's no wonder I haven't seen him since. Why would he come anyway?

I've kept it together at work, but at home, I shed my pain into the pillow, hating that I did that to him. The tears fall silently as they always do. I never let anyone hear me cry, not even myself.

Fixing my white, sparkly bra in the mirror, I'm ready to step out on stage. My hair falls with spiral waves, pinned on one side, and all I want to do is rip it all off. But instead, with one more quick breath, I head out. As soon as I do, I see him.

A panicked gasp falls from my lips as my gaze stays glued to him, seated in one of the areas closest to the stage, with Kora grinding on his lap.

He doesn't notice me at first, but once he does, he grabs her hips, his features hardening with a glare riddling his face.

My insides curl with disgust at seeing him with someone else, someone who isn't me. I know this isn't him. He doesn't care for this. He's doing it to punish me, and it's working. My heart, it literally aches.

I climb the steps onto the stage, seeing her facing him now, his eyes on her breasts, and all I want is to scream, to break everything in this goddamn place!

I begin my dance, every one of my movements quick, jerky. My spins are sharper, my legs whipping out with a violence so raw, it fuels me, my pulse pummeling quicker.

He's mine.

My breathing intensifies, the song's melody attaching itself on to me. I bleed the words, the beat. It consumes me, driving my anger to new heights.

As I twirl down the pole upside down, dangling with my legs gripping the metal, I find him standing up, Kora grinning as she leads him away.

As he goes with her, he holds my gaze, his exhales roughing through the heavy climb of his chest. A muscle in his jaw twitches before she pulls him away, where I'm sure he won't be doing much talking like we once did.

It's really over.

Whatever we had is now gone, burning our fairy tale into the nightmare from which it came.

PART II
THE PRESENT

JOELLE

TEN

I tighten my hands on the steering wheel, beeping the horn at the slow driver before me.

Damn it! I'm going to get there even later!

I texted Chiara earlier, asking if it's okay that I show up a few hours late to work, but she never responded. I found that strange. She always responds right away. But I couldn't come in to work earlier no matter what. I had the worst headache, the kind you can't even function through, the kind that has you heaving into the toilet. Migraines suck. The meds have finally kicked in though, so that's a relief.

I'd never taken a day off, knowing that if Faro found out, he'd be furious. But I had to take the risk. I'd be no good up there with how badly I felt.

That's what I'd tell him if he confronted me. That he needs me at my best, and I wouldn't dare disappoint the master.

Insert eye roll.

Faro is the type of man who enjoys someone bolstering his ever-growing ego. I know exactly what to say to him. Not that it works all the time, but I've gotten lucky and tempered his anger a time or two.

Finally arriving, I find four black SUVs parked beside one another.

That's odd.

The place is normally packed at this late hour. There's always a bouncer stationed at the side entrance, but I don't see one now.

Oh crap, maybe Faro found out about me being late and shut the place down so he could kill me. Okay, I'm probably being a tad dramatic. He wouldn't stop business just to kill me. He would've sent someone to my house by now. But something is going on. The fact that Chiara never responded to my text worries me even more. I have to make sure she's okay.

My legs weigh a thousand pounds as I shut the car off, swinging my feet out onto the concrete. With a tightening in my chest and the crashing of the anxiety in my stomach, I trudge toward the entrance.

As I get closer, I don't hear any music. I hear nothing but male voices in the distance as I open the door. Who the hell are these men? Did they hurt her?

I gasp as the voices get closer, gently closing the door as multiple footsteps march from the back, ready to come face-to-face with me.

I slap a hand over my mouth to stifle the fear crawling up my throat. Tiptoeing away, I hide behind the bar, hoping whoever the hell is here won't find me. I can't afford to get caught in whatever is happening. If I'm dead, Robby is truly alone, and that can't happen.

"Stay here," a man whose voice I never heard before says. "The boss said we're gonna be here all night until they show up. We kill every one of them and bring their heads to him."

"I ain't chopping someone's head off."

"Cool. Then I'll be chopping yours off because if you don't fucking do what Faro wants, you'll die for it, my friend."

"Fuck. Fine. Yeah," the guy grumbles weakly.

Shit. Shit.

Whatever's about to happen is going to be bad.

Where the hell are you, Chiara?

My heart pounds so heavily in my rib cage that a thick sense of nausea churns in the pit of my stomach.

Closing my eyes, I pray that they don't find me. If they do, they'll kill me. There's no question.

I'm a witness, and the Bianchis don't like witnesses. I may make them a lot of money but they'd get rid of me without hesitation if it meant they were protected.

I stay motionless for what feels like an eternity, losing all sense of time. My pulse thrashes endlessly every time I hear the men walking right beside me, every time another happens to march out from the back. I wrap my arms around my trembling knees. My foot rattles, bumping into something with a low thud.

My eyes bulge as I suck and hold my breath, my lungs burning as I do, but that exhale is paralyzed within.

"Did you hear that?" one asks another.

Hairs on my arms prick across my flesh, my heartbeats thundering in my ears.

"I'm gonna go check it out."

Thump. Thump.

He comes nearer.

An ache builds behind my eyes.

This is it. I'm going to die.

My poor Robby.

I finally release that breath, tears trailing down my cheeks.

I'm so sorry, baby. Please forgive me. For all of it.

My attention lands on the thing I hit with my foot, a black bag with something that looks like the barrel of a gun sticking out under it.

Crunch.

The man, he's closer now. Too close.

Just as I'm about to reach down and grab the gun, in a last-ditch effort to die with some damn dignity, a loud bang sounds off, and instantly, chaos erupts.

"They're here!" someone yells.

Pop.

Pop.

Gunshots ring from all directions, a bullet landing into the wall right in front of me, my eyes popping wide.

What the fuck is going on?

Tentatively, I reach down, slowly sliding the gun from under the bag, and grip it in my shuddering hand. I don't want another murder on my conscience, but I will shoot if I have to. Bullets fire while I cower deeper into my hiding spot, thankful I have some protection.

The people continue to fight, the groans and loud scuffle slowly easing, the shooting finally diminishing until it ends. But the men, they're still here.

"Fuck," someone groans, "I'm hit."

Oh God. I hope that means they'll leave soon.

I need to get out of here before they find me.

My heart tosses inside me as some of the men continue talking about getting their friend some help.

"Let's load up and get the fuck out of here!" one shouts to the other.

Relief washes over me, and without realizing, I let out a small whimper.

Oh no! What have I done?

"Did you hear that?" a man says, but that voice...

It can't be...

My skin tingles, a sudden coldness hitting the very core of me. The fear, the shock, it all comes to the surface.

I refuse to believe that the man I've grown to care for, the one I was forced to let go of, is the one in the midst of all this violence.

I'd seen him at the club in these last months, with a different dancer on his lap each time, taunting me.

He'd show up with the same man he's normally with, both of them always with Carlito and his crew. Why he hangs out with those men when he's never been anything like them still makes no sense.

Every time I was forced to dance for Carlito or one of his people, the look on Enzo's face was one that could kill. I was kinda afraid he would.

Is him having two names related to this? Is he a cop or a rival mobster? So many questions swirl into my mind and I'll probably never get the answers.

Say something again.

But hushed whispers are all I hear now.

I hold the gun tighter in my palm, swallowing away the dread coursing up from the tight knots in my stomach. Would he harm me?

Before I can even compose my thoughts, there's a loud crash over the bar, and the next thing I know, someone leaps over it, his black pants and matching sneakers the first thing I see.

My eyes go round, my hand jittering, the weapon almost slipping out of it. "Get away from me!" I scream, before looking up, finding a man wearing a black ski mask.

Clutching the gun in the jerkiness of my grip, I slowly raise it to him, aiming it at his stomach. Whoever this is, he better leave because I *will* shoot.

Where's Enzo? If he sees it's me, I'm sure he'd let me leave. No matter what he thinks I did, I refuse to believe he'd hate me enough to cause me harm.

The man raises his palms out but I keep the gun where it is.

"We're not going to hurt you. Come on out."

I suck in a breath.

"Enzo?" I whisper it so low, he probably doesn't hear me.

"I've got my brothers out there," he continues, his tone even. "Plus a bunch of the men who work for us. We swear we won't do anything to you."

Is he serious? I'd never go anywhere with him knowing what I know now. "I don't care! You need to leave before I blow your fucking brains out."

I raise the gun a little higher, aiming it at his face this time. If they leave, I can finally get out of here before Faro or Agnelo shows up.

"As much as I love a hot woman with a weapon, especially when that woman is you, you need to stop pointing that thing at me, Joelle." I can see his mouth move into that well-known smirk beneath his mask.

I should shoot him. I should make him pay for lying to me or more like omitting all the facts about himself. He's a damn criminal. He's no cop. "Fuck you, Enzo."

He continues to smile in that way that would set me on fire. But now, I want to set him on fire instead. How could I be so stupid? Why did I think a normal man would want a woman like me?

He leans his back against the edge of the other side of the bar, staring over at me, and those eyes, I wouldn't even need to hear his voice to recognize the vivid blaze of bright green.

"You should know by now the main reason I come here is for you. The way you own that pole…" He pauses, practically growling. "Damn, girl. You're like a snake on that thing."

Did he really just say that? The back of my nose burns. That's all I was, just someone to look at?

But he never wanted me to strip. He insisted I didn't, so why is he talking to me like that? But it's not even worth asking. It doesn't matter. We're over. He's clearly dangerous, and I don't need any more danger in my life or in Robby's.

Any man I bring into our world, if I ever have a life of my own, will be someone who could be a father to my boy. Someone good. Safe. Not whoever this Patrick or Enzo is. He's a fabrication. Someone I manifested. Someone that doesn't exist.

"How about you put that gun down and come out with us," he says coolly. "I'll drive you home."

"I'm good here." I tip up my chin, narrowing my eyes into a tight glare, hoping the gun gets him to leave me alone. "You can go."

"Okay, sure, babe, you stay." He shrugs, pulling back from the bar. "But it'd be a real goddamn shame to see all that beautiful skin burn to a crisp when we torch the place down. Wouldn't want all that talent to go to waste."

"Fuck you!" I shout, the anger crashing over me.

He shakes his head mockingly. "Such a pretty mouth saying such dirty things."

You should hear what I actually want to say to you, asshole.

I almost have hope that he'll give up on me and go, but instead, his leg snaps out and he kicks the gun right out of my grasp.

A gasp rushes out and I back into the end of the bar wall, my chest heaving with fear. He stares sharply as he lowers himself, gripping my forearm softly. "Stop fighting me, baby." His voice falters with emotion. "I'm not tryin' to hurt you."

My heart seizes with a beat, my eyes watering for a fleeting moment, wanting that connection we had in what feels like forever ago. But no. I can't fall into our trap. He's not a safe choice. He's a violent one.

"Don't fucking touch me, you asshole!" I bellow, and he groans with a shake of his head before he roughly yanks me up. I kick out my feet, fighting him off, but it's no use. He's way stronger than I am. He stands me up, my chest rising harshly.

"Asshole?" There's humor there, his free palm landing against his chest with feigned shock. "That was me being a gentleman. If I were an asshole…" He fists my hair, tugging my face right up to his. "I'd drag you out by your throat."

I narrow another glare filled with vile contempt, frozen with the rage sheathing me. His breaths are even, unlike mine, as his jaw pulses through the fabric.

His gaze darts to my lips, and mine goes to his mouth. Is it wrong that the fire still burns for a man I shouldn't want, not anymore, not after this? But I want him. I want us. I do. And I hate myself for it. What kind of woman am I for desiring a man such as him?

I can tell he feels it, that anger, but that wild attraction too. I can't turn it off and neither can he.

We continue to stare at one another, battling without words, without weapons. I feel the rousing in my gut, that fear turning into awakened desire.

It's sick. I'm sick. I want to rip away his mask and kiss him. Tell him how sorry I am for lying, for kissing that man he believed was my boyfriend.

He's the only one I want, despite knowing what he's capable of.

But it's too late now.

We're too far gone.

"Come on, man. Dante needs help!" someone hollers.

That causes him to rip away his eyes from mine. And I feel it. That loss. It burns.

"Yeah, shit. My bad." He rubs the back of his neck for a moment, then pulls me away from around the bar.

As we walk away, I hear his hushed words, probably thinking I can't hear a thing as he talks with a man beside him. But I hear it all.

"Do you realize who we have?" he tells him.

"What are you talking about?"

"She's the Bianchi brothers' favorite toy. She makes them a crap ton of dough."

My hands tighten into fists, my eyes narrowing. How dare he say that about me.

"What do you wanna do with her?"

"I'm gonna keep her," he says on a laugh. "What better way to fuck with them? We burn their club and take their favorite girl."

"What!" I utter with a huff.

But they both ignore me, like I'm an invisible ghost.

"Fine," the man grates. "She stays with you."

"Hell no!" I yell. "I'm not staying with him!"

If Faro finds out Enzo has me, I'm as good as dead. He'll think I talked about the members-only club, then he'll kill my son. I have to be back home in case they check.

"Wouldn't have it any other way." Enzo chuckles. "I have a

feeling she and I will have *lots* of fun together." He roughly pulls me against his side.

I groan, the anger permeating my every cell as I stare ahead.

I'll figure out a plan. I will get out of this.

I know fighting him right here is no use. He's going to have me no matter what I do. I'm well versed in knowing when to battle and when to play dead. I'll play this game until he's the one lying on the ground with a dagger in his chest, the one I'll put there.

Then, I'll find my boy and we'll run until we can't run anymore, even if I die trying.

ENZO

ELEVEN

With my brothers back in their own homes, I drag a fighting Joelle to mine.

"Let me go!" she screams, clawing my arm. But I take every ounce of pain, ignoring the useless fight burning inside her.

I didn't need to take her. I could've gotten her safe passage out of here, somewhere the Bianchis would never find her, but I was too selfish for that. I want her all to myself. That shit I told Dom, about her being valuable to the Bianchis, I don't give a fuck about any of it.

It was all bullshit, a way to cover up the reason I had to take her—because I fucking missed her. She messed with my head, my damn heart, but still—shit. She has me.

I have to know if anything between us was real. A part of me doesn't buy that she'd be so callous. No one is that convincing, or maybe I'm just a fucking idiot who let a woman crawl under his skin and poison his mind.

I hope her boyfriend, or whoever he was, misses her because he'll never see her again. I'll make sure of it.

If the Bianchis think she talked, they'll kill her. She's gotta know that. If she doesn't, she'll learn soon enough. Her only option will be to hide under a new identity, one I can provide her with.

"Joelle, it's me. Stop fighting like I'm your fucking enemy," I grit as I finally get her up the steps and into my house, kicking the door closed with my foot.

My men are stationed inside the premises, every door with multiple bodies, guarding, watching, making sure the Bianchis don't think twice about coming anywhere near where we live. Not that they know where we are. We purchased our homes under an LLC.

My brothers and I all live right next to one another, each owning his own mansion in our small, gated block. The homes are separated by acres of land and my brothers' houses are right next to mine. We know the few neighbors we have, but they keep to themselves. Lucky for them.

"I don't know you at all!" Her breathing makes her chest rise heavily as I maintain my hold on her. "Who the hell are you, really? How about we start there?" She yanks her arm out of my grasp and I let her.

"I can't believe I had feelings for you!" She paces around the foyer while I lean against the door, arms folded over my chest. She bumps into the small table in the middle, almost knocking the sculpture there, too pissed to pay attention. "All this time, I thought you were a good man." She huffs, and damn, it's sexy as hell. "But you're like every other guy who's gotten good at hurting me."

She pauses, finally staring my way, brows frowning, her face so damn sad. I just wanna hold her.

"Wait." My mouth deepens into a calloused smirk as I lift a finger in the air, treading over to her. "Hold up." She doesn't resist me when I curl my arm around the small of her back, and tip her chin up with my knuckles, needing her eyes, needing all of her.

"You had feelings for me?" I raise a single brow with a snicker.

She scoffs with a roll of her eyes. "Of course I had feelings for you, asshole."

Damn. Dante was right. I do have it bad.

In all this time we've been apart, I haven't been able to get her out of my mind. She was all I thought about. All I wanted. I imagined her telling me that guy meant nothing, that what we had was real. But it's all bullshit, isn't it?

"There's that damn word again." I drop my hand from her face. "But we'll address your dirty mouth at a later time." I clutch her tighter with both arms, our chests slamming, my lips dropping, almost brushing past hers. "We have more important things to discuss, like your so-called feelings." She pants, her frayed breaths cruising over mine.

I stare down into her lust-filled gaze, wanting to kiss her so damn bad. I fight the depravity climbing up the walls inside, to stop myself from doing just that.

"So those feelings," I whisper. "Were they before or after you were fucking your boyfriend?"

She sucks in a sharp breath, her features bending with a scowl as she pushes her head back, teeth biting into the softness of her full lower lip. But it only lasts a moment, the harshness now back on her face.

"Never mind all that," she fires. "Let me go." As she fights my grip, I hope she realizes it'll do her no good. My palm fastens firmer over her hip, a smile sliding to my mouth.

"What the hell do you mean never mind?" I inch my face closer, narrowing a sharp gaze. "Never mind that you were playing games with me? That your pussy was riding my cock, while another man's dick was actually inside you?"

My hand climbs up her spine until it sinks into her soft waves, fingers twining, pulling, yanking back hard until her jaw is parallel to my lips. I suck on her skin, biting until she squirms, fighting the moan set deep in her throat.

"Do you know how fucking insane that makes me? How badly I want to pin you up against the wall and fuck him out of you until all you know, all you feel, is my cock?"

My other palm slides to the front of her neck, rough calloused fingers enclosing around the delicate flesh. I shouldn't touch something so soft, so damn beautiful. But here I am, doing it anyway.

"I'm not yours. I never will be." Her voice wavers, like a flame, igniting what we could've been.

I miss the woman I had at the club, the one she was when we were alone. She was real then. It couldn't have been a lie.

Fuck! I don't know what to believe anymore.

She doesn't realize how much she meant to me. How significant my feelings for her were, considering I never felt that shit for anyone before.

"What will you do to me, huh? Don't you realize I can't stay here?"

"Why not? I've got everything you'll ever need. And unlike some others, I'm not trying to kill you." I lower my lips, brushing them over her throat, inhaling her scent as she breathes heavily. "I'll do my very best to make sure your stay at Casa Enzo is tolerable. More or less." The chuckle comes from deep in my chest as I look back at her, finding her gaze turned to a narrowed slit.

I grin. Wider. I've realized I like fucking with her a little too much. The harder she glares, the harder my cock gets. I'm a depraved fuck, aren't I?

"Just let me go," she snaps. "I'm nothing to you. If Faro doesn't know where I am, he'll kill someone I care about. If that ever happens..." She shoves at my shoulders. "I'll kill you myself!"

"Such a big threat from a woman in your position." I ease my hold on her. "Who will he kill? Maybe if you tell me something true for once, I can actually help you, which is all I ever wanted to do, Joelle."

She sneers. "Why the hell should I trust you? We know nothing about each other."

"We could. If you were ever honest. Who was that guy at the club you were..." I can't even say the damn word.

"I told you. My boyfriend." She pops a hand on her hip, a brow arching. "Now, are you going to let me go or not?"

"Sorry, baby, but you're not going anywhere. Better get comfy." I wink, not really believing she's got someone to save. Once a liar, always a liar.

"Fuck you!" she snarls.

"Mmm, I wish you would." My gaze trails over her tits as I back away to see their shape hidden behind her white tank. "I keep thinking about that day, you on top of me, rubbing your pussy, except now, when I think about you, you're not wearing any clothes."

"Oh, is that what this is about?" Her mouth curves into a sardonic smile. "I can take my clothes off for you right now. It's what I do best. I'm sure you know that by now."

The vein in my neck throbs, wanting to grab her and show her just how special she truly is. "It's never been about that for me and you damn well know it."

Her eyelids drift to a close, and that's when that vulnerable side, the one she fights to hide, slips out. Her chin shaking, brows furrowing, she can't escape it, no matter how badly she may want to.

"Joelle..." I whisper.

Instantly, her gaze zaps to mine, but her mask, it's back on as she clears her throat, her attention scattered behind me.

Her eyes swell before she looks to me. "Why do you have people everywhere? What is this place?" Shock pulls at her features.

"Bodyguards. They're not gonna hurt you." I cut through the distance, palming her cheek, my heart strumming with intense emotion, hoping she stops resisting once and for all. "I wouldn't hurt you either. You've got to know that, baby." I can barely contain how I feel for her. It's fucking impossible. One second I want to hate her, the next I want to kiss the living hell out of her, to remind her what we were.

"Right. Sure. Of course you wouldn't harm me." She shakes her head, slipping out of my hand, her face turned with revulsion, making me wince. "So, you storming into the club, murdering people, that was what, you being a good person?"

"I didn't say I don't hurt *other* people. I just said I wouldn't hurt *you*. And you suddenly care what happens to Faro's men now?"

"No! But a man like you, with an army of your own, must not be any different than the Bianchis are."

"You know what, Joelle, if that's what you really think, then fuck this. Let's go." My hand shoots to her upper arm, but she pulls away, taking a step back.

I groan with irritation, marching forward, but she continues to move away, her glare zeroed in on me.

"Where do you think you're going? Hmm?" I take another step. "My men are all over the house."

"Let me out of here and you'll never see me again," she swears, continuing to trek backward.

A reluctant chuckle breaks from my throat. "See, that's where the problem lies. I want to see you. All the damn time. It's a problem I didn't know I'd have, but here we are."

Her lips flutter as though she's trying to formulate a response, her movements halted, and I take that opportunity to quickly catch her, circling my arms around her thighs.

"Hey! What the hell are you doing?" She fists her hands, slamming them once into my chest, her gaze furious as I hoist her up and over my shoulder.

"Put me down!" She pounds her fists against my back, causing a deep laugh to roll out from me.

"Nah, baby." I smack her ass hard, walking up the stairs. "You won't be going anywhere until you learn some fucking manners. I promise to teach you."

She growls like a wild cat, someone I'll gladly tame until she falls in line, until she realizes she's much safer here than returning to her previous life.

I get her fear, being taken by me, but I'm not the enemy. I'm the friend she needs. The one who could stop the pain the Bianchis have inflicted, if only she'd quit being so stubborn.

Once we reach one of my unused bedrooms, I open the door and take us inside, throwing her on the bed.

"Don't fucking move," I warn, my steely gaze on hers.

"You can't keep me here," she pants, propping herself on her elbows. At least she's a good listener.

"Haven't you noticed yet?" I walk over to the dresser, rummaging through the kink drawer, finding a pair of soft, black cuffs I frequently use on the women I bring home. "I can do whatever the hell I want."

Turning back, I spin them on my finger, inching closer. She sits up, staring hard at them.

"What are you going to do with those?" Her eyes pop wide.

"What do you think I should do?"

My footsteps lightly thud over the bare wood floor until I get to the bed and sit beside her, my gaze trailing down her body, from those pair of stunning blue eyes to her soft thighs, covered in a pair of tight jeans. "You fight me at every step." I move my hand toward her, roughly cupping her jaw. "Maybe you'll learn to behave if I restrain you."

"Screw you, Enzo." She pushes at my chest, that gaze firing angrily, but something else too, something I recognize well in a woman, something that looks a lot like hunger. And not for food. She likes this. It's too bad I like it too. Very much.

A smirk lines my mouth as I glance at the spot she just hit, her eyes veering down to my lips. Before she can try any more of her shit, I'm on top of her, my body pinning hers, my knee slicing in between the warmth of her thighs, my one hand trapping her wrists over her head.

I circle my hips around her pussy, knowing she can feel how damn hard I am for her, a woman who lied to me, fucked with my feelings, the way I'm going to enjoy fucking with that body. By the end of it all, she's gonna want me deep inside, and I won't give her an inch.

Her lips part, and a soft groan slips past her defenses, my cock rocking against her in slow, sensual circles. "See…" My lips lower to her neck, stroking up gradually, my breath hot, riding over the curve of her jaw. "I knew you'd behave better once you're tied up," I whisper into her ear, her moan enough to send me straight to hell.

My tongue rolls up the base of her neck, my lips on her earlobe now, my cock aching to be inside her as I arch deeper, her whimpers mingling with the harshness of my breaths.

"Enzo," she gasps, needing this as much as I do. It'd be so easy to stop the madness, rip off her goddamn clothes and show her that her fucking boyfriend is nothing more than a forgotten piece of trash.

But I can't. Not until she's honest with me about it all. The Bianchis. Her job. Everything.

I retreat, looking down at this goddamn perfection lying on my bed, in my house, and for the first time, I'm not gonna fuck a woman.

Who knew I was capable of that? I sure as hell didn't.

"That ache you feel in your cunt, maybe call your boyfriend and have him take care of it. If that's really who he was," I spit out, my tone marred with ire.

I climb off the bed, her eyes melding with want, yet rage is there too in her tightened gaze. "I hate you," she hisses.

"Well, baby girl, I can connect you with some women from my past. Maybe you can start a club."

"You think this is funny?" She sits up, getting off the bed, stepping up to me on her tippy-toes until her face is a fragment away.

Fuck. She's hot all pissed like this.

"Fight me, baby." My palm snaps to the base of her nape, pulling her in as I grit my teeth. "I like it rough."

"This is all a joke, huh?" She glowers.

"Do I look like I'm laughing?" I drop the cuffs onto the floor, walking her backward, my free hand rounding her hip until her body hits the wall with a harsh thud.

We lock eyes, my thumb rubbing over the pounding pulse in her throat, her gaze piercing, brows creasing. There's so much unspoken on her face, and it pulls me in where I want to confess every goddamn feeling of mine that she owns.

"When I came that day," I admit weakly. "When I saw you with him, I came to tell you I wanted you. I wanted to try. I was gonna fuck it all for a chance with you. Did you know that?"

She draws in a sharp inhale, her eyes flooding with tears. I tighten my grasp around her neck, leaning my forehead over hers.

"Enzo..." She sighs brokenly, and that one word punches straight into my chest.

"Don't do that." I swallow against the lump in my throat. "I don't need your pity." I slant my mouth to hers, but not close enough to taste it.

I pitch back, letting her go completely, unable to take another second of being this close to her without feeling like my goddamn soul is being ripped away. "I fell for you. I wanted you. And not just to help you. But you pissed it all away." My hands flip in frustration. "Tell me why, Joelle. Why?"

She bites into her lower lip, tears fighting to fall. "I-I'm so sorry."

"Don't be." My chuckle is cruel. Empty. "You were the biggest fucking mistake of my life."

She pants, tears rolling down her face, and I instantly regret what I said. It was the pain talking. Fuck, I'm an asshole.

"Add it to my collection." She sighs, defeated. Shattered.

We're both the same that way.

"What does that mean, Joelle?" Damn her tears, I want to take them away. I want that smile on her face; the real one she'd give me back at the club.

"Never mind." Her shoulders slump as she eyes the floor for a mere moment.

"Was any of it real? Just tell me the truth." The question comes as a whisper, tasting bitter on my tongue, but I need to know.

She swipes a finger under her eye, her face straining as her gaze holds mine. "It was all real," she breathes. "Every moment. Every second. We *were* real, Enzo."

"Then why?" I rush over, palms cradling her face as I stare deeply. "Why the fuck were you kissing him?"

Her eyes go downcast, her lips clasp shut, tears drifting down her cheeks.

"Still won't tell me, huh?" I drop my hands, moving toward the door. "I'm leaving. You're gonna stay here until I can trust you not to try and run away. Not that you can." I shrug a shoulder. "There are cameras all over my property, including this room, and my men will be instructed to restrain you if you get out of hand."

She flashes me a gaze filled with the aching of her heart, and I hate that I'm giving her more of it.

"I'll be back later with some food."

Hopefully when I come back, she's in a more cooperative mood.

"Shove that food down your throat!"

Or maybe not.

I shake my head with a laugh as I lock the door behind me. I never had a woman beg to leave me before. I'm going to savor every damn second of that fight inside her, up until the moment I send her away.

Retrieving my cell out of my pocket, I fire the app I use to see the live feeds from my home. My brothers and I all have cameras installed in every single square inch of our places. Right now, seeing Joelle running for the window to try and pry it open is making me damn happy I have them.

JOELLE

TWELVE

How do I always manage to get myself stuck in these shitty situations? I don't know how long it's been since he left. Hours definitely, if the morning light piercing from the dark gray curtains is any indication.

I'm tired as hell, but not tired enough to fall asleep while trapped here in this damn room. I couldn't even close my eyes, the adrenaline keeping me awake this whole time. I tried to escape through the two large windows, but it was no use, they were shut with a key. Who the hell has locks on their windows?

No one normal, that's for sure.

When I think back on everything he said, how he spilled his feelings so freely, God, it made me want to tell him everything. And if it wasn't for my boy, I would've. If he's even still alive.

By now, Faro probably already knows I've been caugh

considering he has cameras everywhere, including the club, but I hope he realizes I'd never talk for Robby's sake.

Once I figure out how to get the hell out of here, I can look for my son. Maybe I can bribe one of Faro's men into telling me where Robby is? What do I have to offer them, though? Nothing but my body. But I'd give that up willingly. What's one more man? At least it'd have a purpose. I feel dirty at the thought, but there's nothing I wouldn't do for my son. *Nothing*.

I wrap my arms around my knees, tucking my head down, recalling all those good memories from when Enzo would come and see me at the club. I miss us—the way we were together. My feelings for him are still there, buried under piles of ash and dust. With only a slight flick of a hand, it'll all uncover, reminding me of the days I thought I finally had someone I could trust. But that was all a lie. The truth is, there's too much standing between us to find happiness in each other's arms.

Even if he weren't a danger to Robby and me, and even if he could overlook that I'm a killer just like him, I don't think a man like that would choose to be with a whore.

The clicking on the doorknob jars me from my thoughts.

Enzo struts in, fully put together, donning a dark navy suit, straining at every single hard spec of muscle on his body as though tailor made for him alone.

There's a large paper bag in his hand and I almost want to ask what's inside, but don't want to act like I care.

"Aren't you gonna ask me what I brought?" A lazy smirk crawls up his lips as he runs a hand through his combed hair, tousling it a bit.

"Not really." I turn my gaze to the wall, but side-eye him as he treads over to me, sitting at the foot of the bed.

"Fine, tell me," I huff out in defeat.

"You're looking at the bag like I've got a torture device with your name on it inside."

I pop a brow. "Wouldn't shock me if you did."

His palm falls to my knee, sliding up to my inner thigh. "The kind of torture I normally use on a woman, is the kind they beg for."

His words slam hot in between my thighs, my heartbeat quickening, pussy clenching. I squeeze my knees to quench that ache he put there, but it's no use. He has a strong effect on not only my body, but my heart. There's nothing I could do to tame the wildness of my thirst for this man.

He notices my movement, a sultry grin captivating the corner of his mouth. His hand falls away as he goes to open the bag I have now forgotten about. He pulls out white containers, a few bottles of water, and some paper plates.

My stomach growls immediately as he reveals crepes, fruit, and croissants.

"My brother's cook made all that."

"I figured it wasn't you," I tease with a smile, the first real one I've had since I got here, his eyes beaming up at me.

He hands me a fork, then adds some food to the plate before giving me that too. He treats me better than what I'm used to. Locked in a cage with scraps for food is a lot less humane than this.

"I'm glad you're in a better mood this morning."

"Yeah, well." I chew as I respond. "Don't get that excited. It's only 'cause I'm starving."

He picks up a bottle, opening it before handing it to me. I guzzle half as soon as I grab it, placing it on the nightstand once I'm through.

"Continue to behave and I may consider letting you out of this room." His tone is light and teasing.

"Is that so?" I cut into the blueberry crepe, stuffing a huge piece into my mouth. "And how shall I behave?"

"By not calling me an asshole for one." He quirks a brow.

"I guess I can manage that." I shrug, my mouth twitching. If I can get out of this room, my chances of getting out of this house are a lot better.

"Was that a real smile or are you playing me again?"

My mouth drops open in contrived disgust. "Wow. Low blow, Enzo. Real low."

He chuckles, his big, strong palm landing on the top of my thigh and squeezing so deliciously, my insides quiver.

"Shut up and eat," he drawls with a raspy beat, and I almost drop the fork from the electric shock that playful demand sends to every nerve ending on my body.

He keeps his hand there while I eat, like he can't stand the thought of not touching me in some way. I move mine over his, liking this, and wanting more of it. Just touching him feels like it's enough to remind me of the better days we once shared.

He closes his eyes, shaking his head, a harsh exhale falling from his chest, a battle storming within him. I can sense it brewing in the air. "I really thought you needed help," he says. "That the Bianchis were hurting you, but I was wrong, wasn't I? That was a game too?"

The change in mood whips me into reality, one where he'll never forgive me. As soon as he lets his guard down, it's like something comes back and reminds him he shouldn't.

He gets to his feet, his hand no longer on me, and I miss it already—the warmth, the safety of it. Because no matter how dangerous he may be, being around him is the only time I ever feel safe.

He gives me his back as he heads for the door.

"Wait, Enzo. Just wait, okay? Please." Remorse twines into my voice as he stops only inches away from leaving. I get off the bed too but stay far enough away where I can't jump into his arms and cry into his chest, because that's all I want to do right now.

"I didn't play you. I—I really did care for you. It wasn't a game."

He slowly faces me, his expression stoic.

"You don't have to believe what I said yesterday," I continue. "But my situation, it's complicated. There's so much you don't know about me, and you don't want to know. If you knew, you'd never want me." I pause, gathering the courage to continue. "And even if you did, I can't be with you. I can't have any more danger in my life. You're a complication I can't afford."

He grasps the back of his neck. "Don't judge me, Joelle. You don't know what the Bianchis took from us. They're the reason I am who I am. I never wanted this life either."

The agony's riddled there in his words. I can practically feel it coursing through his veins.

"I'm so sorry I caused you pain." My heart shatters over what I did, over caring for someone who'll never be mine.

"Don't worry, baby." His expression turns hard. "We all hurt each other in the end." My bottom lip trembles as he continues. "We'll both have to learn how to tolerate each other until I send you somewhere safe."

I gasp, my inhale trapped in my lungs. "Send me away? What?"

"That's the plan. They'll kill you if you stay. But don't worry, I'm keeping you for a while. You won't be going anywhere until we destroy the Bianchi brothers. May as well get comfortable."

My chest rattles as I choke on my own breath.

Oh God, I can't go anywhere without Robby.

"What will it take for you to just let me go? Would you like me to beg? Is that it? Is that what gets your cock hard?" I clamp my teeth. "A woman begging."

"Mmm..." His gaze narrows. "Oh, you'll beg..." He strides to where I stand, towering over me, his thigh slicing in between my legs as he pushes me up against the wall. His thumb brushes past my parted lips. "But when you beg, it'll be for something else entirely."

I'm caught in his gaze. Unable to move. To respond. The chemistry. That attraction between us, wrenching the words right out of my mouth.

My core tightens, thirsty for this man. A stranger. My once friend. My would-be lover. Except now, he's nothing but my kidnapper and I'm his living prey.

JOELLE

THIRTEEN

I didn't mean to fall asleep, but my body, it was wearing down, breaking from the events of last night. Rubbing my face, I let out a yawn, finding it dark outside as I push away the container and bag of food I left on the bed. I was so exhausted, I forgot to put it on the nightstand.

I spent a while thinking about my son, in between trying the damn windows, hoping I could jump down into the bushes and then run wherever my legs would take me.

But there are men everywhere. Armed, I'm sure. They'd never let me go, even if I were to get past the damn window.

"Ahh!" I scream, tugging at my hair.

My entire body aches, my throat throbbing. The tears, the pain I've spent my life trying to hide is nearing the finish line. It's hard to keep it all locked away, feeling alone every day. It's too much.

Robby is by himself and I'm here. Helpless.

I grab the pillow, soaking my tears into it. It hurts. I want to be free. I want to live a life with my son, the way I never got to.

My shoulders rock as I cry silently, knowing no one will hear me. No one will see me. No one ever does. I'm alone. As always.

My friends and I have been on the road for the second day now, living our best life. I'm using some of the money I saved up from working at a music store close to home. I've been there since I was sixteen, so I have some cushion money.

Both Elsie and Kayla come from a lot more dough than we ever had, so their parents have funded their adventure. Elsie's mom is a plastic surgeon and Kayla's father owns a few wineries. Their parents were more than willing to help me out, but I refused, wanting to pay my own way.

I left some extra cash for Mom, so that way she can use it if she needs it. She hates taking money from me but sometimes she has to. Supporting a family by herself hasn't been easy, and it was part of the reason I began working.

Elsie switches on the radio as soon as we get back into the car from having just eaten at a nearby diner.

I look over my shoulder, back at the restaurant where a man, probably ten years older than me, wouldn't stop talking to us. He was giving me major creep vibes. He's still there, watching our car from the window.

I shiver, every hair on my arms standing on alert. Finally driving away, I ignore the remnants of the eerie feelings left behind by that man.

"I love this song!" Elsie bops her head to the tempo, her fingers drumming on her jeans-clad thigh, her long black hair flipping

around the tops of her shoulders.

"Me too," Kayla chimes in from behind us, curling her arms around the back of my seat.

With the deserted stretch of the two-way road in front of us, I take us to our next stop, a popular karaoke place across state lines. We should get to the city in a few hours.

But suddenly, my Jeep stutters, and slowly the car rolls to a stop.

"What the hell?" I holler, jerking my head toward Elsie, her eyes marred with the same confusion.

"Shit," Kayla whispers as we all hop out, noticing the hood with smoke billowing out of it.

"Let me call for a tow." Elsie rummages through her bag, finding her cell.

"Oh my God," she mutters. "There's no reception."

I swallow harshly, a chill running down my spine.

"We're so fucked," Kayla practically cries, her trembling fingers going to her lips, worry etching her gaze below a set of thick brows.

"It's gonna be okay," I reassure, clasping her hand with mine.

But it isn't okay. Not at all. We wait on the side of the road for what feels like an hour before we see a car. When we do, it's like seeing a light in a dark tunnel, but we don't yet know that while climbing out of one, we are about to drown in another.

"Stop!" we shout, running into the middle of the road, jumping up and down with our hands waving in the air.

The black SUV gets closer, drifting to a stop.

"Thank God!" Elsie says, Kayla breathing a sigh of relief, and I feel it too.

Finally. We're saved.

But when the driver's door opens, when I notice who gets out, my chest grows heavy, my pulse drumming so loudly, I don't hear a word he says, but his mouth, it's moving.

The man from the diner.

I grow dizzy as he approaches, black spots flashing in and out, yet I still see that huge grin on his face. When two others step out of the car, that's when full-on panic sets in. They're older than him, maybe in their forties.

"What seems to be the problem, ladies?" the younger man casually implores, while another marches over to my Jeep.

"Just some car trouble." I force a smile, my legs growing shaky and weak, a thick ball of anxiety slamming into my stomach.

"Lucky for you," the guy next to my Jeep says. "I'm a good mechanic." He strides around, pops the hood from inside, and before we know what's happening, the other older man grabs a hold of Kayla's light brown hair, his arm curled around her neck, her back to his front.

She screams, eyes widened in full-on terror, kicking him, attempting to claw her way out.

"Please, let her go!" I cry, tears raining down my face, and I'm unsure whether to run or to help her somehow.

They only laugh, the other two setting their sights on me, their glares darting to Elsie behind, and I'm bathed in the most paralyzing fear.

My breaths harshly pummel out, my eyes bulging as I step back, needing to get away, but knowing I have nowhere to escape. The man holding Kayla retrieves a gun from his pocket and knocks her on the side of the head, her eyes rolling before she goes limp.

"Run!" Elsie shouts, her voice drifting from the rear. My heartbeat thrashes with every quickened beat, the men crawling nearer now, slithering slowly, knowing they will have us. Yet I run anyway, because running is all we have left.

But we don't get far. A bullet rips into Elsie's calf and she falls instantly, sobbing on the concrete as the man from the restaurant drags her away.

Her teary brown eyes are the last thing I see as someone knocks me on the head from behind, my world turning hazy, a voice saying, "The boss is gonna love you," before everything goes black.

ENZO

The following day, after stopping by work and hanging with Dante for a bit, I got a text from Marissa asking to hang out, which is code for—*please, Enzo, bang my brains out.*

I would, under normal circumstances, but we're definitely not in normal anything right now. I told Marissa I was busy working, hoping that gets her to lay off. She can be persistent as fuck though.

The women at the dance clubs all know me for my reputation and they're not shy about wanting to experience it for themselves. These girls tell their friends and those friends bring more friends…

But my focus is elsewhere. I've got a hostage in my home who hates my guts. Well, that is when she's not playing mind games, like telling me everything between us was real. How the hell am I supposed to believe that when some other man's tongue was down her throat, one she swore was her boyfriend. Yeah, didn't need that fucking visual again.

I'm torn between wanting to hold her in my arms and wanting to rip off her clothes and punish her for ruining what we could've had. It was worth trying. She was worth trying for. Now—it's too late.

After I left the office earlier, I called Colleen, our personal shopper, who hooked me up with all kinds of clothes and more girly shit than I've ever seen in my life. I guessed on the sizes, but

Colleen won't have a problem with exchanging any of it. I hope this gets Joelle smiling.

Readying to enter the room with the six bags I'm holding, plus some food, I stick the key into the door and shove it open.

She sits up as soon as she spots me, the same glare on her face, the one I'm becoming too familiar with.

"Hey, I brought you some clothes and stuff," I say, placing the items on the floor at the foot of the bed.

She crosses her arms over her chest and my eyes instantly zero in on her tits, those nipples hard beneath her tank top.

I grind my jaw.

Fuck. Stop looking.

One of the containers of food is empty, sitting open on the nightstand

At least she's eating.

I clear my throat, my gaze dropping to the bags as I retrieve some of the clothes—dresses, leggings, shirts, shoes. I got her too much shit, considering we won't be going anywhere, but she can take them with her when I send her away.

But the thought of her leaving, fuck… It sets a pain in my chest. I shake it off, not wanting to feel this way for a woman who never really gave a damn.

Getting sick of her silence, I walk up to her, a shirt clutched in my fist, a thumb tipping up her face. "You can say, *thank you, Enzo. That was so nice of you.*"

She scoffs, shoving my hand away. "Thank you, Enzo. Thank you so much for kidnapping me and not letting me leave. You're all kinds of wonderful. I can't wait to introduce you to my mom. She's gonna love you."

My lips wind up at the corners. "I bet she would. Maybe we should call her and ask."

Her face drops, eyes widening. "Ahh—no. We—we can't," she stammers, quickly shaking her head. "Don't ever do that."

I can smell the fear rippling off her.

But why?

I clasp her cheek. "Babe, I wouldn't even know how to. And I wouldn't do that, not unless you wanted me to. I'm not here to hurt you."

Her brows drop with the frown settling on her face. "You say you want to help me, so help me. Let me go, Enzo," she pleads. "That's how you can help! Every moment I'm in here is a chance that the person I love will be killed."

"Fuck, Joelle!" I roll my thumb over her mouth, my chest tightening. "Tell me who it is. I will find them and bring them back to you. And whoever is after them, will die. Believe that."

"I can't take that risk." She exhales a long sigh, gazing up at me with a shadow of her pain.

Lowering with a bend, I kiss her forehead, my eyes falling shut before I right myself. "And I can't take the risk of the Bianchis killing you. As soon as you step a foot out of here…" I look back at her. "They'll find you and kill you, and whoever you care about. So if I can keep you safe, then I damn right will."

"You don't understand," she pants with a soft cry.

"Then you have to help me understand."

"Just go." Tears stamp over her voice as she roughly shoves them away.

"Baby. Talk to me."

"Go!" The word rips into me like a knife. "Leave!" She gets off the bed, pushing at my chest with her palms. "Get the hell out of here!" She shoves harder, but I haven't moved an inch. "I want you to fucking leave!"

I place my hands over hers. "I'll go. I'm sorry. I mean that." Her breaths climb out rapidly, her eyes level to my chest as I continue. "I'd do anything for you, Joelle, even protect you when you don't think you need it. I hope you get that I'm doing this for you."

"You're doing this for *you*!" She finally stares up at me. "Don't act like any of this is for me." She pivots, returning to the bed and gives me her back.

With nothing else to say between us, I leave her, hoping like hell she finds it in her heart to forgive me one day when she's alive enough to do it.

ENZO

FOURTEEN

I've left her alone most of the day, wanting her to calm down a bit before she sees my face again. As I pull up to my house, my cell vibrates with an alert coming from her room, the app letting me know there is increased movement.

My pulse quickens as I fire up the app, parking the Bugatti, then running out. As I storm into the house, my eyes on the phone, I see Joelle is just fine. But the guest room, well… The clothes I bought her are everywhere as she grunts with fury, banging on the windows. I'm surprised she hasn't tried to lift the television—or maybe she has. I should rewind the recording and see for myself.

Just when I think she's about to throw one of the armchairs into the window, she drops against the wall, lifting her knees, hiding her face, and rocks gently. I can't hear her cry, but I know she is, and fuck that makes me want to rip out my very own heart.

I run up, two steps at a time, unlock the door and push it open, needing to hold her, to ease her pain. As soon as I'm inside, she captures my gaze, brushing under her eyes, the red streaks within them slamming into my chest.

I did that. Me.

Fuck.

My hand runs through my hair as I tread slowly, every step seeped in cement. Heavy. Burdened. Knowing she won't want me. She doesn't want my arms to make her world right. I'm the one who set it on fire.

But I go anyway. I go because she needs me, even when she fights it. Even when she thinks she doesn't. Because her heart, it knows me, even when her mind forgets. The ghosts of who we were then—they're still here, trapped in the bodies of who we are now.

If only she'd remember.

"Joelle," I whisper, extending an arm. "Come here, baby."

Her shoulders tremble, eyes watering over, those brows pinched so tight as she looks at me. But she doesn't move, and I don't give up. I lower to the space beside her, stretching an arm around her back, pulling her closer. Her head falls to my chest as my palm brushes up and down her arm.

We stay that way for a while, her body convulsing, her tears soaking my shirt as she seizes it tight in her fist.

"We'll probably need to do something about this mess you created." The words roll out with a faint smile.

She sniffles, her laughter weak. Seeing her this way, it breaks my resolve. I don't want her locked in this room all alone anymore. If she decides to break every damn thing in my house, so be it. I can always replace that shit, but her—there's no replacing that.

"How about we go downstairs and get some snacks? I have all

the good stuff."

"Like what?" She lifts away from me, cheeks stained with a shade of pink, wetness clouding over them.

"I've got like three different cupcakes." My eyes dart to her mouth. "Maybe four ice cream flavors. Wait, make that three. I may have finished one last night."

She squints. "The whole thing?"

"Well, there wasn't that much left."

She stares at me with huge, bright eyes, thinning her lips to conceal the laugh bubbling out.

"Fine." I throw a hand in the air with a chuckle. "There was a shit ton left. What can I say? I'm a sucker for chocolate fudge."

"Is that so?" She hikes a brow. "So if I smeared some on my body, you'd lick it all off?"

Fuck.

My jaw twitches, a fist curling at my side to stifle the image going to my dick. Yeah, too late on that. My cock jerks.

"Really, baby?" My hand clasps the side of her neck, fingers roughing into her skin, eyes delving into the endless ocean of her gaze. "Don't do that," I groan. "I can't think about your naked body dripping with chocolate ice cream when I'm supposed to be comforting you."

"You're doing just fine." She places a hand on my knee. "This is distracting me, and I kind of needed the distraction."

"Well then…" I jump to my feet. "I'll distract the fuck out of you."

Just as she tilts her head to the side with a curious glint in her eyes, I scoop her up by her hips and throw her over my shoulder.

"Hey!" She giggles adorably. "You probably don't want to be this close to me. I haven't even showered."

"You smell good enough to eat, baby girl." My palm lands on

her ass on instinct, and I test the waters, squeezing tight, and her breath hitches.

Her hot panting skims across my back, and knowing how much she wants me, knowing that maybe all those feelings I had back at the club weren't just mine, only makes me want her more. Maybe we were real, however fucked up it was.

I walk us down the stairs, my hand still on her ass, needing to touch her everywhere. Goddamn, I've never wanted to fuck a woman this badly. Hell, I've never waited this long to do it either.

They're more than willing to get into my bed, or anywhere else really. But none of it meant anything, not until Joelle.

We make it to my kitchen and I reluctantly put her back on her feet. She fingers her hair, fluffing it up as she clears her throat, her cheeks a deeper red now as she looks up at me.

"Where's this ice cream you promised?"

"Damn, woman. You've got no patience." I pull out a bowl and spoons from the cabinets, placing both down before strolling to the fridge and opening the freezer.

She follows me, standing too damn close as her attention flows to the cartons of ice cream surrounded by a crap load of frozen veggies.

"So that's how you manage to keep all those muscles in check? Ice cream and broccoli?" Her face lights up with laughter.

"You're a real damn fucking comedian." I bump into her with an elbow on purpose and she does it back, pushing past me to kneel and retrieve the coffee flavor.

"I've got what I need." She eyes me playfully, opening the carton as she heads back to the counter to get her spoon. "You may go."

"Damn, I've been replaced by dessert, huh? I see how it is. Okay. Well, I know when I'm not needed."

"I was kidding." She sucks on the spoon, then dips it in for more. "I kind of need you to show me around first."

"Brat." I move toward her with a chuckle, grabbing the ice cream from her grasp and taking a spoonful into my mouth.

"Hey! I never said I share."

"You do now." I fill the spoon. "Open your mouth." And she does, slamming her gaze to mine. Gradually, I slip the spoon inside, and without my eyes leaving hers, I watch her suck on the cold metal until it's licked clean.

"How'd that taste?" My thumb replaces the spoon, stroking her lips.

"Good." Her whispery breaths got my cock in a chokehold. I inhale deep, dick throbbing for her lips. Both sets of them. I need inside this woman. Need to watch her come. For me, and me alone.

I grit my teeth.

"Come on." Grabbing her hand, I thread our fingers together, stepping away with her next to me. "I'll take you on a small tour, then I have to go to work for a little, so you'll have to manage alone without me."

"I promise not to die from boredom."

"Just try not to break the sculpture by the door." I pull her flush to my side, curling my arm around her hip. "I kinda like it."

"That'll be the first thing I break."

"I shouldn't have said anything, huh?"

She side-eyes me with a tiny flicker of a smile. "Now you're catching on."

JOELLE

He's taken me through some areas of his luxurious place, from the high-tech movie theater to the game room with a huge trampoline in the center, to the outdoor tennis courts and cabanas by the pool.

He's introduced me to all the men who work for him too. They seem decent enough, but people can't be trusted.

But my heart, it trusts Enzo. I don't know why, but it does. He may not be allowing me to leave, but I believe he's doing it to protect me, even though I'd rather die if it meant Robby was safe. But I don't think anything will convince Enzo to let me go. Even the truth.

If I tell him about my son, he'll try to save him. If he's too late, if Faro finds out I talked, Robby is done for. No. I have to figure this out on my own.

"Okay," he says as we return to his pristine, white kitchen, stepping onto the dark wooden floors set beneath. "Now you can enjoy as much ice cream as you want while I'm gone."

"And hopefully a nice, hot shower after I clean the apocalypse that is your room," I grumble, remembering what I did. His hand snakes around my hip, that powerful body slamming to mine.

"Shower, huh?" His eyes turn heavy-lidded, and he leans close, so close a shudder races up my spine, his mouth hovering over my ear. "I kind of wish I had a camera in the bathroom right about now."

My body grows warm and tingly, my core achy, growing wet in the way it only does for him. His gaze bores into mine, and that feeling of lust—it's back with a vengeance.

How would it feel to be touched by someone whose touch I crave? Would it feel good that first time he enters me, knowing all the other times have been to hurt me? Would I want him in that moment, or will I be clutched in everlasting fear?

I want to know. I want to feel with him. The way only he makes me feel.

But what happens after? I'll still need to run. I'll still need to let him go. Again.

"I really gotta go, babe." His voice beats with a sultry rasp, his knuckles brushing along my cheek. "Even though the last place I want to be is anywhere you're not."

"Enzo…" I murmur his name, wishing the intense connection between us was enough to make me whole again, but I'm ruined beyond recognition. He still doesn't know me and all my hidden scars. It's easy to remember, he may reject me once he does.

"I'm still mad at you," I tease, tethered with an emotional edge.

His gaze wanders tenderly over every inch of my face. "That's the way I like it, baby." Those full lips dip to the corner of my mouth, and he kisses me there so lightly, one would barely feel it, but I do. I feel everything. The force of it. The touch, tingling over my entire body. He makes me feel this. Always. And with him, I never want to stop feeling.

JOELLE

FIFTEEN

After he left, I wandered through the house for a while, familiarizing myself with my surroundings should danger strike and I'd need a place to hide. That's how my brain thinks these days, always looking for a hole to disappear into.

Wrapping my arms around the oversized cozy sweater he bought me, I saunter past guard after guard, their stoic expression enhancing the air of danger surrounding them.

As I walk down a large corridor, I freeze when I pass a room he never showed me. The grand piano is visible through the glass door, and my fingertips tingle with reminiscence of once playing the keys so well I'd drown in the music, the world around me slipping away. Could I still play or have my hands forgotten?

FOURTEEN YEARS OLD

"Play that again," Mom says from behind me, her palms clasped to my shoulders as I peer over at her, a smile brightening her face.

I place my fingers back on the keys, the music drifting, the sound of "Prelude No.1 in C Major" bathing us in tranquility. It's my mother's favorite. And it's mine because of it.

We never had money for a piano of our own, but we didn't need one, because this one, it belonged to my grandma. She was a classical pianist, and Mom likes to say I inherited her natural talents.

I've always loved to play. Once, when I sneaked into the music room at school, I played when no one was there, or at least I thought I was alone. I caught the eye of the music teacher who took me under her wing and taught me everything else I didn't know.

"You're truly amazing," Mom whispers. "Don't ever forget that, Jade."

"I won't."

Thinking about her still causes a jolt of pain, knowing she's out there, believing I'm dead, never getting closure. It's an agony I can't describe.

I swipe under my eyes, the wet drops soaking up my fingers. Mom would understand why I couldn't contact her though. She spent her life protecting her children. She'd never want me to put Robby in danger.

I continue to stare at the piano, unable to pull myself away, wanting so badly to know if I could play again, but I won't try. That'll only remind me of the good days, and I can't think of them right now.

I keep moving, even though my heart and soul are still in that room, wishing I could pour myself into every keystroke.

The room beside it seems much safer—a large office by every appearance with its door set open. A black contemporary desk sits in the middle with a high-back leather chair. A long teal sofa stretches across one side, the walls painted a pale gray.

Stepping inside, my feet stride past the soft ivory carpet, the shaggy threads sliding in between my toes, my hand gliding over the polished desk, not a speck of dust on it.

Curiosity sets in and I slip around the desk toward the drawers, wanting to know what a man like that keeps in his office. Maybe I'll find something that'll tell me who he really is.

I pull out the top drawer, finding two blue folders and a small note pad lying on top. Reaching for the pad, I don't expect to find anything in it. But as I open it, my head snaps back.

"How the hell did he know…?" My voice drifts as I read the first page.

Hey, Joelle. Nice snooping.

I flip to the next page, my pulse speeding.

You're looking especially sexy today.

I read through the two other notes, not understanding how he knew I'd wander in here.

You won't find anything too exciting, I'm afraid.

Or maybe you will.

Quickly dropping the pad back into the drawer, I take out the folders. My gaze roams around the room, looking for cameras that I know are here. He could be watching me right now. A smile slinks to my lips and I flip a middle finger right before I go into examining the contents of the first folder.

I find receipts with no business name on them, amounts in the thousands. Rifling through the rest, I move on to the next folder. But just as I open it, something slips out, wafting onto the floor.

Kneeling, I retrieve it, turning it around, finding a photo of a man I'd never thought I'd see again. My shock's hidden behind a rough breath.

I can't stop staring into Roman's bloodied face. So much of it, I could barely recognize him. Why does Enzo have this photo? Did he beat him? For me? Now it makes sense why I haven't seen him since the night Enzo saw us together. Is he dead?

I need answers, and when Enzo's home, he's going to give them to me. Taking the picture, I place the folder back inside, closing the drawer and heading back to my room.

As I do, I pass the foyer, the jangle of keys clinking from the outside has me staying exactly where I am.

Enzo walks in, tight gray trousers and a dark navy button-down conforming to his body like they've been permanently sewn to him, the taut muscles of his arms, his chest rippling under his clothes as he finds me standing before him.

His brow bends in question, probably noting my tight expression.

"We have to talk," I say, the photo dangling from my hand.

"Sure, baby." I'm met with an amusing smirk ticking up the corner of his mouth. "Might this have to do with you snooping through my office?"

"You didn't exactly tell me not to."

"You're right. I didn't." He attempts to lock the door behind him, and when he's about to, a car comes screeching down the street right outside.

He instantly hardens—his face, his body, everything goes on alert. "Stay here and don't move," he demands as he runs out of the house, one of his men beside him, whispering into his ear. Enzo shakes his head, saying something in return, but I can't hear it.

I stay by the door as the tires advance from beyond until a white Mercedes comes to a stop right in front of the house. Two women in short dresses hop out.

My body goes rigid, a burning sensation rolling into my chest.

He has women coming here? While he acts like I matter? Calling me baby. Making me think... I don't know what.

My stomach recoils with a fury I hadn't known I had.

He talks to them with his back to me, and I can see his hands moving as they each gaze up at him, the blonde one running her nails up his arm while the one with the pink streaks in her hair bites on her lower lip, her dress matching the color of her strands.

My feet are moving before I have a chance to stop them. A smile falls to my face as I step out, the same one I gave the crowd that filled the club every night. Walking over, I come to stand beside Enzo, my palm roughly catching his shoulder as he glances questioningly at me.

"What are you ladies doing out here?" I ask innocently, while inside, disgust swirls. "It's cold. Come in," I continue, gesturing with a hand toward the house.

"What the hell are you doing?" he growls into my ear.

I ignore him, my lips winding up.

"We'd love to!" the pink-haired one practically chirps.

They rush past me, marching right in, with Enzo and me following them.

"What the fuck are you doing?" he snaps again, his hand reaching for my hip, his fingers harshly nipping at my skin, but it only makes the fire inside me burn brighter.

I narrow a glare. "You wanted them here? Well, who am I to stop you?"

"I didn—" he tries to explain but I peel his hand off me and join the women inside, who've already made themselves quite at home, their stilettos still on, a tanned leg crossed over the other.

I take my seat opposite them, while Enzo runs a hand through his hair, his forehead furrowed. He's looking uncharacteristically nervous.

"Would you girls like some water or a glass of wine?" I ask, passing a glance at Enzo, whose eyes look like two large bullets aiming right at me.

My pulse beats faster as we stare each other down, my nails biting into my palm.

"We'd love some wine," the blonde tosses, curling her lips as she stares at him.

He's fucked them both. That much is obvious. My body grows numbingly cold, but I have no right to be jealous. He doesn't owe me a thing. In fact, I've hurt him, turned him down more than once, and he's still here, trying to help me.

He's beaten Roman for merely putting his hands on me. What would he do if he knew what the Bianchis have done? What the men who pay them have done? Would he kill them? For me? A girl who means nothing to anyone anymore? An invisible soul trapped in a body burned with scars. That's who I am. He can't possibly fall in love with a woman like that. No. A man like him doesn't want a girl who's sold her body for money.

Shaking the thoughts out of my head, I revert my attention back to him, his gaze still glued to mine, the anger weaved within it.

"Be a good host and go get them some wine," I taunt, gripped with a feral possessiveness for a man I wish I could have.

His jaw twitches. I swallow against the ache in my throat, hating that these women got to have something I desperately want.

His chest roughly expands, then he marches out of the room. The last thing I want is to be stuck here with these women. I don't even know why I did what I did, but with the envy swirling through me, I couldn't control myself.

"So, who are you exactly?" pink hair asks. "We've never seen anyone else here before."

"Yeah," blondie chimes in. "Are you his sister or something?"

No, Joelle. Don't do it.

But the thought to piss him off further is a lot more thrilling.

"I *am* his sister. We're actually *very* close, maybe a little too close if you know what I mean." I pop up a shoulder, leaning my face in with a flirty arch of my brows.

"Wha— Ugh. Do you mean you guys…" The blonde one bulges out her eyes.

"Wow." The other flips her hair back. "You two look nothing alike."

I think that just went past her tiny brain.

I shrug. "Our mom must've had too much fun with the mailman."

In that moment, Enzo stomps back in, three glasses in his hands.

"Babe," the pink one calls. "Oh my God, you never told me your mother had an affair with the mailman."

The blonde woman keeps looking from Enzo to me, like she's trying to imagine us fucking.

I bite the inside of my cheek to stop myself from laughing.

"Don't call me babe." His reply is a sharp bite as he hands them each a glass, looking back at me over his shoulder, his teeth clamping.

The women chug their wines as though it's a shot, while Enzo steps up to me, his body towering, his eyes holding me captive. "Drink." He stretches out a commanding hand, and I tentatively retrieve the glass, my heart flipping around like it's come undone from the grip of my body.

I take a seductive sip.

"I don't know what the fuck you're doing, Joelle." He leans into my neck, a gruff whisper twining up my insides, warming every inch of me. "But you're gonna answer for this."

I stand, my body flat against his, my breasts licking over the buttons of his shirt. "For what exactly?" I sneer, my voice lowered. "I'd never want to get in between you and your extracurricular activities." My eyes are hard on his, while his pin me with a thicker glare. "Now, excuse me." I rush past him. "I'll be upstairs while you entertain your friends." Taking a final look at him over my shoulder, I find him oozing with fury. "Have a *great* time."

I don't give him a moment to reply, heading for the stairs, and as I climb up, I hear one woman say, "We should go up too. We really missed you, Enzo." As I enter my room, I hope I don't hear him fucking them through the walls.

ENZO

SIXTEEN

She's the one who turned me away, telling me how dangerous I fucking am, but now she's jealous that *she* invited women into my goddamn house? I have every right to do whatever I want, whenever I want it. But doesn't she realize I don't want to?

I may have never hesitated to bring women home before Joelle, but now, I have no desire to. No matter what I tell my brothers, what they assume I do, I haven't been with a woman since Joelle and I met. I've come close, hell, I'm only human, but nothing ever happened. I couldn't go through with it.

None of them were her. Because when Joelle and I were together, I felt something real for once, something that I never felt with any woman I wasted my time with. But Joelle found me, the real me, and I never want to share that part of myself with anyone else.

"Are you coming, handsome?" Marissa clasps her hand through mine, pulling me behind her.

We climb up the stairs and I have no intentions of fucking either one of them. I still have no idea why they came, nor do I care. It's probably because I ignored Marissa's text earlier. All I want is to kick them out, but not before I have my own fucking revenge.

Joelle wanted this, did she? She wanted them here, with me. Well, I'll be happy to give it to her. I don't have to do a damn thing for her to think I am.

I pull them into the bedroom next to the one Joelle sleeps in. It's the only room I use for the women I bring home, never allowing any of them into my bedroom. That shit is sacred.

Marissa immediately falls on the bed, her palms fisting the comforter, her pink hair in disarray. Tatiana giggles, climbing on top of her, kissing her neck, both of them hungrily eyeing me. But neither I nor my dick gives a shit, because the one woman I want keeps fighting me.

"Aren't you going to join us?" Tatiana purrs, running her long fingernails over Marissa's now exposed tits. "Come on, Enzo," she continues as Marissa's hand disappears in between her thighs. "You can't possibly tell us you'd rather fuck your sister over us."

I snap my head back. "What did you just say?"

"That girl downstairs. She was your sister, right? Is that why you avoided us today? Were you too busy with her to entertain us?" Tatiana's voice drowns with a moan as Marissa fucks her with her fingers.

Joelle told them I'm her brother? That we fuck? My jaw aches with how hard I grind my teeth. *Wait until I get my damn hands on her.*

"We won't judge," Marissa whimpers as Tatiana returns the

favor, slipping her fingers past her panties. "We'll even let her join us."

"Excuse me, ladies." I march toward the door. "I just remembered I have a business call to make. But you two enjoy yourselves. I'll join you when I return."

Bullshit. I have no intentions of that.

"Mmm, okay," Marissa moans just as I shut the door behind me, heading a short distance to Joelle's room. I don't even knock as I practically tear the door off its hinges, finding her on the bed with a pillow over her head.

As soon as I come in, she jolts with alarm. "What are you doing in here? Shouldn't you be with your fan club?" She lets out a feisty snicker as she sits up. "I heard the cheers all the way here."

"I'm exactly where I need to be." The words come out harsh as I move closer to where she is, so beautiful and so goddamn stubborn. "What did you tell them downstairs while I was getting drinks?"

"Don't you have cameras?" She folds her arms over her chest, the skin of her one shoulder exposed, making me want to yank it all off, to remind her how good we can be together, if only she lets go and lets me in. "Maybe you can press rewind and find out." Her luscious lips tilt up with amusement.

A crude smirk lands over my mouth as I cut all the distance between us, standing right before her.

"I want to hear it from you." My hand falls to her jaw, jerking her head up. "Tell me, Joelle. What did you tell them?"

"Well…" A smile teases the edge of her lips. "I may or may not have insinuated that you fuck your sister." She shoves my hand away, lying back down onto the bed.

"I don't have a sister."

"Surprise." A brow curves up. "You do now."

"Are you cockblocking me, baby?" I lower onto the bed right beside her, my hand trailing up her leg, from her ankle, further, until my palm settles on her inner thigh, and I squeeze enough to get her shuddering.

"No. Just having fun at your expense." Humor settles on her face, and I'd very much like to wipe it off with my dick deep down her throat.

Her gaze skirts to my cock, and I know she can tell how hard I am.

"Like what you see there, babe? Want to touch it and make it feel better?"

"Yeah, sorry, I don't want something that doesn't belong to me."

I scoot closer, my hand now fledging to her waistband, fingertips riding under her shirt, stroking the skin there. "You think my hard-on is for them?"

"I heard you all." Her breath goes all hoarse and wispy, her skin waking with goose bumps from my touch. "I'm pretty sure I know what happened. What I don't know is why you're here."

"Let me clarify some things." My fingers climb higher, her chest rising with my movement, lips parted with soft exhales. My hand lands right below her tits, brushing right under them. The swell of each one has me wanting to feel them in my palms. "I'm hard *for you*, Joelle. I'm always hard for you."

She sucks in a breath, and I look deep into the calmness of those tranquil eyes, barely keeping it together from how badly I want to kiss that wide-eyed look from her face. "And that shit you heard, had nothing to do with me. As you can hear"—I tilt my head toward the noise still very much happening—"they're fine without me. But you…" My fingers track up the side of her body, bare skin on bare skin. "I have a feeling you need me more than you want to admit and I sure as fuck need you."

Her expression turns wanton, cheeks flushed. "Enzo," she whispers, her brows creasing.

"Yes, baby." It's not a question because I know. "That thing you feel deep inside, I feel it too."

My hand falls back to her thigh as her hand lands on my knee, cruising up until she holds my cock in her grip, her hand stroking once as she draws her body near mine, until her breath storms over my mouth.

"Fuuuck." My entire body comes alive, not wanting her to stop touching me.

My gaze narrows. "You have no idea what I want to do to you right now."

"Do it, then." She sighs with a raspy moan.

Oh hell.

"If that's really what you want, then tell me. Was he your boyfriend?" I squeeze my hand, a finger brushing up her pussy.

"You first." She tightens her fingers around my cock. "Did you fuck Kora?"

"Who?" I groan as she massages my hard-on.

"The girl at the strip club. The one you went to the back with."

"Joelle, no. Fuck, baby." I hold her cheek in my hand, my face twisted up. "That's what you thought?"

She nods.

"I haven't touched anyone since meeting you. I don't want to."

She bites into her lower lip and I want more than anything to kiss this woman.

"Your turn." A hand falls to her jaw and I grip it tight as I stare into her eyes. "Was he your boyfriend, Joelle?"

"No." She shakes her head, those eyes glossing over with emotion. "He was nothing."

In a flash, I'm on her, my body pinning hers onto the bed, my knee in between her thighs, her wrists caught in a tightened grip above her head.

"No one has made me feel what you do," I confess, slowly lowering until the tip of my tongue traces up her lips, my breath weaving over the curve of her jaw, down to her neck.

A sigh wrapped in the smallest moan makes it out of her, like she's fighting hard not to show me how badly she wants this. Wants us.

Gently, I kiss the delicate skin of her neck, right over that rapid pulse beating against my tongue. "I sure as hell wouldn't kiss my sister like this." A smile fits over me as I pepper her with more tender kisses.

Her hands break free from my grasp, a palm clutching the back of my head, nails grating up my scalp, her hips rocking against my knee. "Enzo…" The whisper of my name has my cock surging to feel her wet and tight around me.

"If I didn't know you were hurt before," I say, lifting my eyes to the tortured look of desire on her face. "That you were treated roughly by a man whose hands you didn't want touching you, I'd have torn off your clothes and fucked you like a savage already." I clasp her cheek, my heart damn right shredding from the mere thought of what Roman did to her, what others may have done. "But I won't be another man who hurts you. I'd never fucking do that."

"Is that why you beat up Roman?" Her eyes glisten with the tears hidden behind them, her voice imprinted with vulnerability she doesn't always show. I consider it a gift when she feels comfortable to let me see it.

"I didn't just beat him, Joelle. I killed him. Painfully."

Her sharp intake of breath, those brows stitching closer, doesn't stop me from telling her the rest. "I'd kill every last goddamn one who dared to lay a hand on you."

She gasps from the shock of my confession. "Why do you care so much?" Her words tremble out as she looks at me with so much sadness there. "I don't deserve any of it."

"You deserve everything." I drop my lips to hers, leaving a barely there kiss.

She palms my face, both of us holding each other in more ways than one, both of us broken in our own messed-up way. "I wish we could've met before…" She trails off as her eyes blur with tears.

"Stop wasting time trying to find something we'll never have. This is us, baby. Right here. Right now. And there's no one I'd want more than you. This version of you." I kiss the tip of her nose, breathing her in. "Stop building walls when all I've ever wanted to do was break them."

Her chin trembles as I wipe under her eyes. "What do you want, baby? Stop overthinking, just say it. What do you want?"

"You, Enzo. I want you."

"You have me. You always did."

I capture her lips, inhaling her, feeling my body fill up with life as she kisses me back. The gasping breaths, the groans, they hungrily tear from our hearts, my tongue spearing into her mouth with a maddening frenzy, her hands clawing up my back, lifting the shirt tucked within my waistband.

I never want this to stop.

My hand sails down her hip, wanting to feel her come on my fingers. I can't fuck her. Not yet. I want this to be slow. I don't want her to regret a moment between us.

Reluctantly, I pull back, both of us breathless. I sit up, tugging at the top of her leggings and I start to peel them off. "I know how to be gentle too, Joelle. I'm gonna show you."

She holds my gaze, arching her hips, letting me slip them all the way down, my depravity zeroing in on the white lace thong covering that sweet pussy. I want more than anything to taste her, to know how she sounds while quivering on my tongue, but that'll wait too.

"You're so beautiful," I say, gliding back up her body, my lips returning to hers, moving gently, sucking on her tongue as my index finger pulls her panties to the side, stroking up in between her soaked softness.

"Baby," I growl. "You need this bad, don't you?"

"Please. I want to feel what you do to me. What you always do."

"Fuck." I suck in a long inhale, circling a fingertip around her clit, adding a second. "I'm gonna protect you, every gorgeous inch of you." Without my eyes leaving hers, I ease a finger inside her, slow. "No one will dare touch you again. From now on, my hands, they're the only ones you'll ever feel."

"Yes," she cries, her hands fisting the bedsheets, her back curving as her eyelids flutter. "More. I want you deeper."

"I'll always give you what you want." I thrust both fingers all the way.

She squirms, her heavy pants, those tantalizing moans of pleasure have me ramming harder, hitting her G-spot in a way that has my name spilling from her mouth, her walls clutching me tight.

I crash my lips to hers, never wanting to kiss another woman as long as I live. This is what it should feel like. I had no damn clue before—not until her. Nothing will ever compare to this. If she leaves me. *When* she leaves me. I'll never be right again.

Maybe I could convince her to stay. That this home, with me, is where she needs to be.

"Harder," she cries as we separate, her exhales fanning over me as her gaze bores into mine, her hand clasping the back of my neck. "I need it harder."

So I give it to her, my curled fingers slamming inside until she quivers. "You feel so good, Joelle." My thumb strokes her clit simultaneously. "You're gonna feel so good wrapped around my cock."

"Fuck me, ple-please just do it." The words tumble out of her in a hurry, and the tremor behind them has me wanting to do just that.

"Not tonight, baby. I want to take my time getting to know your body." I drive harder. "And I want you to get to know mine."

"Oh God, yes," she cries, her walls clasping around me, pulling me in, my cock stiff and twitching against her thigh, needing inside her warmth.

Her body convulses, her whimpering coming stronger now, her pussy shuddering around me in waves.

"Yeah, that's it, baby. Let me feel you. Let me hear it." I prop myself on my arm. "Let me see those eyes as you come."

"Enzo, yes..." Her voice falters, her gaze fastened to mine, and when she crashes, she doesn't hide it. She lets me see it all, and I savor every moment.

JOELLE

SEVENTEEN

After he touched me, made me feel pieces of the girl I was, he held me in his arms for what felt like hours. The women next door long forgotten, sent home by his men, the ones he instructed to get them out of his home.

I've never been held by a man before. Not really. The one boyfriend I had when I was eighteen was just a boy. We didn't last more than a few months, and the one after him was more of the same. They were nice guys, but no one I really remembered or longed for.

Not like Enzo. He's carved out a piece of me. Owning it. Consuming it. As though it's been his all along. As though I've been his forever.

With him, I'm weightless, lost in a world I didn't know I could have. But he makes me want it. The normalcy. A life—with hi with Robby. And maybe he can protect us. Maybe I was wrong about it all. He's done so much for me already. Maybe I could trust him with my secrets. If anyone could help me, Enzo may be the one to do it.

But I need time to be sure this is the right move. If Robby is still alive, then I have to be absolutely positive that telling Enzo won't harm my son.

Enzo rustles beside me, his large arm draped over my hip, pulling me closer as he groans. His mouth lands on my shoulder so softly, it doesn't belong to a man as hard as him. Yet, that's who he's always been with me, hasn't he? A myriad of faces, an angel, and the devil too.

He fell asleep beside me all night, not wanting to go, and I didn't want him to go either. He makes all the ugly fade away, finding the beauty I once possessed and bringing it out onto the surface.

I could love him. Really love him. The thought hurts, my heart heavy, bleeding for the music we could create. But can it really be our song? Can we sing the words out loud, or are we destined to beat to a melody that never quite fit?

After he brought us food last night, we ate in bed, laughing like long-lost friends, lovers awakened to the colors flooding from a world that was once so dark, so lonely. Until now. Until he came into my life and changed everything. For better or worse. I don't yet know. I'm too afraid to find out.

Fear, that's what I've known these past nine years. My only real friend or enemy. They're one and the same. In my world, people are hard to trust.

But I trust him.

Don't I?

"Good morning, baby," he says, the gravelly rasp of his voice seeps with male power, wrapping me in its safety, something foreign, yet something I crave badly.

"Morning." I turn toward him, an adoring smile spreading wide across his face.

"I hope you slept well, because I sure as hell did." He squeezes the hand on my hip, kissing the tip of my nose.

My heart lurches.

"Never better." I grin, meaning it. Sleeping while my enemies watched my every move, entering my home uninvited, isn't what I'd call quality sleep.

"Good. Maybe we can make this permanent." His palm cruises around to my ass, massaging it as he kisses my neck.

My nipples pebble in the wake of his touch, my moans beating with a hum, my fingers lacing in his hair. Waking up beside him every day, I don't know if I'm ready for that. I'm already falling deep for this man, without knowing a thing about him.

"I need more time," I whisper, and his lips still, his breath warmly drifting over my neck. He draws back, those eyes trapping me in the evergreen forest, into a maze full of temptation.

"I'm not the enemy, baby."

"I know that. But…" I trail off, not wanting to reveal more than I'm ready to.

His hand fastens around the back of my neck, his gaze softening. "It's okay. Don't need to explain."

"I feel like I do." Emotions grip the back of my throat. "I feel like I need to tell you everything, but there are things holding me back."

"You tell me when you're ready because I'm not going anywhere." A crooked smile lands over his face. "And neither are you, baby girl."

"Thanks for the constant reminder." I roll my eyes playfully as he scoots me up and places me on top of him, my cheek against his chest, the hurried beats of his heart pounding underneath me, matching the quickening of my pulse.

"Tell me that being here in my arms isn't better than wherever you were, and I'll let you go right now. No questions. But don't lie to me."

My breathing hitches, my skin awakening with prickles running down my back.

"I can't tell you that."

He lets out a sigh, pushing my body up languidly as his mouth lands to the top of my head, the kiss so beautiful, I burrow further into his chest, not sure when the nightmare turned into a dream.

But Robby, he's still out there, and I still need to find him.

JOELLE

EIGHTEEN

The following night, I go to bed alone, missing those arms around me. The chilly comforter feels even colder as I slip under it.

Closing my eyes, I envision the last time I saw Robby, his brilliant blue eyes so vivid you'd think the whole world was within them. Even with all the awful around us, seeing him in those short minutes every month, managed to make my whole world brighter.

I drift off, remembering him, remembering those fleeting moments we managed to smile together, and I never want to forget them. They're the only pieces of him I have to cling to. The only things that submerge the nightmares that haunt me still.

I stand before them, naked, body trembling, hands covering my breasts, my knees clasped so hard, my bones ache. Tears drip down my cheeks as they stare at me, their gazes putrid, rotting thoughts filling them.

"This is our new one," a man says, resting on the black velvet sofa, the sides of his hair peppered with gray as he swipes the side of my bruised cheek with his hardened knuckles. "I broke her in already."

"Looks like you did more than that." Another laughs, his face just as old as the one who beat me earlier when I fought back. But he took what he wanted anyway.

I wobble on my bare feet, still coming down from whatever they drugged me with.

"Does she dance?" the third man asks, staring past me at the pole centered in the room. "I'd pay to see that body work."

"She'll do whatever the hell we tell her," the one who harmed me chimes in, his sinister tone like spikes across my flesh.

I swallow through the pain in my throat, where he held me while he threatened to kill me if I didn't obey. He said his name was Faro, and that I was his now.

I tried to look for Kayla and Elsie when I was first brought into the cage where I'm held, but they're not there. They would've answered when I called out for them, screaming so loud that the other women there told me to shut up. Where could they be? How will I ever find them?

"Dance, girl," one barks, a snarl turning up his upper lip.

But I don't. I can't. My body is numb, shivering, my breathing so rapid, I'm afraid I'll pass out.

"Is she a mute, Faro?" he continues. "You get us a fucking dummy?"

"Nah." Faro laughs cruelly. "I think she needs some more encouragement."

I gasp, shaking my head. "N-no. Please," I stammer.

"Oh, look," the third man says. "She speaks. It's a damn miracle."

They advance on me, rising off the sofa while I fall back a step, almost tripping, my hands uncovering what I didn't want them to see.

They grin, their eyes on my breasts, the tears streaming down my face and I know what's coming.

As they get to me, as their hands greedily gnaw at my skin, my cries turn to screams, and I don't stop, not until they finish, leaving me on the floor like I'm discarded already.

ENZO

Sleeping beside her, it's the soundest I've slept in forever. She does that, and I hope I do that for her too.

I arrive home after spending a couple of hours at Viper, taking care of some business Dante and I were supposed to handle together. I admitted to liking Joelle, and I caught Dante off guard with that. But I meant what I told him. If Joelle wanted me, I wouldn't hesitate to make her mine, but she's got too much holding her back. If only I could shatter that wall and show her what's behind it. Maybe then she'd stay.

The house is quiet as I enter, my men around the premises as always. Joelle must be asleep by now. The last time I saw her on my cell was while at the club, and she was curled up on the sofa watching television.

Taking the stairs quietly, I make it to the door of my bedroom, but instead of going in, I walk down until I get to hers. I want to sleep next to her again. Does she want me there too?

Gently, I turn the knob, hoping not to wake her. As I start to push open the door, her scream rips through the walls, so loud it causes my pulse to jump, my feet moving with alarm, some of my men already upstairs, marching toward us.

"Sir?" one says behind me. "Is everything good here?"

I find Joelle huddled up against the headboard, knees up to her chest, arms wrapped around them, her body trembling, her exhales loud.

I hold out a hand, indicating for my men to stay back. "It's okay. Close the door."

It clicks behind me as I continue toward her, but she doesn't even look at me, those large, unblinking eyes staring ahead.

"Joelle, baby?"

I near the bed, almost at the foot.

"It's Enzo. I'm here."

When she doesn't answer, I round the corner, sitting close, letting her feel my body heat. She keeps shuddering and her cheeks are glossy from tears.

How long has she been like this?

If I hadn't been busy at the club, I would've done a better fucking job of watching her on the camera.

Did she have a nightmare about what that prick did to her? Were there others? How fucking many?

My jaw pulsates hard, teeth rattling at the thought of what could've been done to her.

My Joelle.

A hand inches toward her knee, barely touching at first, testing her reaction, slowly lowering it, clasping in reassurance. "I'm here, baby. I'm not gonna leave you."

Her head slowly drifts toward my voice, as though she's only just hearing it for the first time. She stares, but it's as though she sees right through me, her lips shuddering like she wants to say something.

Fuck. I'm gonna kill them. If there are more. If they touched her. I'm gonna torture their fucking souls before I end them. Every single one.

Unable to stand another second of watching her so broken, I scoop her up into my arms, cradling her against me as we walk out the door.

Her breathing slows as she lays her head against my shoulder, and once we get to my bedroom, I reach a hand for the knob, quickly opening the door, before shutting it with my foot.

She shouldn't be in that room. She should be in mine. And from now on, she will be. Yanking the comforter up, I place her down on the bed, tucking the blanket around her before resting a kiss on her forehead.

"You're safe here," I whisper. "No one can hurt you anymore."

I slip out of my shoes, pulling the shirt from beneath my pants, unbuttoning it as I start to move. Suddenly, her palm clasps around my forearm, her pleading eyes peering up at me. I see her. Finally, she's there, the clouds shrouding her eyes now fading.

"Stay," she asks, her brows bowing.

"I'm not going anywhere, baby. Just gonna take this shirt off."

"O-okay." She nods with a tremor, dropping her hand away. I quickly snatch a T-shirt and some sweats from the drawer, changing into them.

Placing my nine on top of the nightstand, I get into the space beside her. Shifting closer, I curl one arm under her hip, dragging her body to mine.

"You wanna talk about it?" My fingers stroke up and down her arm.

"Not tonight."

I kiss the back of her head.

"Could you just hold me? You're the only one who makes…" The rest of the words die out, but I'll do anything to hear them.

"Makes what, Joelle?"

She sighs. "Makes me feel safe."

My inhale comes deep. Those words, they mean so much. "You'll always be safe with me."

"I know that now."

"Sleep, baby. No one is coming for you, not while I'm here."

Her fingers slice through mine, curling into my palm. "Goodnight, Enzo."

"Goodnight, baby girl."

Once her chest drops with a steady rhythm, and she's asleep, only then do I allow myself to go there too.

JOELLE

NINETEEN

The nightmares come more often than I'd wish, like an ocean crashing over the shore while I lie there, dragging me into its deep demise, over and over, until I lose the ability to scream.

That first memory of Faro and his two brothers violating me still causes the panic to swell. Underneath my skin, I feel them tearing at me until there's nothing left. Even still, they take more, like scavengers, unsatisfied until they've consumed every bit.

But it was nothing compared to what Agnelo did, over and over, nor the cruelty I endured at that club for the sake of money.

It's been three days since Enzo found me on the bed, trapped in my nightmare. He rescued me from the panic, from the darkness, calling to me while my fingernails dug at the sand, scrambling to climb out.

In these last two nights, sleeping beside his warm body, I've been without a hint of those visions, held prisoner within his arms, casting them away.

If only Robby was with me, I could truly be happy. I could finally live. That's assuming Enzo would still want me after he learns the truth about my child and my past.

The scalding water sluices down my body as I lift my face to it, wanting the burn, the steam enveloping the sprawling master bathroom.

I've got to tell Enzo everything. It's my only option. I have to ask for his help. He's waiting for me right outside the door. All I have to do is start at the beginning. But I just don't know how.

Shutting off the shower, I open the glass door, grabbing one of the white towels stacked on the marble stand beside me, drying off, then wrapping it around myself.

My feet prod over the warm tiles beneath before I get to the mirror, wiping off the steam and looking at my reflection. The woman there, it's as though I'm seeing her for the first time. She may be broken, but there's courage inside.

So much of my story is difficult to imagine, even for me, someone who's been through it. I never got to experience all the things many people take for granted. College. That first apartment. Falling in love. Holding my child after he was born.

The center of my chest turns heavy when I remember the day I gave birth. The day my pain was far worse than anything I'd endured.

Gripping the edge of the vanity, my knuckles strain, that awful day playing right in front of my eyes as though it's happening all over again.

I was only twenty when I became a mother. And I was only twenty when they took him away.

"It's okay, dear," Angelina reassures, sitting beside me on a bed I've never been on, her slightly wrinkled hand clasping mine as I groan from the pain of the contractions.

"Can you please give me something? It really—ahh!" I scream as another one comes.

She tsks with a shake of her head, patting my hand. "I'm sorry, but Agnelo won't allow it, and I have to do what he's instructed."

My scream turns to a gasping sob, the torment unbearable. I can't do this. I can't have a baby like this. My lower back spasms with sharp, stabbing pain as the contractions grow more consistent.

"I want my mother. Please!"

But Angelina doesn't say a word, her expression somber.

When I picture Mom's face, I start to cry even harder. This isn't how it was supposed to be, being taken, getting knocked up by a monster. I don't even know if it's a boy or girl.

As soon as I got pregnant, Agnelo had Angelina check on the baby's heartbeat, throwing some prenatals my way. Angelina saw me a few other times, but they haven't told me anything. I don't know if the baby has all her fingers and toes or how much she weighs. They never allowed me to see a real doctor.

But supposedly Angelina is an OB/GYN, or so she says.

"It'll be over soon, dear. I promise."

But it won't be over. Agnelo won't let me keep my baby. He's told me he's going to take it from me. And if I don't start behaving, he's going to kill my child.

This poor baby will belong to a monster. What will he do to him? Who will care for him when I'm not around? Maybe he'll allow me to keep him. Maybe I can beg.

My chin quivers as I snivel, heavier with every wave of agony.

The contractions come faster now, and I know the end is coming, I can feel that baby pushing down inside me, wanting to break free.

I grasp my protruding stomach, closing my eyes for a moment.

Stay a little longer, little one. The world is cruel. No place for you here.

Angelina checks me, and this time when she looks up, it's with a tentative smile. "It's time. You're having it now."

"No! I can't do this!"

"It's only a temporary pain and then—"

She realizes what I already know. There won't be a forever after for us. He won't be mine. My entire body feels like I'm being gutted with a knife, stabbing me over and over. I can't lose my baby. Another wave of pain hits behind my eyes.

"Maybe you can talk to him," *I plead.* "Ask him to let me keep my child. I'll be good. Tell him. Please!"

Her brows dip and her lips thin as she comes to my side, peering down at me with sympathy. Leaning into my ear, she brushes away a sweaty strand of hair glued to my face. "I wish I could help you, but my hands are as tied as yours. I'm sorry."

Then she's back at my feet. With her guidance, and with complete reluctance, I push that baby out of me, screaming with all my might. When a high-pitched cry slices through the room, my heart bursts with happiness, and then the grief comes.

"It's a boy!" *Angelina announces, cradling him in her arms with a blanket wrapped loosely around him as she wanders to me.*

When I see his little nose, that tiny hand bunched up into a fist, like he's ready for the fight that's about to be his, I slap a hand across my mouth, weeping for the days we'll never get.

I have a son. My son. How could I ever let you go?

Robby. That's what I'm gonna call you in honor of your grandma.

Her middle name was Roberta. It feels right.

I'll protect you, *I vow right then and there*. I'll do everything I can for you, even when I'm not there to do it. I'm sorry for this. I'm sorry I've ruined your life. I didn't mean to. *The tears fall silently as I stare up at his angelic face.* It's all my fault, my sweet baby. You don't deserve this.

"Do you want to hold him?" Angelina asks, gazing between him and me, a grin etched on her face.

I nod, my breaths shuddering from the tears, my mouth curving into a smile, my heart beating so quickly, needing him against me forever.

I stretch out my hands for him, for that little boy who made me a mother, my heart never feeling so much love in my whole life.

But just as she's about to hand him over, a door pushes open. I widen my gaze, inhales fighting the exhales as I see him coming, the eyes of hell, the face of demons. The father of my child.

"Give him to me," Agnelo roars as he marches up to my beautiful boy, grabbing him away from Angelina, her expression as horrified as mine.

"No!" I lift myself up in the bed, ignoring the burning pain as I try to get off. "Please don't take him! I'll do whatever you want!" *I swing my feet onto the floor, fighting to stand, holding on to the mattress as I do.* "Just give him to me, please!" *I wail, hoping for an ounce of his sympathy, but he doesn't even look at me, staring down at my son like he's holding a piece of junk.*

Angelina walks up to him, rubbing the baby's head. "Agnelo, let the girl hold him at least. Babies need skin to skin."

He glares up at her with a snarl. "Shut the fuck up. This is my kid. She's nothing."

His eyes focus on me as he steps close, as I stand there, helplessly watching him with my son. "You're never gonna hold *him. He's mine now. Just like you are."*

"No." I violently shake my head, the wails coming from my mouth sounding inhuman. This is what hell looks like. Feels like. This is agony.

Arms are around me, holding tight, but I barely feel them. "Shh, I've got you," Angelina whispers. "This isn't right," she tells him.

"Wh-who will care for him?" I sniffle, pushing away from her. "How do I know you'll keep him alive? What reassurances will I get that he won't be harmed?"

"Reassurances?" he howls. "Is that some kind of fucking threat? Because if it is..." His hand reaches into his pocket and he retrieves a gun. "I'll kill him right now." He raises the barrel to Robby's little head.

I gasp, panting wide-eyed, hands reaching out for my boy, but Agnelo moves back so I can't even touch him. "No, no, no. I—I wasn't threatening you! Don't kill him, please!"

"Oh my God, this isn't necessary," Angelina says. "How about you give me the baby before you—"

Pop.

It takes my brain a second to register what just happened, my ears buzzing. She falls onto the hard wooden floor, a bullet hole at her forehead, blood oozing out from around her as she lies there dead, staring at the white, unassuming ceiling above.

"See how easy that was?"

He's talking but I can barely hear him.

"That's how easily I can kill this kid of yours."

That gets me to pay attention. My son lies still in the arms of a monster, not realizing the danger he's in.

"Yes, I—okay. I'll do whatever you want. Just don't hurt him!"

"Get yourself cleaned up. The men will pick you up in thirty."

He turns away, taking my entire heart and soul with him, every step he takes slicing at the wound that'll never close.

"Robby!" I call. "His name is Robby."

Then they're gone.

And I don't know if I'll ever see my son again.

ENZO

TWENTY

I wait for her in our bedroom while she takes a shower.
Our bedroom.
It has a nice ring to it. She didn't resist when I told her my room is now hers too. She actually seemed relieved.

Every day in the past three days that I go to work, I hate leaving her, checking the cam feed while I'm there, making sure she's okay. I can't stop replaying her scream in my head. I find myself waking up in the middle of the night to check on her.

The bathroom door opens, and she walks out, a white towel wrapped around her, showing her long, toned legs I very much want wrapped around me. I'm in a permanent state of blue balls but it's gotta be that way until I'm sure she's ready. I've never done slow before, but I've never been with Joelle before either. She's not like the others. Never was.

Her eyes go to mine and— "Were you crying?" I'm instantly off the bed as she gives me her back, rummaging through a drawer to find clothes to put on.

"I was," she says faintly, her shoulders rising heavily as she grips the clothing in her palm.

"What's wrong, baby?" My mouth is on her shoulder, leaving a tender kiss behind, hands stroking up and down her arms.

She sighs, and her body tenses. I reach for the top of the towel. "Let me help you get dressed." Once she nods, I undo it, letting it fall to the floor.

She rotates, and one look at her has me spiraling, needing her so fucking badly I'm ready to get on my damn knees for a taste.

I hold her cheek in my roughened palm, looking so deep into her eyes, I'm almost lost inside them. "I'm gonna take care of you. In all ways."

She smiles brokenly, that lower lip trembling, and it makes me want to cause carnage to every man who's made her this way.

Taking the shirt from her hands, I bring the tank top over her head, her arms raised as I slip it down.

The shorts come next, and I kneel, guiding each one of her legs inside, then I pull them up. As soon as I'm upright, her arms jump over my shoulders, her face burrowing into the crook of my neck.

My hands wind around her lower back and I hold her to me, so damn tight, I'm afraid she can't breathe. But in that same moment, she tightly squeezes her arms around me. I kiss the top of her head, never wanting to let her go. I can't let her leave me.

My fingers coast up her spine, finding the softened strands of her hair. As I pull away, I take a moment to stare into those eyes. I can feel it, right in the pit of my stomach. That sensation I've been experiencing these last few days. The one I know is real. The one I know will only get stronger.

Her pink lips part, gaze misted, cheeks flushed, and I damn right hope she doesn't think I'm crazy for what I'm about to say.

"You've always been too good for someone like me." My knuckle lands on her cheek, brushing back and forth. "I don't deserve you."

When she tries to say something in return, I place a finger against her lips before the same hand goes to her hip. "I need to get this out. It's been killing me not to say it."

Her mouth thins.

"I'm falling in love with you, Joelle."

Her face drops. "Don't say that. You don't mean it." She tries to pull away, but I don't let her go.

"Don't tell me how I feel." I grip her hip tighter, my mouth brushing over hers. "I love you."

A small cry escapes her, hands on my back, sinking her nails into my flesh.

"I've never felt this way for anyone, baby. I'd do anything for you."

With a heavy sigh, she leans in some more, lips touching mine, just staying that way. Just feeling one another.

"You say that now," she breathes. "But when you hear what I'm finally ready to tell you, you may change your mind."

I draw back. "I promise. Nothing you say will change how I feel."

"You don't know that." She lowers her eyes, a bout of sadness behind them.

I grab her wrist and pull her palm over my beating heart. "I do. And when I say something, I mean it."

"I just don't want you to feel you have to be with me after everything you'll hear today."

"Joelle, baby. Give me some credit."

Her shoulders sag, and with a long pull of a breath, she starts to speak. "It all started with a road trip."

I stand there listening as she recounts the day she was taken, and all the women and children who fell victim to the Bianchis. Balling my hands at my thighs, I try my fucking hardest not to react, but inside me, their blood's already spilling. The Bianchis are not only killers but they're sex traffickers too. They hurt *my* girl, and no one hurts my girl without answering for it.

"They made me do a lot of dirty things, Enzo. There were men, a lot of them. They did whatever they wanted for the right price." She lowers her eyes to the ground. "I get it if I'm not the woman you thought I was." Her attention darts back to me. "Because I'm not. I'm a whore, Enzo. And you can't love a whore." Moisture builds in her eyes as they drift to a close.

I tip up her chin with the back of my hand and she tentatively looks at me. "Nothing has changed. You hear me?" I kiss her hard and fast, so she can feel the truth of my words. "I *love* you." I brush away her tears with my thumbs. "I love you more now than I did a moment ago."

"N-no. You can't. Why?" Her expression saddens, ripping right into my soul. "Doesn't it bother you to know the woman you're…"

"Sure it fucking bothers me." I clasp the side of her neck, leaning my forehead over hers. "It bothers me that every man who's touched you without your permission is still breathing."

I lift my gaze back to her, wanting her to see in my eyes what I feel in my heart. "That's the only thing that bothers me, Joelle. All that other shit, it makes no difference. You're mine. That's all that matters."

"You shouldn't love me," she whispers in a shaky breath. "You're the one who deserves better."

"Well, I'm sorry." I force a grin. "You're kinda lovable."

She lets out a tearful laugh.

"Baby, they don't get to define you. Don't let them have that kind of power."

Her tears come like a heavy storm, crashing down her cheeks in waves as her panting grows heavier. "Who are you?" She gapes at me, ragged and breathless.

"Just a man who loves you." I tighten my hand around her neck, lips grazing hers, and I can't handle another second. I take her hungrily, raw passion dripping from my mouth, needing her to feel it, to remember how good we felt together.

My lips fall to her neck as she moans. "There'll never be a day that you don't know how much you matter," I say in between hungry kisses. "Not when I'm alive to show it."

Her hands grasp the back of my head, tugging me closer, my mouth sucking her lower lip now as she groans.

I bring her roughly against me, arms clasped under her thighs as I carry us to the bed, lowering on top of her as my mouth drags savagely down her neck. She claws my back, my cock hard and heavy between her thighs.

"Wait," she gasps as I suck her earlobe into my mouth. "Wait, there's more."

I growl, propping up on my forearms, but not before I leave a quick kiss on her lips.

Her face lights up with a slow grin, but just as quickly, she turns serious.

"Whatever it is, I can handle it." I move off her and lie on my side and she does too. "Nothing will make me leave you. Not even some fucking boyfriend I now know you made up. Why did you anyway?" It's been weighing on me, especially when I picture his smug face.

"Oh God." She huffs. "I forgot I have to tell you that too."

I roll a reassuring palm over her arm.

"I'm just gonna say it." She grimaces. "I'm a murderer."

I don't even stop. No reaction. My fingers still brushing up her skin.

She takes me in with a widened expression "Aren't you going to ask who?"

"No. Because whoever it is, I'm sure they deserved it."

"I—I didn't mean to hurt her." Her voice shudders. "But that night Paulina saw us, she told Faro. He dragged me to his place the next morning, and Paulina was there. We got into a fight, and…" Her shoulders jolt.

"Hey." I cradle her chin in my palm. "It's okay."

"It's not," she cries low. "Once she was dead, he told me I had to get rid of you because you were getting too attached. And…" She catches her breath, talking faster. "And h-he doesn't want the men thinking of us as human beings. So I came up with the plan to kiss someone else and he sent the random guy and… I'm so sorry." A fresh coat of moisture builds in her eyes.

With two hands at her hips, I bring her on top of me as she weakly cries over my chest, my palm on the back of her head. "Shh. It's okay. You had to do it. I get it."

"Why aren't you mad?" She pushes against my hold. "Be mad at me. Hate me! I deserve it."

"No, you don't. Plus…" I smirk. "I think I was pissed at you plenty when I thought you had your tongue down your boyfriend's throat. We're good."

She plops her face back down against me.

"Joelle, you gotta stop hating yourself. That's what this is. I'm not gonna let you do that to yourself."

"How could I not hate myself, knowing what he's been through," she mutters into my chest.

"He, who?" My pulse slams.

Fuck. It better not be some real boyfriend.

She looks up and sighs, the fight gone from her face. "I have a son, Enzo. His name is Robby."

My eyes widen on instinct. I swallow the shock away.

"Where is he, baby? Who has him?"

"Who do you think?" she trembles out. "They took him from me the moment he was born. I only get him for ten minutes once a month. Now, I don't even know if he's alive."

My thumbs erase the dripping of her tears running past her cheeks. "Where's his father?"

"I—" Her eyes scan mine for a second before she swallows harshly. "Ahh, I don't know who it is."

I'm not sure how much truth there is to that, but I'm not gonna push her right now.

"Do you know where they're keeping him?"

She shakes her head. "They never told me. Neither did Robby. They watch us, making sure we don't say anything important to each other. The only thing I once got from him is that he's in a house, which is nothing to go on." She tips her head to the side. "I'm never gonna find him, am I?" The way she asks that, the sound of her pain, it kills me.

"I'll burn the rest of this damn city to the ground until someone tells us where he is. My brothers and I, we'll get him, baby. We'll bring him back to you."

"Thank you." Her lips drop to my cheek, and she kisses me tenderly like she did that one time at the club. Her gaze stills over mine with pounding emotions, wrecking her, and wrecking me too.

The shit she's been through, it raises that sadistic bastard in me, the one who needs to maim, to kill, to brutalize all those who've dared to brutalize her.

There's one thing I gotta know, something I hope she tells me. "Who caused those bruises on your thighs the night I saw them? Was it Roman?"

She sighs. "You don't want to hear this, Enzo. I promise."

The muscles in my jaw flinch. "Tell me."

Her eyes squeeze shut. "There were three of them, and I'll never forget their faces."

My chest heaves as she recounts the night of her torment. I hate that I put her through the trauma of reliving it, but I had to know. Fuck… If I ever find them, the shit I'll do. I let her fall over me once more, holding her, my hand stroking her back for a while.

"There's something else I know, and it could maybe help find Robby," she says, rearing back some more. "The Bianchis' lawyer is Joey Russo. He's in deep. He was at the club a lot, talking to the Bianchis, huddled in corners, exchanging documents. If anyone knows where they're keeping Robby and the others, he will."

"I'm gonna kill them all, baby. And once I find your son, no one will come after either one of you. When he's safe, I want you to both stay here with me."

Her brow arches, her mouth falling open. "Really? You'd do that?"

I let a faint smile settle over my lips. "Did you really think you were gonna run from me? There's not a chance in hell of that, baby girl. Wherever you go, I'd find you and I'd bring you right back to me, where you belong."

Through the haze of her pain, her breathing turns hard, those eyes on my mouth. "Enzo…" Her voice trails, a finger drawing a path down the side of my face. "I love you too."

I draw in a sharp breath, a lazy smile forming. "Say it again," I demand, skirting a hand up her back, fisting her hair as I roll it around my wrist, yanking until my lips are on her neck.

"I love you," she hums as I kiss her softly. "I love you with everything I have." Those words, they fill the void in my heart that I always thought would be empty. But meeting her, falling for her, it changed me, even when I hadn't realized at first.

Gentle kisses are replaced by the grating of my teeth until I reach her jaw, nipping, biting, finding her mouth and kissing her with every ounce of my being.

She groans, rocking her hips over my already straining hard-on. With a growl, I rise, flipping her onto the bed, my body pressing over hers.

Her cries of pleasure grow louder as my cock rubs her pussy, my tongue diving deep into her mouth, sucking hers into mine.

My hand falls to her tits, rolling a hardened nipple between two fingers, my mouth moving south now, down her neck, until my lips replace my hands on her breasts.

I clamp her nipple with my teeth through the tank top, watching her as she watches me suck them. Lowering her shirt with the free hand, I yank it past her arms, her sultry moans only urging me on.

"You want this, don't you, baby? You want my mouth on these tits?" I squeeze both, looking up at her, my tongue swiping across each pebbled bead.

"Yes, touch me, please," she cries, her body rattling underneath me. "Fuck me, Enzo."

"Shit, baby, I want to." I kiss the center of her chest. "I want to feel that tight pussy gripping my cock, but it's all about you right now. I'm gonna make you feel so damn good."

Then I'm on her, my lips on that soft skin, kissing down her body, teeth edging toward her hips, nipping each one as my fingers find the waistband of her shorts, and slowly, I drag them down.

She eyes me hungrily as I slip them completely off. Her bare body like an offering. She locks her knees, and I grab her ankles, legs clasped tight as I lift them in the air, giving me a damn good view of those lips I can't wait to get my mouth on.

"Spread those thighs for me," I tell her as I lower her feet back down. "Let me see you."

She parts them without an ounce of resistance, confidence settling in her gaze.

"Mmm, good girl." My middle finger falls in between her slit, winding it down slow. "My girl."

Her body jolts, thighs itching to close around my touch, but I stop them, a palm on the inside of each, pushing them apart.

Settling on my knees, I grab under her hips, raising her to my mouth, my tongue taking a swipe from her ass all the way to her clit.

Her hands fist, quivering around my bedsheets, my breath blowing against her core. "No woman has ever been on my bed before. No one but you."

"Enzo," she pants, and with that pleading look in her eyes, my mouth wraps around her and delves inside, tasting her, wanting to own every single one of her orgasms.

I thrust two fingers inside as my tongue rolls around her clit, and she squirms, crying out my name, speaking in riddles, the small of her back curving as her eyes roll, body jerking.

"Yes, please don't stop," she begs with a strain in her voice, her walls clasping around me, my fingers soaked, her pussy dripping down into her ass.

Goddamn, she may be too good for a fucked-up man like me, but I want her. Above everything else, I want this. Even if I have to fight like hell for her, I'll gladly do it.

With a curl of my fingers, I add a third, thrusting faster. Deeper. "Yeah, that's it, baby. Grip that pussy tight around me."

"Shit," she swears, her exhales uneven as my tongue envelops her clit, sucking hard, stroking roughly.

Her eyes shut, causing me to pull away. "Look at me. I want your eyes on mine when you come."

"Yes... Oh God," she cries as I flick my tongue over her sensitive clit. And those tremors to her body... Fuck. She's almost there. Her panting riding higher, her mouth round, eyes on me, and with another hard slam of my fingers, she falls apart.

I'm there to catch her, eliciting every last whimper as she stills, the jolts softening to a whisper before I climb on top of her, the throbbing of my cock falling between her thighs as I kiss her frantically.

Her hands bite into my back, her moans on my tongue. The need to fuck her is overwhelming, but I gotta do right by her. I have to be sure she's ready. With everything she went through, it's the only way.

"What about you?" she asks, her face engraved with the echoes of her release.

"I'm fine, right here." I kiss the tip of her nose, my pulse racing as I flip to my side, tugging her to my beating heart.

She fits perfectly, like she was made for me—the missing piece to the puzzle I never knew was incomplete until I found her.

JOELLE

TWENTY-ONE

I understand why he's holding back, why he won't sleep with me. After everything I've revealed, it makes sense. But I'm not some delicate flower he has to keep in shatterproof glass. I may be breakable, but I'm strong. I want to experience everything together.

When I first told him about what I've been through, my biggest fear was his rejection, but he proved me wrong. He wants me still.

Finally, I'm wanted.

Finally, I matter.

ENZO

As soon as I got to work today, I told my brothers what Joelle told me about the Bianchis. We didn't waste any time. Dante and

I went after Joey Russo, but he wasn't in his office, and according to his secretary, he took a long vacation. We knew what that meant. Joelle was right. He has info.

When we couldn't find Joey, we captured two Palermo men instead. Jared, their accountant, and Victor, an associate, hoping they'd tell us something of value, but neither told us shit.

Jared was too scared of the Bianchis to give us a location for the women and kids, while Victor was a real son of a bitch, refusing to talk on principle.

But he did tell us one thing—Faro killed our mother. He was more than happy to rub that in our faces, recounting how Faro arranged her murder.

It was all over money. My father wouldn't pay for protection, so he decided to pay my father back by taking the love of his life. That's what my mother was to him.

Besides us, she was his whole life, and the Bianchis managed to take her from him three years before taking one of his sons. Their cruelty is far-reaching and unending, and it's time they're stopped. It's time for their reign to end, once and for all.

I didn't have time to get cleaned up after Dante and I took care of Victor and Jared. My knuckles still covered in their dried blood, my black hoodie concealing the crimson soaking up the material.

I hope like hell this doesn't scare Joelle off, even though I told her what we were up to. I wanted her to know how far I'd go to find her boy.

I step up to the house, the night wind gusting past my face as I enter, finding Joelle asleep, curled up on the sofa, hugging one of the soft, fluffy pillows I bought from one of those late-night shopping channels. It looked comfortable and was a total impulse buy, but I'm kinda happy I did, seeing how good she looks with it tucked against her.

As though attuned to me, her eyes flip open, and she instantly sits up, noticing the blood on my hands.

She rises, stepping to me, clasping her hands around my knuckles. "Anything?"

I shake my head, already despising the disappointment on her features.

"This is hopeless, isn't it?"

"No." I cradle her cheek, lifting her eyes to mine with a tilt of my thumb. "It's not nearly over. No one's giving up and you won't either." I lower my lips to her forehead, kissing her affectionately, never realizing I could be this way with a woman. "If they had killed him," I continue, peering back at her, "Faro wouldn't be shy about letting us know. My gut says your boy is still alive."

"I hope you're right." She lets out a deep sigh. "I need him, Enzo. Without him, I won't make it."

"I know, baby." With my arms around her, I hold her tightly against me, because right now, that's all I can do.

FIVE DAYS LATER

Once we got rid of Victor and his pal, Jared, we wasted no time following some of the other associates of the Bianchis, capturing those we could. But none talked. It's like they're more afraid of Faro and his brothers than they are of dying, and their deaths were fucking painful. We made sure of that.

In these past days, Joelle has grown more anxious, the fear of never seeing her son is all she thinks about and talks about. I feel damn useless. But today, I decided to get her mind off the search, even if it's for a few hours.

Dom would have my head for this if he knew, but he won't. No one's there to tell him. Dante doesn't even know. If he thought I was putting us in danger, he'd beat my ass too.

I knock on the bedroom door, knowing she's behind it, getting ready for the dinner I arranged at a five-star restaurant, overlooking the water in New York City. The place is exclusive, and not the area the Bianchis or their clowns hang out in. No one will spot us there.

"Come in," she says from a distance. I enter, not seeing her at first until I step into the walk-in closet and find her staring at herself in the full-length mirror.

The tight black dress hits right above her knees, her ass snugly wrapped beneath it, her long hair curled at the ends, reaching her lower back. The red heels make her taller, only a few inches shorter than me.

"Damn, baby." I whistle. "Turn around. Let me look at you."

She does, a sheepish smile creeping over her.

My heart stills as I gaze at the woman I love, my attention swinging from her full red lips to those firm, tanned legs I'd like clasping my face right about now. "How are you this perfect?"

"Oh, shut up." She waves a hand in the air dismissively. "This is too much." She fingers the diamond studs I bought her.

I cut through a few steps until I'm near enough to kiss her, my mouth brushing softly over hers. "It's not nearly enough." I reach a thumb up, flitting it down the side of her face, careful not to ruin her makeup. "You deserve everything, and I'm gonna be the one to give it to you."

Her brows dip, exhales a harsh pant, her eyes glazing over. "If I didn't know any better, I'd think I was dreaming."

"Not yet, baby. But you will be. When they're all dead, you, me, and Robby, we can be a family."

"You'd really want that? Because I don't want you to feel like you have to take on a child. I'd understand if—"

"What did I tell you?" I cut her off, leaning in, whispering low with a hover against her ear. "I don't say anything I don't mean." I pitch back. "I want this. I want us to be a family."

She grins wide, blinking through the thick tears threatening to spill down her face. Her arms fold over my shoulders, lips landing on my cheek, and damn, I feel it everywhere.

"So what exactly do you know about raising a kid?" she asks, eyes narrowing with a tease.

"Nothing whatsoever." I chuckle. "But you'll be there to teach me."

"Not sure I know much either." A weak laugh stitches through her voice.

"Then we'll learn." I clasp her hands in mine. "Together. You're not alone anymore, Joelle. You've got *me*."

She sniffles. "You're an incredible man. You know that?" Her features ride with adoration and it warms every fucking part of me. I never knew how good it could feel to fall in love.

"Yeah." I shrug with a smirk. "I know."

"Cocky bastard." She shakes her head with a playful sigh.

I plant my palms on her hips, pulling her up against me with a groan as her lustful gaze aligns with mine, the mood shifting. Her hand crawls down my stomach until a finger swipes over my hard-on, thick, straining within the confines of my pants, wanting inside this woman like a damn beast.

"Shit. What are you doing?" My words turn gruff.

"I need you to stop holding back, Enzo." She doesn't turn her eyes away. "I'm not scared. I'm not broken." A tight fist wraps around my cock. "I want to taste you."

"Fuck, baby," I grit. "If you don't stop moving that hand, I'm gonna fill that filthy mouth of yours."

"Is that a promise?" There's a light in her eyes, a devious one.

She wants this. And I'm not about to deny her.

My hand jumps to the back of her head, hair rolling around my wrist as I yank hard, my teeth grazing the edge of her jaw. "You wanna be a dirty girl for me? Don't you?"

"Yesss…" The word crawls with a whispery moan.

"You wanna suck my cock and let me fill that mouth?" I let my free hand slink down her body, sliding under her dress, two fingers roughly yanking her damp panties to the side, stroking her soaked clit.

"Yes, Enzo…" She throws her head back as I slowly ease two fingers inside her.

"Such a wet pussy." I fuck her harder, fingers thrusting rough with deepened strokes.

Her breaths hitch, gasping. "Oh God, just like that…."

"Mmm, want my cum dripping down your chin, don't you?"

"Enzo!" she cries as I ram into her G-spot, harder each time. She clamps around me, damn hungry for my dick to stretch her. "Fuck me… I want you so bad," she gasps. "Don't treat me any different. I need this."

But she is different. Not just because of what she went through, but because she's the only woman I've ever loved, and the last thing I want is to fuck this up. But if she really wants this, then I'll give it to her.

"Want me to stuff my cock down your pretty little throat?" I tug her lower lip between my teeth.

"Yes, please," she groans, rubbing her thighs against my touch as I increase the tempo.

"Mmm. So desperate for me." I stretch her as I widen my fingers inside her. "I think we can be a little late to dinner." I run a thumb over her clit, and her hands jump to my arms, nails clawing my biceps.

"So fucking desperate." She sighs, her thighs trembling.

"Yes, you are." I slide my fingers out of her, slipping them into my mouth and suck them dry while she watches hungrily.

"Get on your knees," I growl, and she exhales my name, her eyes aroused, cheeks flushed. Fucking sexy as hell.

I tug on her hair, my lips brushing up her neck, teeth nipping her earlobe.

"I said, get on your knees and open your mouth."

Her breaths are heavy, groaning as I drop my hand away and she lowers herself onto the floor, looking up at me. The eagerness in her gaze has my balls on fire.

Undoing the belt, I yank it off, wrapping it around the back of her neck, pulling each end until her lips meet my cock, still trapped within my pants.

"You feel how hard I am for you? Hmm? That's how badly I want you. Now, you're gonna show me how badly you want me."

A luscious moan slips past her lips and over my hard-on, her tongue darting out, licking up, our eyes locked as she does.

"Pull it out." I loosen the belt from around her, and she quickly works my pants, dragging the zipper down, shoving the slacks and boxers past my thighs and onto the floor.

My cock springs free, and her hands immediately surround it, her silky palms stroking my length from root to tip, tongue swiping around the crown. "Fucking hell. Nothing and no one has ever felt this good." I yank both ends of the belt, my cock cramming down her throat with a gag and a moan. "Yeah, that's good, baby. Swallow that shit."

I thrust my hips roughly, ramming further down her throat, her eyes watering, her hand grasping my balls, massaging as her moans vibrate down the length of me, spearing me with her tantalizing gaze.

"Shit, baby," I hiss, my head shooting back, eyes drifting closed as an ache builds up my spine, my balls tightening.

I drop the belt, spiraling my fingers through her hair, holding her against me, wildly fucking her mouth, the need to spill into it unquenched. "You're gonna take every damn drop into your pretty throat."

My hips drive faster. The sensation from those sexy whimpers, the way she feeds my ravenous appetite with those eyes, turns my vision hazy and I crash, hot spurts shooting out.

"Yes, fuuuck," I growl, clutching her hair even tighter as my cock pulses, spilling into her throat.

I twitch against her tongue, giving her all of me, in every damn sense of the word. I tug her up to me once I'm done, capturing her lips, kissing her with a frenzy as I edge her backward to the bed.

My cock stiffens again, hungry for her as my hand lands in between her thighs, finding her even wetter than before. Knowing how badly she wants me has me needing to finally fill her pussy. I've waited too damn long for this.

Her legs hit the edge of the bed and I pull back, my hand greedily gripping her jaw. "I can't be gentle right now. If it's something you can't do, just tell me and I'll stop."

She shakes her head with determination, her hand clasping the back of my neck. "Fuck me, Enzo," she whispers, her lips falling to mine, feathering over them as she continues to speak. "I want you to show me how good it can be."

With a groan, I take her lips with a hard kiss, unable to hold on to my self-control anymore, my tongue slipping inside her mouth, right before I flip her around and throw her down onto the bed.

Her cheek hits the comforter, my body falling over hers, pinning her to the bed, my hand slipping between us, finding her wet center.

I thrust three fingers inside her, fucking her so good, she can't catch her breath.

"Yeah, that's a good little pussy. Gonna come on my hand before you get my cock." She writhes beneath me, captured, imprisoned by our all-consuming intensity—this love and devotion I never want to be rid of.

With a twist of my fingers, I let her have it all—every rough beat until she fastens around me.

Soaring.

"Oh, fu-fuck, yes, oh my God, I'm coming." Her walls ripple around me, her release hitting her in wave after wave, pulling me inside her.

I drag my soaked fingers out, drawing up the dress past her ass, not giving her a second to recover, fisting my cock and lining it at her entrance, before sinking inside with a single thrust.

"Yes, more," she cries, my hips driving into her, my hand clasping around the front of her throat, fingers dipping into that soft flesh as she lets out a loud cry.

Sex has never felt this goddamn good. Not with anyone. Being with her is on a whole other level. And even before tonight, I knew it'd be this way.

I slip out, clasping her hips as I stand, hauling her up in the air, lowering her back onto my cock as I grip my hands around her ass.

"Yeah, that's it, bounce on that cock," I grit hoarsely as she begs me to give it to her faster.

Her fingers cling to my shoulders for support, her brows bending, her mouth round. Our eyes connect, caught in wild pleasure, in that magnetic force between us.

"Fuck, Joelle. I love you," I say, growling low, my hard-on spearing her so fully, all she can respond with are her broken moans, her thighs quivering, her cunt throbbing around me.

Without separating, I place her down onto the soft rug beneath our feet, my length slipping out of her, replaced by my fingers, fucking her so hard, her eyes roll back.

"Oh God, Enzo, I'm…yes!" she screams, spilling over my hand like a damn fountain.

"Good girl. That's it." I rub my palm all over her clit, slapping it once as she screams. "Just like that." I thrust my cock back into her as she continues to quiver with the last few drops of her orgasm. "You're perfect."

Lifting her legs, I pin them around the sides of her face. Pounding into her in this new position has her gasping as I impale her with roughened strokes, another release clawing through her. I can feel it around me as she tightens.

"Come for me, baby." I pummel her harder, rolling my cock with every thrust, my own release creeping. "You're mine." I nip her lower lip with my teeth. "Your pussy is mine. I can't wait to fill it."

With another drive of my hips, she falls apart and I join her, spilling into her warmth, falling beside her as our bodies finally still, our breathing rapid as I spoon her close, her fingers sliding between mine.

"That was—wow." She sighs, trying to catch her breath.

My chest is heavy from the firing of my inhales. "It was."

She clenches my hand against her stomach. "We should probably talk about the condom situation."

"Shit, I'm sorry, baby. I always use one, but with you, fuck, I forgot."

She pivots my way, facing me. "I just want you to know, um…" Her gaze diverts away this time, like she's too nervous to say whatever it is.

"What is it?" My knuckles trace the contour of her jaw. "Don't be shy with me."

"I'm more embarrassed than shy." She rests for a second before she huffs out an exhale. "The men, they always used condoms. I needed you to know that. It was a rule at the club, like the pill they shoved down our throats so we don't get pregnant."

"I believe you." I press my mouth to her lips. "If you're more comfortable, I can wear a condom."

"Maybe I can get the pill instead?" She scrunches her nose in the most adorable way.

"Fuck yeah," I smirk. "I mean, yeah, whatever you want, baby."

She giggles, swatting me on the chest. I claim her lips, kissing her slow, imagining the world we could build together once we destroy the one standing in our way.

JOELLE

TWENTY-TWO

We finally arrive at the restaurant over an hour late, but the owner didn't seem to mind, especially with the hundreds Enzo slipped into his pocket.

Being out, like a normal woman, with a man I love, is an experience I'll never take for granted.

He sips on his whiskey while I drink the burgundy-red wine in a fancy sparkling glass, the tableware as decadent as the rest of this place. The dimmed, overhead lights above brighten the room just enough, working in sync to the sparkling large gold chandelier at the center.

I cut into my steak, tender, delicious. The first one I've ever tasted. I didn't grow up with too many luxuries, such as going out to nice restaurants. Pizza and pasta days were as extravagant as my mother could afford. But I don't need any of that to be happy. I just want my family back, my son, and Enzo. He's family now, a piece of me I'll never be able to let go of.

"How's everything?" he asks, slicing into his own steak, those captivating eyes gazing back at me, making my stomach flip from the emotions he brings out.

Being intimate with him, finally experiencing that with someone who I care so deeply for—it was more than I could imagine.

It's as though I was caught in this bubble, where the rest of my world and everything that happened to me prior, no longer existed, even for those moments in time.

But of course, it did. I know that. I still carry those scars every single day, trying my best not to live in their shadow but in spite of them. I have to go on. I have to move forward somehow. For me. For my boy. For my own survival. Because that's what I am, a survivor, and that's one thing those bastards will never take from me.

"Oh, it's truly amazing," I finally answer him, clearing my thoughts. "We could never afford this sort of place when I was younger. My mother was a single mom raising my brother and me."

"You miss them. Why don't you call them?" He glances to his plate, his eyes wandering up to mine in between.

"I can't do that. They told me that if I contact my family, Robby dies. I can't risk it."

His jaw twitches. "Okay, baby. We'll call them after we get Robby."

I breathe in a sigh. "What will I tell them? How can I look them in the eyes?"

He leans into the table across from me, his hand tucking over mine. "You tell them you love them and that you're happy to be with them again. I promise, they won't care about the other shit.

They'll just be relieved to get you back."

Biting into my inner cheek, I suppress the emotions riding up the back of my nose. I pick up my wineglass and take a few sips. He's right. Mom would never judge me for what I've been through. She'll hate herself for allowing it to happen, but she'd never think bad of me. And when she meets Robby, God, she's going to love him. As for Elliot, I don't know. Nine years is a long time, and he's an adult now. My God, what does he even look like now? Will I ever see them?

Pulling in a long breath, I push those thoughts away. I can't continue thinking about them or it'll eat me alive.

Distracting myself, I dart my eyes around the room, Enzo's hand still clasped to mine, my attention wandering to the soft waves of the river outside our window. I'm instantly transfixed by its tempered beauty, waiting to crash over the world around it. I wonder how it'd feel to be as powerful as the ocean, having the ability to drown all those who've made you suffer, to keep them under, unable to ravage.

Enzo squeezes my hand and I look back at him, at this man who loves me with his whole heart, so much that I feel it every single moment we're together.

But as I lift my gaze away from him for only a moment, just a fraction in time, my inhale seizes in my chest, a tremor running up my arms, my body cold. Naked.

I continue staring. Unable to move. To breathe. I can't rip my eyes away from them, those men tucked in the corner. Talking. Smiling. Like they didn't ruin me. Like they're not the monsters I know they are.

"Baby? What's wrong?" Enzo's voice may as well be distances away. "Joelle?" He's in front of me now, turning the chair, blocking my view of the two men seated there, their dates across from them.

My lungs are heavy, as though I'm the one trapped under that water now, screaming, begging them to stop.

"Tell me." He kneels, his palm possessively cinching around my knee, his thumb under my chin, nudging my face to him and him alone. "Who are they?"

He knows.

With my lips trembling, eyes burning with the tears that don't come, I look up at him. "I'll—I'll never forget their faces," I whisper so low, I don't quite know if he's heard, repeating those same words I used when I recited what they did to me.

But when his face turns with something dark, something cruel, the vein at his neck practically puncturing through his skin, I know he's heard.

"Are you sure?" His nostrils flare.

I nod, my pulse slamming, remembering how one of those men stuck that baton in me. How he enjoyed hurting me. How the others laughed before they all took their turn. I wasn't a person to them. I was a carcass. A toy. A sick game they played. But now two of them are here, enjoying their food as though nothing happened.

"I'm gonna take care of it, baby. I can't take it back, but fuck, I'm gonna make sure they bleed for it."

"Wha-what are you going to do?"

"You mean what are we gonna do?"

I nod, my heart pacing.

"You trust me?"

"Explicitly."

He gives me his hand. "Let's go."

I fumble, grabbing my purse as we both rise. He threads his fingers through mine, glancing at me with breathtaking fervor as we make our way to their table, every step like torture. Like my legs are slowly turning to stone. But I fight it, shoving down the nerves, the mind-bending fear. Because I'm not alone, and where I may be weak, he's strong. And his strength is contagious.

Both men turn as we approach. For a split second, they don't recognize me, but then it comes, that panic, that sheer terror on both their faces, their eyes filled with the same horror I had on my face when they tortured me.

They both glance at one another, the two women beside them oblivious as they talk to each other.

Enzo squeezes my hand once.

"Hey, guys!" he greets them, stepping right behind them, each of his arms falling over their shoulders like they're long-lost friends.

I stand to the side, my eyes on the man who held that baton, his face pivoted to me, his anxiety setting over my gaze. I relish it. His fear. I smell it. Taste it. I want to own it. The utter devastation I felt moments before is replaced by the need for vicious violence. I've never felt this much rage before. It's like someone else is trapped inside me, screaming, and ripping at the seams to get out.

Enzo spins the man's head forward once he notices the asshole gaping at me.

"Hey, pal," the other one says, turning around in the chair. "I think you got us confused with someone else."

"Nah." Enzo's forearms clench around their necks, biceps popping as he does. "I'm pretty sure I have exactly who I was looking for, and there's something important we really should talk about. So how about we send these ladies home so we can do just that?"

I finally peer at the two women, probably not much older than me, their faces stunned, expressions frozen.

"Yeah, we're not gonna do that," the one who used the baton says.

Enzo only chuckles dryly. "Yeah, you are. Because we both know if you don't…" The rest of it he says quietly into the man's ear, and when he does, the color completely drains from my tormentor's face.

Enzo pats him on the head. "That's what I thought."

Reaching into his wallet, he throws some money on the table.

"Are you their girlfriends, wives?"

"No, um…" one answers, her long fingernail pushing her short, brown hair away from her face. "We…" She glances at the other woman.

"They pay you to be here?"

She nods.

"Well, how about I take the trash out of here, because that's what they fucking are, isn't that right?" He forms a fist, shoving it into one of the men's necks. "They hurt you yet?"

Both women glimpse down onto the table.

"That's what I thought. How about this, ladies? We never saw each other. When they go missing, and they *will* go missing, you never speak about me or her." He gestures with a thumb at me.

One can trace the danger on his handsome face, like a path leading to destruction.

"Okay, yeah," she says, swallowing hard. "Whatever you want."

"We're gonna go now," he tells them, removing his cell from his pocket and typing something quickly before he places it back. "There's more than enough money on that table for the both of you."

He drags the chairs out, the men still on them, both slowly getting up, their bodies shifting uncomfortably on their feet.

Enzo leads them out, stepping up behind them, one hand clasped to mine and his other in his jacket pocket. "One wrong move, I'll shoot you both dead. I don't give a shit what happens to me because I'll gladly kill you for what you did to her."

Enzo smiles flirtatiously as two women at the table we pass glance suspiciously at us.

"Listen, it was all a misunderstanding," one of them says. "We didn't know—"

"Didn't know you were raping me? Holding me down while he shoved that baton in me while I begged for you all to stop?" I whisper-shout as we march out the doors and back onto the street. Enzo's car parked right across from the restaurant.

They're both facing me, sandwiched between us and the car, their expressions void of any redeeming emotions. Not that it'd change anything. They're monsters of the worst kind.

Enzo's breath is hot and heavy at the back of my neck, his arm curling around my front as his lips fall to my temple. "I'm going to make them suffer, baby. They're going to bleed," he says against my ear. "For you."

Inhales storm into my lungs, my heart pounding so fast, I can't tame it, wanting them to feel an ounce of what they did to me.

Enzo lets go, opening the door to the back seat and shoving one of the men. "Get the fuck inside."

They both reluctantly enter, and Enzo locks the doors with a click, before grabbing zip ties from the glove compartment and tying their hands together over their knees. "I'm gonna show you what I do to those who hurt my girl." He slams the door hard, then helps me into my seat and gets into his.

With a turn of his key, we're driving off.

"What the hell do you want from us?" one of them asks. "Money? Info? What? How can we fix this?"

"You don't get it, do you?" Enzo finds him through the rearview mirror. "There's nothing you can do. Nothing you can say. You're both gonna die tonight and no one will find your bodies."

We arrive back at Enzo's, a pale blue McLaren Speedtail already parked in the driveway, a man I recognize from the strip club casually leaning against it.

"That's one of my brothers," Enzo explains as we get out, strutting over to him. They clasp hands before his brother raises a chin in greeting.

"Nice to officially meet you. I'm Dante."

"You too." I reach out a hand for his with a smile matching his crooked one.

"So, what do we have here?" He eyes Enzo's SUV, some of the guards already moving to stand around the car. Enzo must've texted Dante from the restaurant.

"The usual shit." He shrugs. "No dicks have been cut off this time though. Not yet."

Dante chuckles. "Your boy has some screws loose," he says to me.

"Yeah," Enzo scoffs, "says the guy who cut out that one dude's eyes."

"True." Dante's lips deepen with a smirk. "We've all got a little bit of crazy in us."

I narrow a gaze. "I'm not sure if I should be afraid or—"

"Nah, you just gotta embrace the crazy." Enzo drapes an arm around my shoulders, pulling me to his side with a kiss to the top of my head. "We're more lovable that way."

"I'm going to take your word for it," I toss with amusement before my expression turns serious.

"Does he know?" I ask Enzo, looking between them. I know he understands what I'm talking about.

"Yeah, he knows." He weaves back to look my way. "I'm sorry."

"No, it's fine." My mouth tightens. "I guess I should be used to people knowing my past."

"I'm sorry for what you went through, Joelle," Dante remarks, the kindness in his eyes is as soulful as his brother's. "We're going to find your son, and we're gonna get him out of this."

"Thanks." My chest warms from his sincerity, though I'm plagued by doubt. Every day that Robby's out there, the chances of finding him diminish.

"Are we ready to do this?" Dante asks, running a hand over the top of his head, fingers snaked past the length of his thick, brown hair.

"Let's go." Enzo starts to move back to his car with me in tow, Dante walking ahead, opening the door.

"Hey, boys!" he tells them. "Welcome to the party." He plasters a facetious grin as he yanks them out by the zip ties like he's dragging cattle to the slaughter. The looks of defeat on their faces tells me they know the end is near.

The girl I used to be would be horrified at the relief I feel knowing they'll die, but the woman I am today, she'll enjoy every moment.

Two of Enzo's guards grab the men by the collar of their shirts and drag them into the house.

We follow inside as they're led into a basement, climbing down step after step before we arrive at a brightly lit room, more like the size of three.

Enzo is before me, a palm clasping the back of my neck, his forehead leaning over mine. "You don't have to be here for this."

"I need to be here." I push away a fraction, wanting him to see me, to see how much truth is in my words. "It may not take back what they did, but at least they'll know what it means to suffer."

"I promise you. They're gonna fucking wish they were dead by the time I'm done."

Softly, I plant a kiss on his lips, and for a brief moment, his eyes fall closed, a lazy smile crawling over his mouth.

"Why don't you go sit down on the sofa," he tells me, affection carved into his gaze.

"Okay."

"I love you," he swears before backing away, moving toward the kitchen set against the wall to my left, a large black pot of water boiling on the stove, bubbles spilling over.

On the counter beside it lies an opened black case, a sizable collection of knives and sharp weapons holstered inside. A shudder drapes over me, even knowing I won't be on the receiving end of them.

I take my seat as my tormentors are pushed into the two chairs neatly placed in the center of the room, facing Enzo, their exhales unsteady, their eyes wandering around the room and the six guards who now fill it. Two of them bind the ankles of the men to the chairs with another set of zip ties.

Dante stands behind them, his arms crossed at his chest, peering at Enzo's back as he runs his hands over the weapons before him.

"This is nuts." The ringleader breaks the silence. "We paid for it. That was her fucking job."

Enzo's shoulders slowly hike up and down, like he's controlling the anger simmering beneath.

"Shut up, Jay," his friend spits out.

"Yeah, shut up, Jay." Dante smacks him on the back of the head.

"What?" Jay laughs mockingly, his charcoal eyes deepening to almost black, the color of hell. "They're going to kill us anyway. Hey, you," he continues, calling to Enzo. "Did she not tell you how good she gives it?"

My stomach churns. That fucking bastard.

"Don't let her lie to you. She loved every second of my dick in her cunt."

The rage balls in my chest, squeezing at me as I jump to my feet. "You motherf—" But I don't finish the sentence, because in a mere blink, Enzo is on him, the blade in his hand slicing wide right across Jay's cheek.

"Ahh!" he cries, blood gushing down his face and into his lap, right over his balled fists.

Enzo removes a gun from his ankle holster, pushing the barrel into Jay's forehead. "You should've never opened your mouth. You're about to lose your tongue for it. But first…"

He aims the weapon at the man's crotch.

Pop.

The bullet fires as a scream pierces the room. His scream. Enzo reaches into Jay's pocket, retrieving his wallet as the man continues to wail.

"How does it feel to be powerless?" I rise, making my way up to him, to both of them, needing to confront them. "How does it feel to know you're going to die?"

Enzo moves a fraction, giving me space.

I lower my head, my face level to Jay's. "I didn't want what you did to me. It's men like you, with your sick depravities that kept the club going. I've never wished death on anyone, but I wish it for you, for all three of you."

When I straighten, I'm met with a face of the man whose love for me outshines every awful thing he may have done. He shares in my pain. Owns it. Feels it. I'm really not alone anymore.

Dante slips a hand into the other man's pants pocket, dragging out his wallet. "Graham Mince. Age forty-two," he reads.

Enzo opens the other wallet. "Jay Singer. Age forty-four. We'll make sure even your mommy can't find your remains."

"I'm sorry!" Graham now begs with the tears of a coward. "It wasn't right what we did. I know that now."

"Fuck you!" My fist connects with his lip, adrenaline winding through my veins as he groans.

"That's my girl." Enzo steps around, grabbing my hand and rubbing my knuckles. It aches in that moment, the rage fleeing, the pain coming, but it felt good. I needed to do it.

With an arm curled around the small of my back, we face them together. "Beg. Scream. It doesn't matter," Enzo says. "I'm going to take bits of you until you die. And right now, I'm gonna start with your tongues."

ENZO

TWENTY-THREE

The things we've done would make most people sick, but it has no effect on me. Not when the blood belongs to those who've messed with the people we love.

Sure, we may be goddamn beasts, but we hurt. We feel. And when one of ours is in pain, we feed the demon that feasts on the vengeance that's been breeding within us, growing with each passing year. It's ours to savor. Nothing will make us stop, not until every one of them dies. All the people tied to the Bianchis, all the ones who ruined the lives of so many.

Dante pries Graham's mouth open, as the man fights it, but he doesn't stand a chance. My brother's strength is no match for him. The shit they did to her would have them skinned alive, but I don't know if she'd stomach that level of savagery.

He rattles on the seat, crying, his thumb missing after he refused to tell us the name of the third man who was with them the day they... I can't even say it.

"Shhh," I mock. "It'll be over soon." I lift the chef's knife, its blade sharp, glistening under the lights as I grasp his tongue in between my fingers. "Well, until I find something else to chop off." My laugh is cruel as I start to slice.

It goes in clean. The gagging, the attempts at screaming, it only makes me want to torture him more. They will suffer for their sins. I will avenge her pain. This is only the beginning.

Once his tongue is disconnected, I throw it on the floor by his feet. I turn to find Joelle staring, her eyes huge, chest heaving.

"Are you okay, baby? If this is too much, I can have my men take you upstairs."

She shakes her head rapidly. "I'm fine."

I nod once, returning to Jay, who groans, still in visible pain from having his dick shot off.

"Nothing to say anymore?" I edge the tip of the knife under his jaw, raising his face to me.

When he doesn't answer, his gasping only getting stronger, I pierce the blade into his skin, right under his chin, the gasps now replaced by weeping. "How many times did she beg you to stop? How many fucking times did you refuse?"

"K-ki-kill me," he sobs. "Please kill me."

"Oh, don't fucking worry, I plan to. Not just yet though. First, you're gonna be a good little boy and tell me the name of the third man."

"Please," he weeps, his body rattling.

"Name!" I swing the knife, piercing it into his shoulder, pushing it deeper.

His shrieks turn into gasping sobs.

"Name!" I pull out the blade, readying to do it again.

"S-S-Sammy Rio."

A triumphant grin settles over my face. I flip the knife in my palm, eyeing the black resin handle, a knife Dante got for me, one for Dom too. They were custom made by a guy he knows. Beautiful work. Perfect for what we do with them.

Dom would've been here too, but he's busy taking care of Chiara after our gun supplier, Cain, hurt her. His end was pretty painful too, but probably not as painful as Graham's and Jay's will be.

"Where's the club located?" That's one thing we haven't yet figured out.

"I—" His snivel is exhausting and annoying as fuck.

"Hurry up," I say, the tip of the blade nearing his throat. "I'm getting pretty antsy."

"I—I don't know." He tries to catch his breath. "We call a n-n-number on the back of a gold card. Guy in a mask shows up, b-b-blindfolds us, and drives us there."

"So basically, you're fucking useless," I grit. "Figures." My chin tips up to Dante and he gets to prying Jay's mouth open. With the blade in hand, I slowly saw off his tongue, the screams of a man who holds no power only getting louder.

But I'm not done. Nearing Jay's ear this time, I grasp it tight. When he starts shaking, I glance up at Dante. "Bro, could you hold him down? I'm trying to work here."

"Hurry up, then." Dante clutches Jay's shoulders. "My brother's pretty good with a knife." He grins. "Just not as good as me. So this may take a while."

"Fuck you, man," I hit back, the blade leveling against Jay's ear, and I get to cutting.

"Mmm!" The asshole attempts a shout, but it comes out more like a mumble. He deserves it. If anything, he's getting off easy.

After his ear is clean off, I toss it over his limp dick, or whatever's left of it, dropping the knife on the floor beside his feet.

Graham mumbles with a cry as I march to the stove, picking up the pot of water hot enough for even Satan to be satisfied.

I walk it over to them. "Enjoy the shower, fuckers." With a faint chuckle, I flip half of the scorching liquid over Graham, some of it filling his mouth, searing over that half of his tongue he still owns.

Drops flick past my own face.

Shit. This is *damn hot.*

As I near Jay, he shakes his head, eyes bulging. I do the same to him, the water drowning out his pathetic attempt at making a sound, tidal waves of blazing heat pouring over him.

Giving them one final look, I make my way back to my weapons, dropping the pot into the sink. My fingers drift over one of the torches we like to use, melting off the flesh of our enemies.

"It's enough." Her voice drifts me out of the haze. "You don't need to do more. End it." She's on her feet, treading to me, her light footfalls getting close, a hand on my bicep as she nears.

"Are you sure?" I turn, rounding a palm on her hip. "You have to be damn sure. There's no going back."

"I am." She takes my other hand in hers, the blood of her torturers smearing past her long fingers as she stares deeply into my eyes. "Kill them."

I drift a gaze to her lips, my heart echoing with affection, and I kiss her. Slow. My blood-stained fingers lace into her waves, silky around my hand as I angle her sideways, deepening our connection.

She wrecks me, then builds me back up again. The consuming way she weaves herself through every part of my existence, it's damn near flawless.

Reluctantly drifting off her, I place one more kiss on the tip of her nose before I'm back to my knives, tightening a fist around another, the blade longer, thinner.

The wooden floorboards creak beneath my feet, the two men still whimpering like dying animals, half caught between this world and the next.

I won't kill them for mercy. Their death comes only because she asked it to. If it were up to me, I'd torture them more, until they died from blood loss, from shock. But if this is enough for her, then it should be enough for me.

Clutching Graham by the back of his neck, I yank hard, until his glazed, red-streaked eyes meet mine. The edge of the blade lands on the side of his neck and I cut right across with a long, drawn-out slash.

Blood. It flows. An unbending river.

The other bastard is next. "I only wish I found you sooner," I say before I slice straight through his carotid.

His eyes widen with a horrified expression, but it's a useless effort. He'll be dead in minutes. They both will be.

Joelle comes to stand beside me. Her hand finds mine in the carnage I've created, and together, we watch the men inhale their very last breaths.

JOELLE

TWENTY-FOUR

I never knew a man to be gentle, not unless he was interested in that kind of thing when he purchased me for an hour, sometimes two, depending on how big his wallet and stamina was. But Enzo, he's the most gentle and loving.

A few weeks have drifted by since he's killed those men, and since then, he's treated me with even more care. It's like he's trying to make up for all the wrongs in my life. Like he can erase them somehow. And though he can't, though no one can give me back those years, it's a relief to know I'm finally safe, that I finally have someone who wants to protect me.

But our time together in these past weeks haven't all been enjoyable. Enzo and his brothers still can't find Robby, though they have done nothing but try.

The hollow ache in my chest grows bigger with every passing

day, fearing I'll never get my boy back alive, that they'll tell me they found his remains instead. I wake up in the middle of the night from nightmares, Enzo's arms lulling me back to sleep.

He's kept me in the loop about everything, wanting me to know that he won't keep secrets between us.

When I found out Chiara was taken only two days after Enzo killed Graham and Jay, I couldn't believe her own father could be so cruel to his own child. But, then again, knowing what I know about him and his family, I'm not surprised either. They got her back though, safe from his grasp. And knowing Faro is dead, gives me a sense of peace.

Not only was Chiara taken, but shortly after, her cousin, Raquel, was too. Of course, her father, Salvatore, was involved. He's dead like his brother, along with Carlito, that sadistic man she was supposed to marry.

I heard about Raquel when Carlito talked about her at the club. I didn't know she was Chiara's cousin until Enzo told me.

She's with Dante now, but none of us will ever be truly free until the Bianchi men are all gone. I can't wait until that day comes.

I've briefly met both of Enzo's brothers, along with Raquel once in the past week, and I was finally able to see for myself that Chiara was safe.

With everything going on with her family, she's really worried about her other cousin, Aida. Neither Raquel nor Chiara grew up close with her, thanks to her father, Agnelo. But they love her and want her to be safe. They don't even have a cell number to check on her. As far as they know, Aida doesn't own a phone. When they've tried to call the house, no one answered. But no one usually does, Chiara told me.

She's concerned Aida's father did something to her. If I know anything about Agnelo, I know what he's capable of. If I were his daughter, I'd run the hell away the first chance I got.

Chiara is itching to head to the house and find Aida herself, but Dom doesn't want her in danger, and who knows what she could be walking into. I can't say I blame him.

I stand under the spray of the warm water, hands in my hair, washing away the shampoo, unable to wait until I'm done so I can curl up next to Enzo for the night.

The bathroom door squeaks, cool air whisking past my body, my skin pricking. I see him then, his thick, brawny thighs strutting toward me, visible even through the steam masking my full view of him through the glass door.

He moves to where I am, closer now, his hand on the door as he slides it open. I squint a playful gaze as he walks in beside me, a smirk on his face as he twists the knob to the double shower next to mine, and the water comes alive.

"Didn't you already take one like an hour ago?" I ask, as I pick up a sponge and lather it up with some bodywash.

"Did I?" The corner of his sinful mouth curves into a sly grin as he stands under the water, eyes shut, his ripped abs flexing as he works his hands through his hair. The veins in the corded muscles of his biceps swell as though trying to rip right through his skin.

My body turns molten as my gaze falls to his cock, thick and so damn hard. My hands itch to touch him, to feel him inside me. He hasn't been shy about showing how badly he wants me.

And he wants me *all* the time. Fast or slow, he knows my body well, bringing out every ounce of pleasure I've lacked.

His head straightens, his heavily hooded gaze trapping me in its tantalizing allure, those sea-green eyes caressing a path down my body, from my lips to the apex of my thighs.

He grabs a bar of soap, rolling it down his chest without looking away, lower, to the pack of solid muscles on his stomach, to the thickening of his cock, stiffening the more I stare.

My nipples turn taut as he places the soap back, his hand falling to his hard-on as he strokes himself. A steady ache builds in my core, my pussy clenching, needing him to take away that pain. My hands fall over my breasts, squeezing them together as he groans, stroking himself harder, the hallows beneath his cheekbones deepening.

He's unable to glance away. The way he devours me gives me the courage to try something I haven't done since before my world was turned upside down. I roll my palm through the slickness of my body, past my stomach, until I find that place I've been used, abused, but I get to claim it now. It's mine. This moment, this feeling—it's mine. But it's his too. I want it to be. It's my choice, and no one gets to make those for me any longer.

I back up against the wall, slipping a finger inside.

"Yeah, baby," he groans. "Let me see those fingers stretch that pussy."

I sigh his name, adding a second finger, his dirty talk like gasoline over my body, lighting me up.

"That's a good girl. Finger your pretty cunt before I fuck it. Let me hear you come."

"Yes," I cry, thrusting faster, my muscles spasming, my core drenched, needing him badly. My exhales turn to hurried gasps as I watch him watching me, and nothing has felt so erotic.

"That's it, baby. Show me how you like it." He fists himself tightly, the water dripping down his heavy, rigid cock, his form rippling as every muscle tenses.

My thighs tremble, clamping around my hand as my orgasm builds, unable to take my eyes off his hand as it leisurely rolls down his length, then up again.

"Can't wait to taste you on my tongue, feel you come around my fat cock." He groans as I move deeper, faster, my body quivering as I almost reach the end. "You want that, don't you, baby girl? You like that pussy spread open with my tongue while you sit on my face."

"Oh God, yes, please," I cry, unable to hold on much longer.

"Come for me, baby. And then you're mine."

My lips part, my moans sounding more like pleading cries, and when I brush my thumb over my clit this time, my release spirals, practically knocking me down to the ground.

He's on me before I can recover, pushing me harder up against the wall, his mouth capturing mine, his tongue fighting its way inside, teeth nipping my lower lip. He's demonic in the way he wields his power over my body, like he knows it better than I do. Maybe he does.

His fingers slip between my legs, and I fight against his touch, still sensitive from the orgasm I just had. Before I know it, I'm rising higher again, his fingers spreading me, sinking inside.

"Yeah, that's it," he groans, his lips kissing past my neck, coasting down to my breast, gripping a nipple between his teeth before continuing downward.

He sinks to the floor, peering up at me as he lifts one of my legs and throws it over his shoulder.

"It's time a man worshipped you for a change." That's the last thing he says before his mouth covers my pussy. I scream out his name, my hand weaving into his voluptuous hair as I pull hard, the tip of his tongue dancing over my clit, the tempo fast yet slow. He brings me to the edge, but never lets me fall. I cling to the orgasm he denies, wanting it so badly, I'm ready to beg for his cock.

"I know exactly what this pussy needs." The vibrations from his warm and seductive voice against my most intimate place has me wordlessly panting, clasping my hand tighter around his hair.

His tongue shoves inside me, two fingers sweeping up and down both sides of my clit. I gasp from the intense sensation, my core quivering as the back of my head falls against the tiles, water sluicing down our bodies.

I'm almost there, falling faster. When he slides his long, thick tongue in deeper, those fingers swirling harshly over my clit, my orgasm bursts to life.

"Yes, Enzo! Oh fuck, yes!"

His approving growl drives every ounce of pleasure from me before he climbs back up, kissing me with a fury to match my own.

Our hands are everywhere at once, practically clawing at each other before he lifts me up by my thighs, my back hitting the wall behind me as he positions his cock at my entrance. Now that I'm on the pill he was able to get for me, we don't have to worry about condoms.

He holds me steady with the power of his grip as the head of his length enters me slowly, but he doesn't move at first, stilling inside me as he gazes deep into my eyes.

"I love you, Joelle. Too fucking much."

And my heart, it winces at the name he uses, the name they all used for me, those men who hurt me.

I should've told him by now, I owe him that, but I was holding back for some reason. I'm done now. I want him to know all of me. I love him enough to give him something else. My real name.

"Call me Jade," I tremble out, so nervous he'll hate me for not telling him sooner.

"Jade?" His brows bend with confusion as he brings a hand up, keeping me steady with his other one, his arm gripping me under my ass.

He clasps his large palm around the side of my neck, his cock tipping further into my entrance.

"Yes." I nod, swallowing the emotions overflowing through me, tears aching with every beat of my heart. Fear and love, they battle for space, for air. What will he think of her? Will he want her?

Then I tell him. I give her to him. The girl. The woman.

"I'm Jade Macintyre."

With hooded eyes, his lips lift softly. "Jade," he whispers as he kisses the corner of my mouth.

"I love you, Jade."

He thrusts all the way inside, and with the tears rolling down my cheeks, he gives me something no man has ever given me—he gives me acceptance.

JOELLE

TWENTY-FIVE

As I inspect myself before the full-length mirror the following day, readying for the barbeque at Dom and Chiara's, I keep worrying about the questions that may come up. How could I answer them? No one knows who Robby's sperm donor is, not even Enzo.

I can't even stomach the word father because that's not who he is. He's nothing to us. I don't know why I'm so hesitant to tell them all the truth. Maybe because it's Chiara and Raquel's family? What if they side with him? What if they think bad of me? I shake those thoughts away. Chiara would never do that.

"You ready, babe?" Enzo strolls out of the bathroom, hair slicked back, short-sleeved baby-blue T-shirt wrapping around his solid chest, his ass tight in a pair of denim. He said he wanted to match my eyes. Yeah, he's corny as hell, and all mine.

"I think so." I turn from one side to another, wondering if high-heeled sandals and a black pencil dress is proper barbeque attire at a mansion. But I don't care. I never had a life before, and I'm liking getting dressed up.

"What's there to think about?" His arms curl around me from behind, resting over my stomach, his chin propped on top of my head. "You look so damn good, I'm about to keep you all to myself."

"Really?" I narrow my eyes at him through the mirror, his lips curving flirtatiously, as do mine. "And what would you do with me?"

"You really wanna know what I'd do to this gorgeous body right now?"

I nod, arching a brow in challenge.

His lips gradually slip down to my neck. "I'd bend you over this mirror and make you watch as you take my cock."

Oh God.

The dirty words send a jolt right to my core, my inner thighs tightening as heat pools between them. "Is that a promise?" My voice turns whispery, filling with want, my hand slipping in between us, finding him hard. I tighten a fist around the stiff head of his cock, my eyes connected to his as his chest rises with heavy beats.

He fists my hair, yanking me back hard as a deep-chested growl splinters out of him. "Yeah, it's a fucking promise. And I'm about to show you how well I keep them."

With the same hand, he pushes my head down, my body bent over, my palms splayed against the cold glass.

My panting is frantic as his fingertips crawl down my back and over my ass, taking their time reaching the hem of my dress. When he does; when his touch rolls up inside both of my thighs, I moan, my hands slipping.

"Don't move." He swats my ass hard, his gaze glued to mine through the mirror, and my core clenches, my teeth sinking to the corner of my lower lip with a cry.

Watching him do this to me, it's sending my body into a frenzy, a complete needy mess. I fight to keep myself upright as he slowly lifts my dress, drifting it up past my ass. Two fingers wander in between my cheeks as he pushes one into the puckered flesh, my breathing rapid as I anticipate what he'll do next.

"Good girl. Stay still while I play with that greedy, little pussy."

"Shit," I hiss, my core soaking my panties.

His hands find me damp, aching lust spreading over my entire body. His fingers curl over the thin strap of my thong, pulling it down, exposing me. Those palms massage the back of my thighs as he brings my panties all the way lowered, until they're around my ankles.

I step out of them, just as his palm moves up the back of my right thigh, so slowly, so seductively, my release builds, the wetness drenching.

"Touch me," I beg, my voice a mess of emotions. "Please." It's the first time he has since I told him my name. He never questioned it. Never asked more. He just accepted that it was me.

"Mmm, where? Tell me where you want it, baby."

"I need you inside me. Please, Enzo, fuck me."

"I love hearing you say my name when you're so eager to have this hole filled with my cock." The next sensation that envelops me is him, two fingers driving deep, the pain and pleasure morphing into something new, something so damn good, I scream as he works me like he's trying to climb inside.

"Harder. Yes! Don't stop," I plead, his other hand reaching for my throat, gripping me in a chokehold as he jerks my head back, my body bending to his expert touch.

"Mmm. You're dripping," he groans with a husky beat, the sound pulsating around the curve of my ear. He drags his fingers out of me, while I pant from the loss. "But I need you dripping down my cock."

I try to right myself but his palm lands heavy against the small of my back, bending me over even more. "Did I tell you to move, baby? Keep that pussy spread open for me. I like looking at it, especially when my cock is stretching it out."

"Hurry!" I squirm, needing him to make me come.

His hand whips out, landing hard over my ass. "You making demands now? Because if so, I'm gonna make you wait it out until we get home." There's a teasing edge trapped in those words and the thought of having to wait has my core clenching on instinct.

"I'll die." I sigh with maddening desperation, pivoting my head toward him, finding a cocky smirk settling over his lips, his hands on the zipper of his jeans, the sound as he drags it down causing my pussy to throb.

The crown of his thick length nudges at my entrance. "Don't worry, baby girl. I'm gonna make sure that doesn't happen." With one single thrust, he's buried inside me, the sensation of his jeans rubbing against my skin, feeling so full of him, it all causes my body to shudder.

His fingers spread into my hair, twisting as they roughly pull, his heavy grunts spurring me on, the need climbing.

He reaches around to play with my clit, brushing over it with merciless strokes. I can see myself in the mirror, see him staring at me, his nostrils flaring, my cries of pleasure rising as he pounds into me so roughly, I scream. His face contorts with desire the more he pins me with a gaze.

"Enzo! Yes!" I'm almost there, falling into the intensity we create together.

"Jade," he growls. The rough call of my name has my toes curling, body firing off like fireworks with the tumultuous waves of my orgasm.

"Fuuuck!" His hot release shoots inside me, his groan rough, making me cry out louder for every bit of him.

His hips ram powerfully until he spills every drop. Once he's through, his exhales are as ragged as mine.

He wraps my hair around his wrist and yanks me upright, drawing his lips to my ear. "I'm never getting sick of fucking you."

"Please," I sass. "Like you have much of a choice."

"Brat." He chuckles, spanking my ass before he's stuffing himself back inside, zippering up.

"You can punish me later." I wink, putting my panties back on, then straightening out my dress before running to the bathroom to get cleaned up.

When I come out, a delicious, crooked grin greets me. "Don't look at me like that." I narrow a playful stare, grabbing his hand. "Let's get out of here before we're late."

"I like being late," he drawls in a deep, sexy way as we exit.

"I bet you do."

We arrived at Dom's a little while ago, enjoying steak, burgers, and veggies their caterer had been busy grilling up.

As we ate, Chiara had shared the news of her pregnancy. I was filled with complete happiness for them, yet a bit of melancholy made its way in too. I can't lie and say it wasn't there, but I did my best not to show it.

After dinner, the ladies and I went over toward the pool, each taking up space on one of the loungers beside each other. As we spoke, as I broke down and told them how happy I was that my son looks nothing like his father, Raquel asked who that was.

At first, I was going to lie, but then I realized they really are on my side. I had no reason to keep it a secret anymore. So, I gave them a piece of my history from the time I was taken, from the moment I became the property of the Bianchis.

They all appear visibly shaken at the news I had just shared, especially Chiara. Her face is stricken with grief as she glances at me, having just returned from throwing up. When she heard who Robby's father was, she didn't take the news well, and neither did Enzo.

"I'm sorry," Chiara says, her eyes briefly closing before she continues. "I'm sorry for all of it. If he were here, I'd kill him."

I know she means Agnelo.

I get up, going to her, gently taking her hand. "I don't blame you or Raquel. You're not responsible for their actions. Don't be so hard on yourselves."

"Yeah." Chiara nods, sliding her hand out of mine, pacing as though she blames herself no matter what I say.

"Sir?" An armed guard grabs Dom's attention. "One of the cameras on the other side of the fence malfunctioned," he explains in a low tone. "The men are looking at it."

Dom hurriedly gets to his feet. "I'll go check it out," he says, starting to rush away with the man.

I'm too busy focusing on him to notice anything else until it's too late. Until a bullet rips through the air, the one coming from the man who's been cooking our food, listening to our conversations, severing the only peace we've had in a while.

But it's not the bullet itself that starts the war, but it's who it's aimed for.

It hits Chiara on the side of her stomach, her body falling as though in slow motion. Dom screams her name, running to her while I'm there, unable to move, as though frozen in time.

My eyes, they won't peel away from Chiara's body floating in the water.

I hear my name as though from a distance, someone grabbing my arms, practically dragging me backward until I land onto the ground.

Hands clasp my cheeks. "Jade, baby. Stay here. Are you listening?"

"Okay," I whisper softly, seeing Enzo clearly now, his gaze doused with animalistic rage and intense worry.

"Don't cry. Shit, baby. I'm sorry. I'm gonna take care of it. Just don't fucking move from this spot."

I nod, tears trickling down my cheeks. I finally feel them now.

"I love you." His lips fall to mine in a quick embrace before he leaves me there, not knowing if Chiara is alive.

More bullets blaze to life, more men arriving. I can hear the taunting, the shouting, the fighting.

I huddle behind a large tree, a tall shrub immediately at my back.

Is this about me? Is that why they came? Did I just cost Chiara a chance at becoming a mother? Did they harm Robby?

The fear from the unknown crashes over me, hitting with the same force as the whip of gunfire around us. Will we lose someone? How many more lives can these monsters ruin?

"Give us Chiara and Raquel. That's all we want," a man I immediately recognize says.

Benvolio.

Someone else's laughter erupts and I instantly recognize it.

Agnelo.

"I want that whore, Joelle, too. Where is she, huh?" he asks roughly, sending a shiver running down my spine.

A guttural snarl woven with a growl erupts from Enzo. "I'm gonna rip your damn head off just like I did to your men, who are lying dead, where you'll soon be. Both of you," he snaps, his voice deadly. "I'm gonna enjoy gutting you like a pig."

I swallow through the bile rushing up my throat, choking on the rancid taste.

"You fuckin' jackass motherfuckers," Agnelo continues. "Who do you think you are, huh? You're all about to join your mommy and daddy. My nieces, Joelle, they'll all be following you there too."

Pop.

A single gunshot causes me to gasp, my body jerking backward.
Please don't let Enzo die.

"Nice try," Agnelo chides with a terrifying tone before the words are replaced with more gunpower, bullet after bullet shooting from all around.

I'm helpless, trapped here, my body jolting every time someone's gun goes off.

I back up further, curling my body in the hopes of not getting shot, but instead, I hit something hard behind me. I try to turn, but a hand buckles around my shoulder, warm exhales creeping against the side of my neck.

All the hairs on my body stand up and my pulse thrashes.

"Don't turn around. Pretend I'm not even here," a voice I've never heard before says. "If you do, I'll fucking shoot you. Understand?"

I nod, but barely.

"Agnelo has a message for you." He drops a piece of paper onto my lap, and as I try to look down at it, he tightens his grasp.

"You don't want to disappoint the boss, Joelle." He says my

name with crass. "He'll be waiting." His hand is gone faster than it came, leaving my body ice cold, the shock of it lacing through me.

Finally, I look down onto the paper, finding a message from the man whose soul left him a long time ago, assuming he ever had one.

I knew I'd find you, eventually. You can't escape me. You better find a way to meet me at this address 1010 Main Street. Come alone. Robby and I will be waiting. He's counting on you. Ticktock.

I read the words over and over, knowing I have to go. There's no other choice. But how will I ever get out of here without being stopped?

The fighting continues for a while, and my panic, it only intensifies. My poor, sweet Robby.

I love you so much, baby.

New tears spring up, my bottom lip quaking.

"Raquel?" Dante calls to her, though I can't see either of them from my position. "Give me the gun, baby."

Why does she have a gun and why is she not hiding?

It's then that I realize, the gunfire has ceased.

"Come on, I'm taking you inside," he continues, and as I slowly sneak a peek around the tree before me, I find Benvolio dead on the ground, and other men lying all around.

Enzo jogs, drawing near, kneeling once he's before me. "Are you okay?" He palms my cheek as his eyes wander over every inch of me, while I attempt to hide the paper now discreetly crumbled in my hand.

"I think so. Is it over? Is everyone okay? How's Chiara?"

"No one else got hurt, but fucking Agnelo ran. The pussy."

He must be heading to this address.

"I don't know anything about Chiara's status yet," he explains. "Dom took her to the hospital."

"Can I go see her?" And then it hits me, that would be the perfect way to escape and find Agnelo. I realize it's probably a trap, but I can't ignore when he comes calling. He doesn't threaten lightly. If I don't go, I know he'll kill my son.

"It's not safe for you to leave right now. I need you where our men can keep an eye on you."

Irritation settles in my gut. "This is bullshit, Enzo. You can't keep me prisoner forever."

He watches me sympathetically. "I'm not, I swear. But I can't risk your safety. We'll talk about it later, when I'm done with those assholes, all right? I love you."

My gaze narrows, locking him with a brutal stare.

His chest widens with a hard inhale. "I've got some loose ends to clean up." He gestures behind us with a tilt of his head to two men being dragged away, their mouths gagged. He gives me a hand as I get to my feet. "I gotta bring you inside. Then I'll take you back home."

"Fine," I practically snarl, already starting toward the house, him jogging after me.

"Don't fucking do that." He grips my wrist, halting me, pulling me right against his body. "It's for your own safety." He throws my arm over his shoulder, his hand now braced around the back of my neck. "Agnelo won't stop until he has you." The way he looks at me—God, those intense green eyes spilling into my very soul, his fingers dipping into my skin. "I'd *die* before I let him have you. You hear me?"

He draws his face close to mine, his lips skimming across my mouth, my eyes watering, my heart hammering. The affection, it kills me.

I've been without it for so long, it may as well be foreign. But with him, it feels like home. But it's incomplete, like the roof has been ripped off.

My son, my mom, my brother, they're a part of me too, and without them, nothing will be the same.

A soft exhale rises out of me, gently caressing his lips with my shaky ones.

"I love you, Enzo. Thanks for loving me," I say, barely grasping to keep all the tears locked away.

"Loving you, Jade, is the easiest thing I've ever done." His mouth finds mine, reminding me just how much he does.

JOELLE

TWENTY-SIX

I'm back at Enzo's. He had just left with Dante and Raquel to go see Chiara at the hospital. My renewed anger at not being allowed to join them has me in a frenzy, pacing around the acres of greenery, Agnelo's note still crunched in my palm. I need to figure out how I can get out of here without one of the guards stopping me.

I spot a few men at the other end of the yard, standing at attention beside the tall gate, leading outside. Maybe if I can cause some kind of disturbance in the house, it'll make them run inside, giving me the chance to escape.

I have nothing to lose. Deciding to try, I head for the kitchen. What the hell could I do to make them all come to my rescue, and how could I dodge them before they get to me?

Think, damn it! It's now or never.

Once Enzo returns, I'll be stuck here. He won't let me out of his sight. As I face the stove, a dangerous idea comes to mind, but one that may work. Taking out a pan, I place it on the stove. I grab olive oil and sprinkle some onto the surface, before turning on the gas. A minute later, the pan sizzles.

There are two exits that lead out from the kitchen—the one through the large glass door closer to the men outside, which is the one I hope they use—and another off to the right, which will be my exit.

I'll rush out of the kitchen once the fire starts, then run like hell. It's a gamble, but escaping from the front door isn't an option. Enzo has way more men posted there.

With no one looking, I move the pan away and spill a few drops of oil onto the stove top, the fire starting to come alive.

Before the alarm rings, I back up, slowly creeping away. As soon as I do, the alarm blares, the men all rushing toward the sound, calling for me.

My heart knocks in my rib cage as I tiptoe out the door, not a soul noticing me as I find the will to run like hell. My dress and high heels long abandoned for leggings, a large black hoodie, and the most comfortable sneakers I've ever owned.

I gently open the fence, my feet hitting the pavement, not seeing anyone as I dash toward the street, with only the main gate and a single man at the booth to stop me. I don't wait. I continue running, even as the guy stands from inside the partition. I barely look at him as I hurriedly near the end, but when I get to the gate, it suddenly starts to shut right before me.

"No!" I scream, grabbing it. "Let me out!"

"Ma'am," the man calls from behind, my hand locked around the bars, fingertips pressing into the cold, hard metal as my breathing ravages from within.

"Get the hell away from me and open this damn thing!" I shriek, shaking the bars, the note caught between my palm, my back to the man keeping me away from my son.

"Please, calm down. Let me call one of my bosses and we can sort this out."

I turn, gritting my teeth, my eyes narrowed as he reaches into his pants, retrieving a cell. But suddenly he stills, confusion branded on his features, his eyes bulging as though he's seen a ghost. The phone falls from his grasp, tumbling onto the grass. He backs away from me. "It's not possible," he barely whispers.

I whirl my head around, wondering if someone is behind me, but there's no one here but us. "What's wrong?" I ask. But he shakes his head like he's in a daze, completely ignoring the question.

"It can't be." He takes a step forward. "I've been looking all this time and—"

"What the hell are you talking about?" My pulse races, a cold rush swarming up my entire body.

"You don't recognize me, do you?" The softness in his voice breaks with emotion. This tall guy towering over me looks as though he's about to collapse.

He must be a customer. That has to be it.

"Look." I swallow harshly, trying to bury this eerie feeling wafting over me. He's seriously creeping me out. "I think I know where we met, and I don't do that anymore. If Enzo finds out, he'll basically kill you, so why don't you shut the fuck up and let me out. I'll keep this between us. Sound good to you?"

He chuckles with sadness piercing through, wiping under his eye. I hadn't realized he was crying.

My stomach churns.

"I don't know what you're talking about, but it's nice to see you haven't changed much."

Goose bumps break over both arms, running up so quickly, it almost hurts. "Who are you?" I breathe.

He comes nearer, a gentle hand tentatively falling to the top of my shoulder. "It's me, Jade." He sighs. "It's Elliot. God, I've been looking everywhere for you. I can't believe you've been here all this time."

I don't know what happens after because I fall, my knees buckling, the lights going out.

I think I faint.

"Give her some room," someone demands as I grumble, my eyelids flickering as I start to see again, the overhead lights causing me to squint. That same man stands over me, the one who claimed he's my—brother. I jump to a sitting position from the sofa, but as my head spins, I regret it.

"Hey, drink some water," he says, extending a glass toward me.

Glancing up, I try to find bits of the sixteen-year-old boy within the man who looks nothing like him.

Could it be him?

"You can't be my brother," I say, grabbing the cup and drinking all of it, now suddenly parched. "I don't know who you are." I shove the glass back his way and he takes it. "This isn't funny."

With a head tilt, he tells the others to go, and they leave us alone in the den. He sits beside me, letting out a hard sigh. "Who else would prank you the way I used to?" He lets out a chuckle. "Like put shaving cream and cinnamon all over your mouth? Remember how we told Mom that day you—"

My body breaks with a tremor, blinking through the large tears welling. He was always coming up with weird and unexpected ways to prank me. "Oh my God," I cry. "It really is you."

I slap a hand over my mouth, staring at him with fresh eyes, both of us gripped with so many emotions, it's too difficult to contain them.

"Elliot?" My chin quivers. "Elliot." I throw my arms around my brother, hugging him so tight, I'm probably killing him.

His arms wrap around me even tighter. "It's me, sis. I'm here."

I silently cry in his arms for a while, and I think he cries in mine. He lost me too. It must've been hard. He said he looked for me, but how did he end up here?

It's a conversation we have to have, but not now. Not when I still have to get to Robby. Maybe he can help. Gently pushing away from him, I look on the ground for that piece of paper.

"Elliot, I have a million questions. So many that it'll take us days to talk, and I'm sure you have them too, but I have to find someone before he's killed. You have to let me out of here."

"Do you mean Robby?"

I jerk back. "How did you kno—"

But as he fishes in his pocket, lifting a hand, I find the note dangling from his fingers.

"Who is Robby, Jade? What are you involved in? Are Enzo and his brothers hurting you? Because I don't give a shit that I work for them, I'll kill each one if they did something to you."

My eyes grow.

Whoa. What happened to my sweet, pain-in-the-ass little brother?

"No. I love Enzo." I clasp my hand over his, releasing an audible exhale. "I guess I have to tell you, but be prepared. You're going to hate this story."

He steels his jaw, nodding once. I tell him everything, skipping the parts filled with the specifics of what those men did to me, but

I recite the important parts, about the Bianchis, how Agnelo raped me, how I met Enzo.

When I'm done, he looks enraged. He's scary like this, even while I know he'd never cause me any harm.

"I'm going to fucking kill everyone who's still alive. Whether they personally laid a damn finger on you or not, they're fucking dead."

"I know you're upset, but I have to go to that address. I have to get my son."

"Jade, they're going to kill you as soon as you step foot there. You'll never get Robby."

An unbearable pain lodges into the back of my throat. "I can't sit here and do nothing."

"That's not what I said. But you're not going anywhere. We are."

"What?"

There's determination on his face as he retrieves a phone from his pocket.

"Who are you calling?"

"Enzo. He's with Dante. I'm telling them what's going on so we can go and get Robby, then kill those fucks once and for all."

I grab his wrist. "What if that doesn't work? What if they see you guys and kill my son?"

"They won't." A flick of a smile etches his mouth. "I'm going to get my nephew back, so I can tell him all about how I would torture his mom when we were kids." Tears swim past my eyes.

"I'm not losing you again." His brows tighten. "Trust me, okay?"

My shoulders drop. "Okay."

I don't have a choice now. Maybe Elliot is right. Agnelo wouldn't hesitate to shoot me dead after killing my boy.

He dials a number. "Sir, listen, Jade was planning on running and—"

He pauses, listening to Enzo, whose voice I hear, but not what he's saying.

"It's a long story. I don't have time to explain. But she got a note from Agnelo saying they'll kill Robby if she doesn't—"

"What?" His gaze focuses on me intently. "Okay. No problem."

"What is it?" I ask in alarm as he climbs to his feet.

"Talk to him as you follow me out to the Jeep." He hands me the cell.

I quickly place the phone to my ear. "Enzo?"

"Baby? I got him. I've got Robby. We found him."

I stop, my inhale locked in my lungs. The shock, it hits me right in the heart. I could barely hold the phone or walk, almost collapsing to the ground.

"He's in the hospital. I just got here a minute ago," Enzo continues. "I was about to call you when Elliot called me. He'll take you to him."

"Hospital? Wha-what'd they do to him?"

Elliot hooks an arm through mine, leading me to a car that's already waiting. The doors open and he helps me inside.

"I don't know what's wrong with him yet," Enzo says as the engine spurs to life. We roll out of the driveway and onto the street. "The woman I found him with said he'd been sick. His pulse had stopped for a few seconds, but—"

"Oh my God!" I gasp, the tears rolling down my cheeks, a weighty ache settling over my chest.

"He'll be okay, baby. He's with the doctors. You gotta believe he'll come out of this."

But I can't.

Hope isn't something I'm used to.

JOELLE

TWENTY-SEVEN

We arrive at the hospital, and as soon as the car stops, I jump out, running inside.

"I'm looking for my son." I huff, my palms flat on the counter of the front desk, a woman no older than me sitting there, peering up.

"What's his na—"

"Jo—Jade." I turn sharply toward Enzo's voice.

"Enzo?" My heart drops from relief as I see him on my left, standing up from one of the chairs. I rush toward him. Our bodies connect hard as his arms hold me with everlasting strength. I sob quietly against him, a hand gliding up my back, soothing me as he always does.

"Have you heard anything?" I ask, just as Elliot makes it inside.

"Not yet, baby. But listen, his name is John Parker here. I didn't want the Bianchis finding out we have him. Don't worry about anything. The staff here will not ask questions. We're good friends with two people on the board."

"Okay." My fingertips jump to my forehead. "I need to sit." Elliot takes the empty chair beside me while Enzo takes the other.

Minutes tick by and we wait in silence until Enzo breaks it.

"I gotta ask…" He leans his elbows on his thighs, his attention on Elliot. "How the hell do you know my girl's real name?"

He's trying to remain calm, but I could tell the beast is roused awake.

Elliot snickers. "She's my sister, man."

He jolts in his chair, sitting straighter. "What?" He runs a hand past his face, his eyes darting between us. "Is he telling the truth?" he asks me.

"Yeah." I smile weakly at my brother. "He kinda is."

"Okay, back up. Someone's gotta explain all this to me."

Elliot's brown eyes grow sad as he momentarily looks to the floor before he speaks.

"Since the moment our mother and I knew she was gone, when the police failed to find her, I was determined to do what they couldn't. But I was just a kid." He shrugs. "Only sixteen. So with help from some friends, I found this guy online who could go into the dark web. He tried to help me track Jade that way, but it was impossible. It's like all traces of you vanished," he says to me. "I decided to join the army at eighteen, wanting to become stronger so I could find and kill the ones who took you. But as the years passed, I regretted it because all that time, I could've been looking for you."

"Oh, Elliot." Tears spring into my eyes with a renewed sense of anguish. "Don't blame yourself." Taking his hand, I hold it in mine. "None of this is on you. You wouldn't have found me anyway."

"I'm your brother, Jade, and I failed you." He's so broken. I can see it on his face, and the pain, it bleeds into mine.

"No." I shake my head, my vision blurry. "The path you took, it led me to you. If you hadn't done everything you did, we probably would've never found each other."

He lets out a sharp exhale. "Maybe you're right."

"I was always right." My mouth cracks with a small laugh.

"Yeah, you never let me forget it." He chuckles.

"So, how did you end up working for Enzo?"

"Well, technically, he's assigned to Dante," Enzo clarifies. "Though the guys work for all of us."

"I got shot last year," my brother adds.

"What?" I gasp. "Are you okay?"

"Yeah." His face sparks with a grin, registering the shock on my face. "That's how I ended up working for them." His head tilts toward Enzo. "I had to leave the army because of it, then a buddy of mine, who I met at basic training, was already working for them, so he put in a good word for me. They tested me hard." He lifts a chin to Enzo. "But I'm here." He grins at him.

"Damn, man," Enzo chimes in with a smirk. "I almost didn't vote for you. You were too fucking pretty. I was kinda worried you were gonna take all the ladies away from me."

"Hey!" I giggle.

He raises his hands up. "That was way before I fell madly in love with your crazy—" I glare playfully at him. "Let a man finish. Damn. Crazy, yet absolutely beautiful ass."

"I don't want to hear about you loving my sister's ass." Elliot gags.

As we all laugh together, I remember that even in the darkest of days, the light shines just enough to remind us it's there after all.

An hour later, a doctor finally walks out. Her long, white coat hits past her ankles, her black-trimmed glasses perched on her slim nose.

"Mr. Cavaleri," she greets him with a serious expression, her dark brown hair wrapped neatly into a bun. "Are you the mother?" Her attention reverts to me.

"Yes." My pulse slams with a heavy pounding.

"Your son is stable right now. He had developed RSV, a respiratory virus, that then resulted in what's called bronchiolitis. That can sometimes happen and is what caused the low oxygen. He's sleeping at the moment, and once he's awake, you may go see him."

"Will he pull through this?" I ask, my tone etched with worry.

"With the medication we've given him, you'll be able to bring your son home very soon."

My knees buckle, and I hold on to Enzo for relief as the doctor leaves us with a tight smile.

"She must think I'm the worst mother." My tears soak through his shirt as I hide in it.

"Nah, baby. She doesn't." He tips my chin up with the back of his hand. "She knows he was taken from you. She won't be calling the authorities. I took care of everything."

"Oh, thank goodness." I wince. "I could only imagine what they put him through."

He leads me back to the chair, and as we're all seated, I turn to Elliot. "Oh God, we have to call Mom! Did you tell her I'm alive yet?"

Instead of appearing ecstatic, his face falls, or more like shatters. He can't even look at me anymore.

"What is it, Elliot?" My heart pounds. "Tell me."

His throat bobs. "I-I'm sorry, Jade." Twined between each

syllable is unexplained grief. I slap a hand over my racing heart, sharp stabbing hitting the middle of my chest.

"No," I cry, tears welling. "Don't. Please." Teardrops pour down my cheeks. "Don't you say it."

But he does. "I-I'm so sorry, but Mom died two years ago from a brain aneurysm. She didn't suffer. I swear."

I slap a shuddering hand over my mouth, my vision swimming with too much sorrow to see anything beyond the need to scream, to cry with the worst kind of pain.

"She never gave up that you were alive. Not once." He's off the chair, kneeling in front of me, his hand on my knee as I hide the tears behind my palms. "She always thought you were somewhere she couldn't reach. Always talked about you. Drove the cops crazy every damn day. She loved you, Jade. *I* love you."

She's gone. She's never going to know I made it out. That I'm alive. She's never going to meet her grandson.

Enzo's touch strokes up my arm, as my sobs get louder, the storm of my anguish raging with deep turmoil, wrecking me until I can no longer contain it. For the first time in the past nine years, I let it out. I cry, really cry. I cry for all the losses I've had, for all the bottled-up agony—sobbing, it all pours out.

Heavy. Loud. Unafraid.

I cry for my mother.

For myself.

For all of us.

It's freeing and painful and raw. With every drop, I am letting go of the woman I was forced to become, welcoming the girl I used to be, the woman I am now.

I found her. I can finally hear her. Feel her. I'm not going to let her go. My mother wouldn't want me to.

I will remember you with every kiss, every hug I give to Robby.

You will never be forgotten, Mom. You will live on forever.

I push the door open a little at a time, worried I'll scare him. His face turns toward the sound as I enter, and when he sees me, his little blue eyes instantly brighten.

The oxygen mask is no longer on his face, taken off as soon as his stats normalized when he woke up an hour ago. Once the doctors were done with their tests, I was cleared to go to him. They told me he demanded to see me as soon as he saw them, and I couldn't wait another moment.

"Mommy!" He coughs, and it breaks my heart to hear how ill he is, how neglectful they've been with my baby, not that I expected any different.

"Hi, my sweet boy." My tone is low as I tread lightly, sneakers softly crashing over the marble floor.

Enzo had arranged for him to get the best room in the hospital. The size of it is more like a penthouse.

I take a seat on the side of the bed, my knuckles reaching down, brushing past the hollow of his cheek. "I love you so much, baby. Mommy will never let anyone hurt you again. No one will separate us anymore."

"You promise?" he asks with a quiver in his chin. "The bad men are gone?"

I don't want to lie, but I owe him some semblance of safety. "They will be, and they'll never get anywhere near you again."

"And you, Mommy? Will they get you?"

The back of my nose burns with a sting of emotion clouding over the words that are difficult to say.

"Mommy?" he questions once more, coughing roughly, those piercing eyes needing answers, needing his mother to be okay.

"They won't get me either. My friend, Enzo, the one who brought you here, he'll make sure we're both safe. Always."

"That's good." He smiles weakly. "Can I live with you now?"

"Are you kidding me? Of course!" I scoot closer, lying beside him, my arm draped over his belly, my lips on the top of his head, kissing the soft waves of his blond hair. "I'm never letting you go. You're stuck with me forever."

He laughs feebly. "I love you so much, Mommy."

"I love you too, Robby."

"I'm tired." He yawns. "Could you hug me while I sleep?"

"Today and every day." I stroke away the hair lining his forehead, hoping that's true, that I can spend all my days with him from now on. "Close your eyes, sweet baby. The monsters are gone now."

But that's not true, is it? They're still out there. Waiting. Haunting us. Until we settle this, until I come face-to-face with that man, this will never end.

I'll be coming for him with an army of my own. I need to do this for Robby. For me. For my friends still out there.

He has to die and I have to be the one to do it.

ENZO

TWENTY-EIGHT

"**A**bsolutely fucking not!" I grit my teeth, trying to calm the pump of rage filling my veins. "You're not putting yourself in any danger."

"Can you listen?" Jade counters fiercely, flipping her hands in the air in despair and frustration. She's yet to convince me while we're all gathered in a small, empty conference room at the hospital. Elliot's here with us, along with Dante and Dom.

Jade called for a meeting, informing everyone of that damn note she got from that piece-of-shit Agnelo, and apparently, she started a fire in my house to run after Robby. I swear that woman—fuck! If she thinks I'm going to let her into the lion's den by her damn self, she must have me confused for someone who doesn't give a shit about her.

"I did listen, baby." I steady my tone, marching a step toward her, holding her face in my palms, staring deep into her eyes. "This isn't happening. You're not making yourself bait."

"Jade, maybe you should listen to him," Elliot throws in.

Her eyes flip to his, standing behind me as my hands drop. "I love you, Elliot, I really do, but you don't understand. None of you do." Her attention scatters across the room. "My friends are still out there. They need my help. What that family has done to us, and the kids, the women…" Her eyes flutter closed for only a moment.

With a long breath, her gaze lands hard on mine. "I'll be safe. You'll be right outside with your men and I'd have the gun and wire on me, plus the vest."

"How do you know he's even there? It's been hours since you got that note. He's probably gone by now, hiding in some rathole once he realized we had Robby."

"Well, I have to try." She sighs. "I have to find Elsie and Kayla and all the other people they're keeping caged up. I know he'll tell me just to rub it in my face."

While she waited for Robby to wake up, I told her about all the other people we saved when we found her boy. But she told us those numbers don't add up, that there are hundreds more.

I slide up a hand, gripping her chin in between two fingers. "Please… I can't fucking lose you, not when I just got you back."

She lays her forehead against mine, both of us clinging to one another in a sea of chaos. "I love you so much, Enzo. You're the heart of my world."

"Then don't go. Let me take care of this."

She pulls away enough to lock her tender gaze to mine. "I have to do this, Enzo. I need him to know I'm not afraid anymore. Don't take it from me."

That damn pleading look in her eyes, hell, it sits heavy on my chest, robbing me of my ability to refuse her.

"After everything I went through," she continues. "I deserve this. Are you going to be the one to take it from me?"

Everyone else remains silent, giving us the opportunity to figure this shit out ourselves. But I know neither of my brothers would willingly put their women in mortal danger. How could I allow her to go? But if I don't give her this, will she ever forgive me?

"I'm giving you five minutes with him before I go in. Not a second more. If I hear anything I don't like, we're going in."

"Deal." She grins like we're going to prom, flinging her arms around my shoulders. I hug her to me, just holding her, my eyes closing. The thought of anything happening to her, it destroys me, but I get the need for revenge. We all do.

"Don't look all that happy, baby." I'm staring back in her eyes with a slow wind of my mouth. "If you die, I'm gonna be super damn pissed. And you do not want the rest of the world to see me that pissed. I promise."

She laughs faintly, her lips hovering over mine. "Then I'll try not to die."

My hand grips to the back of her head, pulling her hair roughly so she can get a damn good look at my face. "Trying ain't good enough, baby."

Then I kiss her, like it's the last thing I'll ever get to do.

JOELLE

My stomach sinks with every footfall. The hospital hallway is dim, the rooms all shuttered as I continue to my destination, to see Chiara. Enzo informed me she had lost the baby when the bullet struck her.

My heart bleeds for my friend, for that loss. It may have been new, she may have not been that far along, but to a mother who wanted her baby, it doesn't make a difference. It's ours. That pain. That emptiness. That what could've been. What would've been.

I gently knock on the door, knowing Chiara has been awake after her surgery, and Raquel opens it, her eyes glazed, mascara running down the outer edges of her eyes.

"Joelle, I'm so happy to see you're okay." She speaks low, and in her eyes, I see the genuineness. She actually cares about me. It's nice to have that.

She swings her arms around me for a quick hug. "I'm so relieved you have Robby back." She clasps my hand in hers. "He'll be okay."

"Thanks. How is she doing?" My eyes dart to Chiara, lying motionless on the bed, attention fixed to the wall in front of her, but she's not really looking at it. I've been there, in that state of heartache, locked inside my head.

"She's as good as she can be." She huffs, shaking her head as her eyes land to the floor.

"What did the doctors say?"

She glances up. "That she was lucky. Nothing major was punctured. The only bright side is that she can have more kids. I'm so grateful for that." She bites the corner of her bottom lip. "If she couldn't…"

I place a hand on her shoulder. "She's going to come out of this. They both will."

"I hope so," she whispers, peering behind her for a second. "I hate seeing her this way." Her eyes grow sad, and my heart, it grows sad with her.

"Is she up for visitors?"

"She'll want to see you." Her lips tighten with a smile, moving out of the doorway to give me space to walk inside. "I'll be with Dante. Just get me when you're done. I don't want her to be alone while Dom is with the guys."

"Okay."

She starts toward the elevators while I tiptoe inside, shutting the door behind me, every step more wary than the last.

"Hey, Chiara. I hope it's okay that I'm here." I'm almost to the foot of the bed. She doesn't look at me, her gaze still glued to the wall, her skin ashen, eyes so cold, I almost shiver. "I'm here for you. Mother to mother. You can talk to me if and when you're ready."

She snickers now, slowly turning to me. "I'm not a mother." Her tone, it's dead. "I was barely pregnant."

She doesn't mean it. I can practically feel the pain she's hiding, like it's there in the room with us.

I take a seat beside her. "There are no rules for this, Chiara. It's okay to feel what you're feeling. It's okay to cry, to fall apart, to hate them. Just don't bottle it up." Gently, I set a palm across her arm. "If you do, it's going to eat away at you until there's nothing inside. Don't give them that."

She rips her eyes away from me, turning to the wall once more, her bottom lip jittering just slightly.

"I love you, Chiara. You're like family to me. I hate that you're hurting."

Those large brown eyes disappear behind her eyelids as they drift shut.

I give her a little squeeze. "I'm going to be leaving in a little bit to confront Agnelo, but I wanted to see you before I did."

That gets the fire going in her gaze, her elbows hitting the bed, helping to prop her up as she winces in pain.

"I wish I were there too, with Dom and you and everyone," she tells me. "I'd fucking butcher him alive."

"I believe you." I grin widely.

A hint of a smile sets over her lips. "Be careful."

"I'll try."

"And thank you for what you said. It meant a lot even though I didn't show it. I'm kind of a bitch right now."

"Well, bitch away. I've always enjoyed your bitchiness."

"Oh, gee, thanks. I wasn't that bad."

"Sure you weren't." I roll my eyes playfully, getting to my feet, knowing Enzo and the rest of the team are waiting for me to go after the last Bianchi bastard still standing. I still have to see Robby one last time in case... My heartbeat thunders in my chest at the thought.

"Look who's being a bitch now." She pops a single brow, and I love to see that spunk back on her face.

"I learned from the best."

"Well, then hurry back so I can teach you some more shit. If you die, I'm gonna be pissed."

"That's what Enzo said." I break out in a hearty laugh.

"I knew he and I would eventually find something in common."

With every turn the SUV makes, my skin crawls, the nerves finally welcoming me into the dark. The sky has long abandoned the blazing blue, now woven with ash dipped in black ink, and serenaded by the stars in the softest of melodies.

Enzo is seated beside me, his fingers linked through mine, his other hand on his weapon, clutching it so tight, his knuckles must've turned white beneath his gloves.

"One minute to showtime," the driver announces.

"Are you sure you want to do this?" Enzo quietly implores. Elliot and Dante are in the row behind us, while Dom is in the passenger side.

"I am. Whether he realizes I'm not coming alone or not, I need to look him in the eyes. I need him to see me. *Really* see me. The way he never did before."

He clenches his jaw. I have every intention of surviving this, but if I don't, if my death can save my friends and others, then it's worth the sacrifice. And leaving Robby forever, God it would be the worst kind of pain, but maybe when he's older, he'd understand why I did it. That sometimes helping others in spite of your own safety is worth it in the end.

"I'll be close," Enzo assures me with a look that says he wishes he could take my place. "If you say the code word, I'll storm right in. Got it?" He wraps the span of his palm around the slope of my neck, his gaze sinking into mine.

"Yeah." I nod against his strong hold, his masculine touch tethering to me possessively.

"Tell me what it is again."

"Spider." I snicker. "Original. Did you think of it?"

"I did." His mouth twists in amusement, tapping his temple with his index finger as his hand falls from me. "This brain wasn't made in a day."

A small laugh bursts out my throat. I clasp my palm around the stubble riding his cheek. "I love you," I tell him. "Just promise if anything happens to me, you'll—"

"Hell no." He shakes his head. "We're not doing that shit."

"Enzo…" There's a pleading in my voice because I need to hear him say it. "Please, let me do this."

"Fuck, baby," he grits, sucking in a deep breath as his eyes shoot to the roof of the car. When his gaze returns, there's so much torment within it. "I'll take care of him," he vows, knowing exactly what I was about to say. "You'll never have to worry about that. He'll always have me and your brother. But I swear to God,

Jade…" He palms the back of my head, gripping it tightly as he lowers his forehead to mine. "You're not dying on me. He and I, we both need you."

But there's a good chance I won't make it out of this. He doesn't know the extent of my plan once I come face-to-face with the man who ruined my life.

"We're here," the driver informs as a heavy sigh leaves the both of us simultaneously.

"Goddamn it," Enzo spits out as the vehicle stops about a quarter block away from the address Agnelo scribbled down, additional vehicles halting behind us.

I glance out the window, finding a silent street with nothing but trees, the forest seemingly endless under the singular streetlight.

We get out, as do the men from the other vehicles, all of them now circled around us. Enzo and his brothers had already sent men to scout the location and the surrounding vicinity before we arrived. There are no homes for miles, and they've shut down all cameras in a five-mile radius.

"Okay, this is the plan," Dom says, his tone commanding. "Enzo will walk Joelle to the corner before she heads the rest of the way alone, with us taking our positions. You all know where you're supposed to be. Radio for assistance if you need it and shoot every motherfucker who stands in your way."

There's a collective nod from the men.

"All right." Dom's eyes dart to each one of them. "Let's end this."

As they all disperse, I go to Elliot. With a defeated look, he throws his arms around me and hugs me tight. "You better not die." His words fall with affection against my ear.

"That's what everyone keeps telling me." I let out a small laugh as we separate. "I love you, Elliot."

"You too, sis." He kisses me on the cheek, then moves to the rest of the guys.

Enzo's there now, grabbing my hand and yanking me hard against him. With this damn vest on me, I can barely feel his body.

He touches around my hip, making sure the gun he gave me is still tucked in the waistband of my leggings, the oversized black hoodie covering it from view. We only had a little bit of time for him to show me how to work it, but I got the hang of it.

"I won't be afraid to use it. I promise."

"You better not, baby. He has to know Robby is with us by now. He'll have no reason to keep you alive, and I hate that I'm letting you do this. It's killing me."

"I know it is," I breathe, leaning over and kissing him softly. His eyes fall to a close as our lips meet, then his mouth devours mine, the passion dripping from the endless vows of forever. His hand holds me captive by the back of my head, his tongue dipping inside, caressing mine with every waking beat of his heart.

Though the kiss had only just begun, it ends just as quickly, ripping us apart, like the Bianchis have done to everyone who's had the misfortune to meet them.

"I'll be back before you know it," I say with a torn-up smile.

"Not soon enough." He inhales sharply. With melancholy filling my every pore, I take his hand as we walk toward the corner where the monster waits in a large, unoccupied warehouse.

I wish there was another way to save my friends, but there isn't. He must know Robby is gone, what other leverage does he have on me except Kayla and Elsie? I bet they're there with him. He'll want to kill them in front of me before shooting me. But what if I gave him another option? What if I offered something better in exchange? Something he's always wanted desperately.

Me.

I'll kill the mic I have strapped to me and offer up myself to do with what he wants, even if that means death. That's been the plan all along. I'm ready for it. I hope one day, Robby can forgive me if I don't make it out, but I can't let my friends continue to live a life of torture while I selfishly enjoy mine. How could I let that happen while knowing I could've done something to help them? I couldn't live with myself.

Enzo and I reach the end of the street, pausing on the corner before I have to make the rest of the way alone, only a few feet standing between me and the devil.

His hands ball into fists as his gaze cuts into mine, fear warring within those eyes, bleeding down his face. But he knows it's a battle he'll lose. I won't let him stop me.

I fight the storm of tears pounding at the wall around my heart, knowing I have to hide them. I can't tell him this moment may very well be the last one we have left.

"I'll see you soon," I say with a tendril of a smile. I kiss him slowly, those lips softly brushing over mine, reminding me of the moments of love and joy I felt every second we spent together.

Gradually, my fingers slip away from his, and with a last look into his eyes, I'm gone, marching away from him and a life we may never get.

JOELLE

TWENTY-NINE

A s soon as my hand hits the doorknob, my throat closes, tightening with every slam of my pulse, fear ramming in my throat so heavily, I almost run back into Enzo's arms.

Shuddering with a long, strained breath, I pull the door open. The loud squealing as it parts crawls up my arms, dotting my skin with terror.

I tiptoe inside the cold, darkened room. Even through my hoodie and the shirt beneath, the hairs on my arms stand up, pinching at my skin.

My breathing is louder than the cautious footsteps I take as I continue inside, looking around against the speckle of light peeking from my left. There's not a person here.

The bastard must've thought I wouldn't come now that Robby

is safe. My stomach drops with disappointment, but relief too.

I don't want to die. I don't want to leave Robby or the man I love. I only just got Elliot back. How could I abandon all that?

But as I start back to the door, a blaring creak pummels through the silence. Abruptly, the entire room erupts with glaring lights, as though the sun has risen from eternal sleep, burning at my eyes.

I shroud my gaze behind my arm, slowly adjusting to the brightness, my body waking with a shiver, knowing the man I despise is here after all.

"I didn't think you'd show," that voice that always managed to fill my blood with contempt says. "I underestimated how stupid you are."

I lower my hand, my glare narrowed at the short man who's spent years tormenting me, the top of his head now bald, the sides sprinkled with tiny, gray strands.

But he's not alone. There are at least a dozen men here, including the one Enzo has been looking for. The Bianchi lawyer, Joey Russo is beside him, strapped in a navy suit as though he's heading to the courtroom right after he's done here. He's nothing but a sick, perverted man. His hand glides through his thick black hair, the sides of his deep brown eyes crinkling as he smirks, probably picturing doing the things he's done to me every chance he got.

Their appetites are as depraved as they are, but looking at Joey, one would never know it. He appears put together, attractive even, a lot better looking than his cousin Carlito. But that means little. He makes my skin crawl.

I never told Enzo what he did to me—the knife he used to prick my thighs while he raped me. The blood. He enjoys it. He especially loved to hear us scream. So I stopped screaming. I did what I could to keep fighting in the only way I had left.

Enzo will rip him limb by limb if he finds out, but I've tormented him enough with the details of what I've been through. Joey will die today. I know he will. And that'll be enough.

"I'm here for Kayla and Elsie. I know they're here. Get them."

Agnelo snickers as his men form a semicircle behind Joey and him. "You think you're making demands here, little girl?" His upper lip curls with a sadistic snarl, his feet prodding toward me, and I unconsciously move back a step. "Where's your boyfriend and his pack of puppies? I can't believe he'd let you come here all alone."

The corner of my mouth lifts into a taunting smile as I reach under my shirt.

"Taking off her clothes for us already, boys." Agnelo rocks with a sinister chuckle, the men all joining in. "We're going to have a show."

But I ignore them, ripping off the wire I have taped to my stomach. That causes them all to shut the hell up for once.

I stomp on the wire, knowing Enzo probably figured out what I'm doing, so it won't be long until he comes rushing in.

"Wired, huh? I should've known," he says, his chest lifting with a heavy, amused sigh. "Are they here?"

"Not yet. But they will be soon. Give me Elsie and Kayla, and you can go before they kill you and your men."

His guys burst into a fit of laughter.

"You think I'm scared of those punks? You think you could make me give them up?" he roars, the anger seething over every part of his face. "Weren't you happy with stealing our boy? Had to be greedy and come back for more? You stupid bitches never learn."

"He isn't *our* boy," I bellow. "He's *mine*."

A chuckle boils out of him. "That's where you're wrong. Did

you forget how he was made because I could remind you. Right here."

They all laugh cruelly, and my stomach drops as I watch them mocking me. The wave of those memories floods into me until my heart squeezes too tight.

"You can have me. In exchange for their freedom. Isn't that what you always wanted? For me to be—"

His shrill cackle of laughter interrupts the rest of my words. "You think you're worth that much to me?" He catches his breath. "You aren't worth shit."

This isn't working. What have I done? He's going to kill me. I'm going to die and so will my friends.

"You don't recognize this place, do you?" His question hangs in the air, thick as the grayed-out beard lining his round jaw. "I guess you wouldn't. You were never up here. Most of your time was spent below, doing everything I made you do."

I gasp at what he's admitting.

We're here. At the club.

At the place where evil was born, residing endlessly. The vileness seeped into its walls, marking them for eternity.

"Ahh, finally. She realizes the significance of all of us standing here." He glances behind him, and at first, I don't understand why, but as more footsteps shuffle forward, muffled crying filling the room, the fear, it grips me raw.

Who is that?

But my question doesn't go unanswered too long. As the men separate, another comes toward Agnelo, and he's not alone. Clutched within his grasp is Kayla, or what I recognize of her.

Her straight, brown hair is ragged now, worn down like the rest of her. The curves of her body have mostly disappeared, but my attention goes to the large red mark on her swollen cheek, her eyelids puffy from crying.

"What the fuck did you assholes do to her?"

"Whatever the hell I wanted." Agnelo sneers. "Like I always do."

"It's okay, Kayla." I look at her, forgetting all of them. "I'll get you out of this."

Her chin trembles, more tears streaming down her face as she whimpers, but her eyes, they stay on mine. Pleading. Lost.

"Shut the fuck up!" The man who's still got his grip on her jerks her hard.

"Don't fucking touch her!"

"Or what?" Agnelo asks.

"I'll kill you," I spit through gritted teeth.

"Fucking adorable. Isn't she, boys?" His chuckle twists with the evil rising from his soul.

"Where's Elsie? What did you do to her?"

"I have no fucking clue." He shrugs. "The little bitch ran off, and this one"—he points a thumb to Kayla—"still won't tell me shit. I've tried, many times. Believe me." He walks up to Kayla and runs his disgusting hand down between her breasts. "Isn't that right, dollface?"

She recoils, sniveling as his hand falls away.

"All this one told me is that your little friend left, leaving her here alone to suffer. What a girl, huh?"

Elsie would never leave Kayla. That makes no sense. If she ran, she would've taken Kayla with her. If Elsie is still out there, how come she never contacted anyone?

Enzo and his brothers looked for both girls. There was not a trace of them. Something must've happened to her, maybe something even worse than this. I won't rest until I get the answers. It's not above Agnelo to lie.

"She's probably dead somewhere," he adds. "Good fucking riddance. Now, I'll watch you, your friend, and all the others caged up downstairs burn alive. I have no use for this place anymore. I'll find another. I'll get more people. And this time, you won't be joining us, I'm afraid."

"What? No! You have to let the kids go. They're just babies! You can't kill them!" My voice slices with a sob, imagining it's my Robby there. "Please," I plead as I come closer. "Just take me. Kill me. Do whatever you want. Let the others go."

Agnelo's men could be setting a fire downstairs already. I have to do something to save them all. I can't let any of them die. Now, I wish I hadn't ripped the damn wire, so Enzo could come and rescue them.

"You're not worth all that." Agnelo snickers. "My only regret is that Robby isn't here too. But I'll find him, and I'll end him like his whore mother."

My hand sneaks under my hoodie, my palm wrapping around the handle of the gun. "You son of a b—" I never finish the rest of that sentence. Glass shatters from around us, the windows breaking, my world erupting in gunfire as I run to hide behind a large crate.

Enzo and more of their men swoop in from outside, their weapons blazing, taking out some of the Bianchi men one by one, before they could even aim their weapon.

Dante kicks one in the face, then puts a bullet in his chest, while Dom kills one more. I look behind me, only a couple of yards away, finding Elliot shooting at a man in front, simultaneously fighting off someone else. He doesn't notice as another comes at him quick, a pistol pointed at my brother's back. Before I know what I'm doing, my gun is in my hand, and I pull the trigger.

Elliot's eyes land on me as the asshole falls, and he mouths *thank you* before he finishes him off. I have no idea where I hit him. I just hoped it was somewhere good.

My heart rams in my rib cage as though ready to split right out of me.

I actually shot someone.

Kayla. Oh my God. Where is she?

My gaze darts around the room, hoping I can find her among the chaos. At first, I don't, but then I see her. Agnelo is dragging her away, his forearm trapping her neck as she tries to fight him off.

With my weapon steady in my grip, I ignore everyone else, muffling the rampage, my focus on my friend and the man who thinks he's invincible. It's time to put an end to him once and for all. He doesn't see me coming, not at first, not until I'm close enough to kill him.

His lips jerk with a sinister promise as he lifts the hand with his weapon clutched in it. He pulls her away little by little, trying to escape. But I won't let him. He doesn't get to come out of this alive.

With my gaze perched to my friend, I hope like hell she understands the unspoken words filling my eyes.

With parted lips, her head nodding once, she bites his forearm and ducks down. The next thing I hear is the pop from my weapon, the bullet aimed for his forehead.

ENZO

She thought she could give herself up and I wouldn't be there to stop it? I had the warehouse bugged. I didn't tell her because I had a feeling she was going to pull some stupid shit like this.

She's damn loyal and selfless. Her bravery is one of the things

I love most about her, but fuck if she thinks I'd let her give herself up to that animal. If anyone is dying today, it's me. I'd take her place without hesitation.

Something slams hard into the back of my head as I fight a motherfucker off. The sharp sting of pain only makes the anger radiate deeper. I kick a guy in front, right in the face, pivoting to find the one who hit me.

"Fight me, pussy," he sneers, landing a punch into my jaw that I let him have with a grin that says, *you just fucked with the wrong person.*

"If you insist," I mutter before—*pop.*

He didn't even see my other revolver, hidden in my jacket pocket. His hands clamp around the hole in his stomach, blood rushing out. The shell-shocked look on his face only irritates me, so I fire another into his forehead, killing him in a flash.

I fight off every living, breathing Palermo man, my brothers and our men all doing the same. But my goal is to get to Jade and take her the hell out of here before she becomes a casualty.

Where the fuck is she?

Dom has Joey Russo in his grasp, punching the shit out of him as the scumbag groans in pain, cowering on the ground, before getting a hard kick in the stomach. But Dom doesn't stop, his shoe pressing down over his throat as he fights for air, his fingers clawing with desperation.

The other men are all at our mercy, more of them arriving from below the trapdoor that has now popped open, the place where the Bianchis have been hiding the club.

As my nine rips into the forehead of another man, I see Jade from the corner of my eye, that bastard pointing his weapon at her, but my girl, she has one on him too.

"Don't, Jade!" I shout, but in the chaos, she doesn't hear me.

I run across the wide space, shoving at the men around me to get to her, to stop her, afraid that his bullet will enter her before hers kills him.

Pop.

Fuck!

I'm too late. She shoots, as I continue to run, to scream her name, afraid he'll kill her, but instead of firing back, Agnelo only laughs.

Jade's shouting slams into my gut as I'm finally beside her. Her bullet, it didn't hurt Agnelo at all. It hit Kayla instead.

She falls to the ground as he lets her go.

"No!" Jade screams, dropping the gun and running toward her friend, whose arm oozes with blood as Jade quickly removes her hoodie and wraps it around the wound. "I've got you," she says with a sob. "We'll go to a hospital as soon as we get out of here."

Agnelo takes this opportunity to try and run, gun raised to me as he steps backward toward the door only a foot away. He may act tough, but he's a pussy. He flees when real trouble comes, and we're as real as it gets. He won't escape us now. Not this time.

I'm on him before he can move another inch, swiftly kicking the weapon from within his grasp, slamming another kick across his ankles, dropping him to the floor.

"Finally." My foot lands over his round stomach, retrieving the pistol from my pocket, pointing it at his chest. "I get to kill you."

My thumb rests over the trigger, and with a final look, I start to pull.

"Put your gun down," a man behind me says. "He's mine." The cold metal of what I know is a weapon is pressed to the back of my head.

"Nah, man. You must be confused," I tell him, turning toward whoever the hell it is, about to kill him too if he doesn't take that pistol away from my face.

He stares me down, fury locked in his eyes, and I do the same. But as I look at him, this kid no older than me, I'm momentarily gripped by the realization that I've seen him before.

"Who the hell are you?" He ignores my question, his glare darting past me and now centered at Agnelo, cocking the weapon at him.

"Ahh, there he is," Agnelo jeers. "I've been looking for you."

My pulse knocks within my head, this uneasy energy rustling in the air, blowing over me.

"Well, you found me," the guy calmly says, though his expression is anything but calm. "Now tell me where she is. Where the hell did you send her?"

I look between them, unsure who they're talking about, trying to place this stranger at the same time, but I can't.

How the hell do I know him? Maybe from one of our clubs?

"Tsk, tsk." Agnelo laughs, his brows dipping with amusement. "You'll never find her. Stupid kid. I told you, she'll never be yours. When will you finally listen?"

The room has gone silent, my brothers and Elliot moving closer from my left, their footsteps crunching over the glass.

The guy growls, kneeling to the floor, the butt of his nine slamming hard into Agnelo's temple. "She's your fucking daughter and you sold her? To who?"

Daughter?

"Are you looking for Aida?" I ask the guy, and that gets his attention.

"How the hell do you know her? Have you seen her?"

"No, man, I'm sorry, but if you need help, my brothers and I, we can help you find her."

His jaw grinds. "I work alone." Then his gaze is back on the scumbag.

"This is so beautiful. Reunited at last and they have no idea," Agnelo taunts. "I only wish my brothers were still alive to witness this miracle."

My throat goes dry. "What the fuck is going on?"

"Why don't you tell them who you are?" Agnelo looks to each one of my brothers.

Dom circles the kid, staring at him for a long, quiet moment, as though for the first time.

"No..." Dom's inhale is harsh as he shakes his head. "It can't be." His hand runs past his face. "I watched you di—"

A heavy, sinking feeling blasts into my stomach.

"Who is that, Dom?" Dante asks, his tone sliced with the same trepidation.

"Don't you recognize your own brother?" Agnelo chuckles.

"Br-brother?" I whisper. But when I look at him again, really look, those large brown eyes... "Fuck." I grip my hair.

Dante faces him now, Elliot pointing the gun at Agnelo in case he decides to run.

"Matteo?" Dom's shell-shocked voice causes us all to freeze.

"Surprise!" Agnelo snickers.

My world spins, my chest erupting with needle-like stabbing as my mind tries to wrap around something I never thought was possible.

"How could you be here? Where have you been?" Dom asks, the words falling unevenly, unable to pull his eyes away from our baby brother.

"He's been with me this whole time," Agnelo interrupts. "Isn't that right, kid?"

"Tell me where she is!" he roars in return.

"You're like a sad, little puppy." Agnelo's expression is filled with annoyance as he tries to sit up, but Elliot pushes him back down. "She's long gone by now. Probably in a different country."

Matteo growls, pressing the muzzle of his weapon to his own forehead.

"Good luck finding her by yourself," Agnelo throws out. "But if you want a shot at saving her, well, you're going to have to take me out of here before your brothers end your chance of ever getting to her in time."

"Matteo, please," Dom practically begs. "Let us help you. Don't fucking listen to him. All he ever does is lie."

"Goddamn, Matteo. We're your brothers." Dante clasps him on the shoulder, but Matteo shoves his hand away. "We'll help you find her."

"I have no brothers." He looks at us, one by one. His eyes used to hold the warmth of our mother in them, but now, they're empty, as though stolen, like he was. "The best thing you can do is forget you ever saw me. I'm still dead where it matters."

His weapon is aimed at Elliot now. "Tell your friend to move," he says to Dom. "Agnelo is coming with me."

Dom jerks his head sideways and Elliot moves back, allowing Agnelo to climb to his feet. Matteo wraps his arm around the bastard's neck, his weapon drawn at us as he starts tugging the old man toward the door.

"Wait!" I shout. "Don't go. We love you, man. We never would've given up finding you if we knew you were alive."

He stops, his shoulders swaying with heavy breaths, his gaze puncturing me with a wound so painful, I almost drop to my knees. If he was with them all these years, who knows what they did to him.

"I'm—I'm sorry." Dom breaks down.

The look of a tormented man is what I find in Matteo's eyes as he stares at us with a cloud of emotion. For a moment, I think he'll actually stay. That he'll choose us.

Instead, he runs out the door, and we lose him for a second time.

JOELLE

THIRTY

The chaos of the two days before is behind us as I sit beside Kayla, luckily fine, the flesh wound now wrapped by a doctor we took her to after we left the warehouse.

I couldn't believe that Enzo's dead brother has been alive all those years in Agnelo's clutches. I kept staring at him, wondering if I ever saw him at that filthy private club, but I don't think we've ever crossed paths.

Raquel is seated next to Chiara, home recovering after checking herself out of the hospital. She wouldn't hear a word of it and told Dom she'd go back if there was a need. And when Chiara makes up her mind, the devil himself couldn't stop her. The fight in her eyes, it's back now. That's how I know she'll be okay after all that she's endured. They can knock her down, but she'll always rise to the top. It's how she's been the entire time I've known her since we met at the strip club seven years ago.

Robby is home too. His doctor was impressed with how well the meds were working, and Enzo assured her we'd take care of him. She didn't object, and even said being with us may be best for him. And here, in Enzo's place, we're finally home. Robby's upstairs, sleeping in his own room that Enzo promises to turn into whatever he desires. The look in that man's eyes when he talks about my son and me, it's overwhelming. I could practically feel his love for me, for a boy he doesn't even know. It's more than I ever thought I deserved.

"We have to find Elsie." Kayla's voice splits through my thoughts. I haven't pushed her to talk about what happened when she saw our friend last, wanting to give her some time to process it all before any of us begin questioning her.

Her hand jitters as she lifts a water bottle to her mouth, taking small sips before placing it on the coffee table before us.

"We will," I tell her, raising my leg onto the sofa, pivoting toward her. "You wanna tell me what happened? Why she left and you didn't?"

She nods as she peers down onto her lap. Elliot, Enzo, and his brothers stand beside each other, their front against the back of the sofa where Chiara and Raquel are seated.

"We were looking out the window," she starts, her brows angled with a frown, "when a dark blue SUV pulled up. We'd never seen that vehicle before, and we made a habit of remembering every person and every car that came." Her gaze sweeps past me, staring straight, her eyes lost to the memories.

"The guards who watched us and the other six girls who lived at the house were stationed on the first floor by the entrance. Elsie and I were on the opposite side of the floor at the time." She strains with a quick exhale before continuing. "A man in a long black wool coat stepped out of the car, his black hair slicked back. I don't know his name, only what he looks like. The man went inside, speaking to one of the guards, asking for Faro, saying something about talking business." She blinks back tears, some caught in her long lashes as she stares at her fidgety hands.

"Something told Elsie that this was our chance to run. She begged me to come with her. She said we could escape out the window while the guards were distracted and hitch a ride in the back of the SUV. But I chickened out." She flashes her tear-filled eyes to me. "I couldn't. I was too scared. I was never as brave as you two were. So, I stayed." She shrugs, lips bending with a scowl. "I have no idea where she is, or whether that man ever found her. It eats at me every day, not knowing what happened, that I never joined her."

The hopeless anguish inside her has my own tears springing. "You did what you felt you had to. It's okay." I take her hand, slipping it into mine. "If I were in your place, I don't know what I would've done."

"Oh, please." She cracks a smile, swiping under her eyes. "You know you'd be in that truck already."

A brittle sigh falls from my lips. Would I go or would I stay? I don't really know. But she's here with us. Finally. And we'll find Elsie too. I can't give up hope.

"Please find her." Her eyes plead with Enzo and the others.

"We're going to," Enzo swears. "We have something to go on, thanks to you."

She nods wistfully.

"We may need you to look at some pictures," Dom adds. "To see if you can spot the guy you mentioned. If he was at that place where they kept you, then he has to know the Bianchis well."

Her eyes suddenly grow huge. "Oh my God! I just remembered."

I scoot in closer. "What is it?"

"His scar." Her voice drowns into a whisper, mouth parting for a beat. "There was a scar on his cheek. It was long, like he'd been slashed across it with a knife."

"Shit." Chiara's brows shoot up and everyone's attention flies to her. "Was it on his right side?" she asks, edging toward the end of the sofa with a hiss, clearly fighting through the pain.

"Yeah." Kayla's gaze narrows as she meets her stare. "How did you know that?"

"Because I know who it is."

My heartbeat quickens.

"Who, baby?" Dom strides to her, his thumb rolling down her cheek tenderly as she peers up.

"It's Michael Marino. The man my father was going to force me to marry."

"Fuck," Dom swears. "You think he's involved in the club?"

"I have no idea."

"Isn't he in the Messina family?" I ask, anxiety filling my lungs, finding it hard to breathe.

"Yeah." Chiara's mouth thins. "He is. His father is the don, and I heard not for long. Rumor has it, he's at war with his older brother, wanting to take over for his father instead."

What has Elsie gotten herself into?

"His door will be the first one we knock on when we go looking." Dom moves a step back as he glances to his brothers. "If that bastard did something to her, I'll personally end his fucking life."

"I guess we may have another war on our hands." Enzo rubs his palms together, his lips rolling with a sneering smile.

The stairs creak behind us, and suddenly Robby's there, rubbing his eyes as he pads to me. "Mommy?" he groggily asks. "I had a bad dream."

"Oh, baby." I get up, lowering before him, wrapping tender arms around my sweet boy. "Want to sit on Mommy's lap?"

That gets him grinning wide, the sleepiness still fastened to his face.

My laughter at his genuine happiness is a welcomed sound. It's still pretty early in the morning and I much prefer he get as much rest as possible, but I'd never refuse snuggles with him for anything.

Slipping my hand around his small one, I lead us to the sofa, scooping him up on top of me, his delicate face tucked against my chest, the grogginess disappearing as he gazes at everyone.

"How about I get you a big-ass chocolate chip cookie?" Enzo asks. "Maybe two."

"Language." I widen a glare with a teasing jerk of my lips.

"Baby, with you two living here, that kid is gonna hear a lot worse shit coming from me than that. I kinda have a potty mouth." He winks with a wicked smirk, and hell, it goes straight to my core.

"I quite like it," I sass.

His gaze smolders, jaw flexing, those eyes finding my mouth and staying there longer than appropriate.

"You two need a minute? Because Uncle Dante can babysit."

"Shit, maybe *you* only need a minute." Enzo shoves his brother playfully across the chest. "But my girl knows, with us, it's more like hours." His lower lip disappears between his teeth as he practically undresses me with warmth caressing over my most sensitive places.

"Dude, that's my sister." Elliot shakes his head, laughing.

"Sorry?" Enzo flips his hands in the air, feigning an apology.

"Do you have any brownies?" Robby asks. "That's what the

nice lady who I stayed with would make me when the mean man wasn't there."

I suck in a breath. Afraid to move. Afraid he'll stop talking. My heart lurches.

Keep talking, baby boy.

I've been terrified to ask anything, not wanting to somehow impede his recovery or harm him by remembering, but I have to know who kept him all these years.

"Wow, that was so nice of her," Enzo says, lowering to the spot next to us, glancing at me, his expression intense. He knows how important this conversation is, and I let him take the lead.

"Yeah, she was really nice. Ms. Greco always made yummy stuff."

"Like what?" Enzo's features soften.

"Muffins and cupcakes. That kind of thing."

"I wish I could have some."

"The other lady was nice too," Robby adds. "She helped me learn to read and did math with me. I love them both."

My heart tugs. *Who are they? Did they love him back?*

"I bet you're better at math than I am." Enzo rolls his eyes. "I'm not very good." He chuckles, eliciting a giggle from Robby.

"Aida always told me I was a genius."

"Did you sa-say Aida?" Chiara stammers, her expression stunned.

"Yeah. She had yellow hair," Robby tells her. "I lived with her and the bad man who sent her away. She said her dad was the bad man, and I had to hide when he came home."

"Oh my God." Chiara's fingers tremble against her chest.

My vision goes hazy. He's been right under my fingertips. No one knew that Chiara and Raquel's cousin had my son this entire time. I never imagined Agnelo would keep him in his own damn home. But what better place to hide him than there?

"Did they ever hurt you?" I caress his forehead with the tips of my fingers, the back of my nose straining with an ache, but I fight the emotional black hole trying to swallow me up.

"No." He lifts his face up to me. "Well, sometimes her dad screamed really loud when I was bad." His mouth drops into a scowl. "He is very scary."

Anger burns white-hot across my skin. "You weren't bad, baby. It's that man who's bad."

"Yeah, buddy. Your mom is right. He's not a good guy, and he'll never come near you again." Robby sits up taller, eagerly looking at Enzo like he's his new favorite person, and it makes my heart all sorts of happy. "You see my brothers over there and your uncle?" Enzo slants his head toward them, and Robby nods.

"Well, they'll always protect you and your mom, just like me."

He sighs with relief. "That's good. I don't want to leave my mommy again."

"You never will." I swear it like an oath sewn into my very flesh, kissing the top of his head, my eyelids slowly swimming to a close as I picture that animal scaring my innocent baby. I could just kill him. I can't believe he's still out there.

"How did you end up in the place we found you?" Enzo continues. "Where did Aida go?"

"She had a big fight with her dad about the man in the basement."

"What man?" Enzo's tone lowers to a whisper.

"I—I can't say. Aida told me to never talk about him, to pretend he was never there, or her dad would punish me."

Discreetly, my hand falls over my mouth as I look at Enzo, who's thinking the same thought as me.

It had to be Matteo.

Right?

"When her dad got very loud, I ran upstairs and hid. He was screaming at her. I could hear him even there. Then I heard a loud boom and Aida was screaming too. I was so scared, Mommy." His arms fall around my middle in a tight hug.

"That was so brave of you." Enzo comforts him with a pat on his head. "Do you know what happened after that?"

"Yeah, I stayed in my room for a long time, and then this man I didn't know grabbed me from under the bed and took me to that smelly place and put me in the cage."

"Holy hell," Dante says incredulously. "You think he's talking about Matteo? What did they do to our brother?"

"That's what we're gonna find out." Dom clenches his fist at his side. "No matter the cost."

ENZO

With Jade next to me, we tuck Robby back to bed. He's been tired with being sick. "Sleep well, little man. We're gonna be right downstairs if you need us."

"Okay," he mutters, already dozing off as Jade kisses his cheek one more time before turning off the lights.

"You're so good with him," she admits as I shut the door behind us.

"You sound surprised." My mouth tips up. "I'm a man of many talents."

"I'm serious." She pauses, her palms clasped around my upper back as she looks up at me with damn near wonder. I've never been looked at that way, and it feels fucking good. "Thank you for that. You being great to my son. It means everything."

"I love the both of you and that's never gonna stop." I bring my lips to hers, sliding against them, groaning as my teeth sink around her bottom one.

"Say it again," she moans hoarsely. "I want to hear you tell me you love me."

"I can do that, baby girl." I walk her backward until she lands against the door of an empty bedroom. "I can do that as many times as you want."

My mouth moves to her jaw, nipping that delicate skin. "I love you," I tell her, my lips falling softly on her neck, my hand rolling down her stomach until it reaches the waistband of her leggings. "I love you," I repeat as my fingers climb inside, cruising lower, until I reach the lace of her panties, two fingers slipping past the thin strap of fabric, finding her warm and wet. "I love you, Jade," I say one final time just as the pad of a single finger slowly rubs her clit once, before slipping inside.

"Oh God, Enzo. We can't. Your brothers are waiting for us downstairs."

"So let them wait." I slam harder, thrusting two fingers all the way in, until her thighs shudder, until she can't help but mask her scream-filled moans behind my shoulder.

"I missed this wet, little pussy." I roll my thumb over her center as I finger-fuck her, and damn, her walls clamping around me only makes me go harder.

She bites into my shoulder, nails clawing at my back, gasps getting louder the harder I thrust.

"You're gonna be a good girl and come all over my hand."

Her breathing goes all shaky as she cries against me.

"That pussy likes when I talk dirty to it, doesn't it?" That gets her groaning louder.

I grab a fistful of her hair, pulling hard, teeth gritting with a growl. "You're gonna look at me when I fuck you. Show me how good you can come."

She pants, riding my hand, nails piercing roughly as her brows tighten.

"Yeah, that's it. Come for me, baby girl. I wanna taste it on my fingers." I ram so deep, her entire body breaks into a tremor.

Her need spirals as I pound into her until she falls apart, her mouth dropping open as she cries my name, those eyes pinned to mine.

I don't let go. This connection, this insane want for a woman I love, it carries me somewhere I've never been and never want to be without.

"If we had more time, I'd fuck you right up against this wall." I cup her pussy, slapping it once, her exhales rough, her gaze still carrying the look of desire I want so badly to own. "I'm gonna save that for later though." My hand reluctantly slips out, and I press my fingers into my mouth, sucking them dry. "Fucking delicious." I grip her jaw, my tongue sinking into her mouth, swiping over hers so she can taste herself on my tongue.

"Mmm," she hums, and my cock grows heavier, stiff, and aching for her.

"I don't think I can walk." She laughs with a sigh.

"Then I'll carry you." I ready to throw her over my shoulder.

"Don't you dare!" She giggles, swatting my hand away. "I was only kidding."

"Really? So you can walk?" My palm captures her throat, gripping tight, my lips catching hers in a quick, rough kiss. "Guess later I'll have to fuck you so hard, you won't even be able to sit, let alone walk."

A frustrated groan escapes her. "That's not fair. You can't say things like that right now."

My thumb rolls over her lips, my hard-on straining against my black sweats. "Then let's head downstairs and be done with it, so we can come back and I'll properly show you all the ways I've missed you."

We've been so consumed with Robby and seeing Matteo that I haven't been inside her since the barbeque.

Grabbing my hand, she practically throws me down the stairs with how hard she drags, and I meet her enthusiasm with a chuckle.

As soon as we're back with everyone, we take the same spots we had before.

"Shit, put on the TV," Dante says, staring hard at his phone. "Hit the news channel. It's on."

Raquel grabs the remote, bringing the screen to life. After a minute of the female newscaster talking about a robbery gone wrong, the story shifts to one we know well. After all, we were the ones to tip them off.

Once Matteo left, we went to the basement of that warehouse, finding even more cages than we had before. Women, kids, both boys and girls trapped in them, some crying, others as sick as Robby was when we found him.

We wanted to take them all, but instead, we decided to document every photo, every file, then call a good friend from the FBI who handles shit like this. We told him everything that those motherfuckers had done and left the evidence with him after taking photos of it for ourselves.

Once he got his unit down there, we left. But not before we emailed one of the biggest news channels, knowing with the proof we shared, they'd run the story, exposing the Palermo crime family once and for all.

Not only did we expose them, but we exposed all the celebrities and politicians who frequented that place. The Bianchis weren't stupid. They kept their names, along with photos of them doing sick things to those kids and women. We hid the faces of the victims when we sent some of the photographs. Only the authorities have all the originals.

We don't know if any of the other crime families had knowledge of what the Bianchis had been doing, but I sure as hell hope not. If they did, we'll kill them all too.

My attention draws back toward the television as the story begins to unfold.

"Today, we bring you a *Channel Three* exclusive. This story and the images that go along with it, may be disturbing. Viewer caution is advised."

The screen changes to the shot deep in the heart of the city as the woman continues. "Deep in the city, in the middle of nowhere, is a horror like no other. We don't want to imagine things like this happening, but every day they do. Human trafficking. Women, young children as little as seven were being abused by dozens of faces at a secret club run by the notorious Palermo crime family."

The clip switches to the warehouse, yellow caution tape around it, men and women with badges now walking inside it. "Some of the faces you'll see in these photos," the newscaster continues, "are people you'll recognize. They're your favorite quarterback." A photo of a football player flashes on the screen, a household name, a little girl we know to be no more than ten on his lap, her face blacked out by us, body blurred. "Your favorite talk show host." Another photo slides down, this time a man has a woman in a chokehold, a whip in his hand.

"The people involved have been wanted by law enforcement for decades, but they've finally been caught in one of the biggest victories of our time. The FBI has arrested over three dozen people who had a hand in this awful tragedy." The video cuts back to the newscaster. "Many of the children were taken from families who owed a debt to the Palermos and have since been reunited by the tireless efforts of both the police and the FBI."

We managed to reunite Serena and the rest of the people we found the day we found Robby with the help from the authorities too.

"I'm glad it's finally over." Jade sighs, rubbing away the tears tumbling down her cheeks. She smiles with sadness seeping from her eyes, but relief, it's woven within them too. I can see it.

And every day, I'll fight like hell to find the pieces of her they tore away and build them back up again. I may never be able to undo what's been done, but I can make it so that she no longer lives it. Her life, *our* life, it'll be beautiful.

"Do you think I could play your piano?" she asks sweetly, those eyes cast with a glimmer.

"You play?"

"I used to." Her face falls. "My mom loved to hear me play."

"She was amazing," Elliot adds, coming toward us. "Mom was sure you'd be accepted to Juilliard. She was saving money for you to go."

"What?" Her gaze overflows with tears. "But she knew I was going to eventually go to medical school."

"Yeah, but she knew you were doing that for her. She told me years later that when you came back from your trip, she was going to talk you into applying so you could follow your passion, instead of doing what you thought was right."

"Oh, Mama." She lets out a cry.

"She loved you so much, Jade. I'm sorry you lost all these years with us."

"Me too." She looks up at him, tears swimming down like a heavy stream.

"Wait, I'm sorry to interrupt this beautiful moment," Chiara bursts out. "But who the hell is Jade?"

That gets Joelle—Jade laughing. Fuck, even I'll need time to get used to it.

"That's my real name," she explains.

"Damn." Chiara considers it contemplatively. "I like it."

"So, you gonna play us something?" I ask, giving her my hand as she rises.

"As long as my fingers still work."

"I'm sure you're even better than I can imagine."

I lead her to the music room, with the rest following behind us. "Our mother loved to play too," I explain. "I had purchased it in honor of her."

"My God, could you be a little less perfect?" she teases just as we enter the room, biting into the edge of her bottom lip while facing me.

"I do kill people."

"I'm willing to overlook that." She shrugs with a smile twining up her lips, and it hits my heart like an avalanche of emotions.

"Damn, woman…" My palm rests over the side of her neck. "I love you."

"I love you too, Enzo." With a soft sigh, she moves to sit on the bench, opening the grand piano. She hesitates at first, her fingers trembling for a moment before they hit the keys, and then, she plays.

And once she does, once that music washes over us, the magnitude of her talent is more than I can even comprehend.

Moving back, I stand beside my brothers, who look just as taken aback as I do.

"She's fucking amazing," Dante whispers.

"I know."

She plays like she's never forgotten a beat, the music permeating the very essence of who she is, her eyelids swinging to a close, her head, her body swaying to the melody I've never heard before. I could watch her play every damn day, even if it's the same song every time.

"Sir," one of my men calls from behind. "I'm sorry to interrupt but I thought you'd want to see this."

"What is it?" I ask Stan.

"We found Matteo on one of our security cams," Stan tosses calmly. "Plus some traffic cams we hacked, and we think we can track him to wherever he went."

"Show me," Dom throws tensely. "I wanna see him."

Stan quickly removes his cell and fires up the video, pressing play. Thankfully, we installed our own cameras around the perimeter of the warehouse.

We see Agnelo still in Matteo's grip as he drags him into a white van. Before he enters the driver's seat, his hand on the door handle, he stops, his eyes transfixed to the exact same spot the camera's hiding, as though staring right at us.

"Fuck," Dom roars in a whisper. "We're gonna go after him."

It must be hard to know Matteo never died. Knowing Dom, he's holding himself responsible. But how the hell could he have known?

Hitting pause, we meet the eyes of our brother, a man who's now a stranger. I hope we get the chance to see him, to know him, to finally be a family like my parents would've wanted.

But what if he wants nothing to do with us? What if we found him, only to lose him for good?

THANKS FOR READING!

What happened to Matteo and Aida? Will he re-unite with his brothers? Find out in *The Devil's Den*!

PLAYLIST

- "On the Rise" by Generdyn feat. BELLSAINT
- "Here We Stand" by Hidden Citizens feat. SVRCINA
- "Hit Me With Your Best Shot" by ADONA
- "Battlefield" by SVRCINA
- "Bad Things" by Summer Kennedy
- "Honest" by Kyndal Inskeep feat. The Song House
- "Time Is Running Out" by Kat Leon
- "Found" by Jacob Banks
- "Lips on You" by Maroon 5
- "Do It For Me" by Rosenfeld
- "Lose to Love" by Madison Watkins
- "Won't Keep Quiet" by Hidden Citizens feat. ADONA
- "4am" by Liv Ritchie
- "World on Fire" by Klergy
- "Bad Boy" by Raaban and Tungevaag feat. Luana Kiara
- "Blackout" by Freya Ridings
- "Power" by Isak Danielson
- "Wicked Game" by Ursine Vulpine feat. Annaca
- "Ready Set Let's Go" by Sam Tinnesz
- "Who Are You" by SVRCINA
- "Youth" by Daughter
- "Rescue My Heart" by Liz Longley
- "New Skin" by VÉRITÉ
- "Don't Let Me Go" by RAIGN
- "A Little Bit Dangerous" by CRMNL
- "Silhouette" by Unions

- "Faithful – Stripped" by BOBI ANDONOV
- "Better Days" by Dermot Kennedy
- "The Few Things" by JP Saxe feat. Charlotte Lawrence

ALSO BY LILIAN HARRIS

Fragile Hearts Series

1. *Fragile Scars*
2. *Fragile Lies*
3. *Fragile Truths*
4. *Fragile Pieces*

Cavaleri Brothers Series

1. *The Devil's Deal*
2. *The Devil's Pawn*
3. *The Devil's Secret*
4. *The Devil's Den*
5. *The Devil's Demise*

Messina Crime Family Series (Coming 2023)

1. *Sinful Vows*
2. *Cruel Lies*
3. *Twisted Promises*

Lilian Harris

For Lilian, a love of writing began with a love of books. From *Goosebumps* to romance novels with sexy men on the cover, she loved them all. It's no surprise that at the age of eight she started writing poetry and lyrics and hasn't stopped writing since.

She was born in Azerbaijan, and currently resides in Long Island, N.Y. with her husband, three kids, and a dog named Gatorade. Even though she has a law degree, she isn't currently practicing. When she isn't writing or reading, Lilian is baking or cooking up a storm. And once the kids are in bed, there's usually a glass of red in her hand. Can't just survive on coffee alone!

Lilian would love to connect with you!

Email: lilanharrisauthor@gmail.com
Website: www.lilanharris.com
Newsletter: https://bit.ly/LilianHarrisNews
Signed Paperbacks: https://bit.ly/LHSignedPB
Facebook: www.facebook.com/LilianHarrisBooks
Reader Group: www.facebook.com/groups/lilianslovlies
Instagram: www.instagram.com/lilianharrisauthor
TikTok: www.tiktok.com/@lilianharrisauthor
Twitter: www.twitter.com/authorlilian
Goodreads: https://bit.ly/LilianHarrisGR
Amazon: www.amazon.com/author/lilianharris

Printed in Great Britain
by Amazon